# Crossroads

To Cathy:
May God continue to use
you as His light in Gibbon &
beyond! Blessings —
Sarah Nordlund

# Crossroads

*Carter Reed*

WESTBOW
PRESS

A DIVISION OF THOMAS NELSON

WestBow Press books may be ordered through booksellers or by contacting:

WestBow Press
A Division of Thomas Nelson
1663 Liberty Drive
Bloomington, IN 47403
www.westbowpress.com
1-(866) 928-1240

Because of the dynamic nature of the Internet, any web addresses or links contained in this book may have changed since publication and may no longer be valid. The views expressed in this work are solely those of the author and do not necessarily reflect the views of the publisher, and the publisher hereby disclaims any responsibility for them.

Any people depicted in stock imagery provided by Thinkstock are models, and such images are being used for illustrative purposes only.

Certain stock imagery © Thinkstock.

ISBN: 978-1-4497-4339-0 (sc)
ISBN: 978-1-4497-4341-3 (hc)
ISBN: 978-1-4497-4340-6 (e)

Library of Congress Control Number: 2012904757

Printed in the United States of America

WestBow Press rev. date: 3/22/2012

*Stand at the crossroads, and look, and ask for the ancient paths, where the good way lies; and walk in it, and find rest for your souls.*

*Jeremiah 6:16*
*New Revised Standard Version*
*(NRSV)*

# Contents

# ACKNOWLEDGMENTS

To my parents, Fred and Kay Reed. This story began with you, while I was growing up in Gibbon, Nebraska, and came to fruition under the palm trees of California. Thanks for providing the oasis.

To Sheryl, who gave me courage to write. You were the first reader of *Crossroads*. Your encouragement helped me press on to finish this project and has given me the confidence to share it with others.

To Cindy, my prayer warrior and accountability partner. You are my cheerleader, who challenges me to never settle for anything less than God's best. Thank you!

To Marty, my husband and friend for over twenty-five years. Your support and kindness have been instrumental. Thank you for helping me cross off "bucket-list" items. I couldn't do it without you!

To my daughters, Jess and Sam. Your lives are testaments to God's faithfulness to our family. You both are loved with an everlasting love!

To my T. P. M. buddies: Kristi, Pam, Kerri, Kim, and Rebecca. God has healed us and set us free. Thanks for being a part of my transformation.

Above all, thank you to my glorious God and Savior, Jesus Christ. You have saved me from myself and set my feet upon your path. May your message of love continue to set captives free.

# Chapter 1

# FRANK

Frank DeMotto sat in his brown suede La-Z-Boy rocker-recliner. It was well worn and dilapidated from years of use. His body imprint was molded forever into the cushions. As he sat rocking, a slow, creaking noise escaped from the decrepit chair. The dilapidated rocker reminded Frank of his own frame: tired, worn-out, and creaking with old age.

Frank stared out of the dirt-streaked sliding door of his apartment at the Santa Clara Mountains. They loomed majestically on the horizon, like a huge blanket covering the valley with its darkness.

Apartment 105 of The Haven retirement home had been his residence for the past two months. His little, one-bed-one-bath apartment felt like a prison to Frank. The white walls and tan carpet were sterile; no décor adorned the walls, except for a lone photo of a beautiful woman nailed onto the wall next to the door. The woman had been his wife. Her long, blond hair was pulled back into a high ponytail. Her eyes sparkled with joy, and her smile was breathtaking. Frank couldn't help but smile each time he looked at that photograph. It was the only bright spot in this whole dump.

Like most things in life, he despised this place. He was a practical man and had no interest in making this place feel homey.

He had all he needed: a television to help him pass the time, his comfortable chair, and a table to hold his newspapers.

Several days' worth of dirty coffee mugs and cereal bowls filled the small kitchen sink. The smell of sour milk clung in the air from some half-empty glasses that sat atop the kitchen counter. Stacks of old newspapers from the past month, stacked like mini skyscrapers, were perched precariously on the oak coffee table in the middle of the room. Unopened mail was tossed carelessly across a small, rectangular dining table that was wedged against the wall in the galley-style kitchen. Apartment 105 was as unkempt as the man who resided in it.

As Frank sat alone, staring out his patio door, the sound of the Fox News channel blared from his television. The light from the television reflected off the patio glass, and Frank caught a glimpse of his reflection. His tired, sunken eyes stared back at him. With a sigh, Frank closed his eyes, trying to escape his reality. Slowly, his mind wandered into his storehouse of memories—and back to happier days.

## Summer of the Tree House (1948)

"Frankie!" His mother's voice rang through the chill of the summer evening. "Where are you, son?" she groaned.

Eight-year-old Frankie sat cross-legged in his fort, atop the mighty oak tree that stood alone in the vacant lot behind his neighborhood. It was his most prized possession. He had built it with his very own hands. Of course, he'd had a bit of help from good old Mr. Druthers, the kind widower who lived across the street. This tree house was the one place he could escape to and be free.

Frankie was an only child, and both his parents spent the majority of their day at work. DeMotto Delivery occupied his father's every waking hour. Stan DeMotto delivered cattle and hogs throughout the Midwest. He owned his own rig and took pride in being his own boss. He rose early in the morning and worked late into the night.

"Ain't nobody gonna get these bills paid if that truck sits in the driveway," he said almost daily to his wife.

Sometimes Stan made deliveries to Colorado or Kansas City. Then he would be gone for several days. Frankie liked it the most when his dad wasn't around, because Stan was always tired and crabby when he was home. The policy "children should be seen and not heard" ruled the home whenever his father was present.

Frankie's mother worked as a secretary at the local dentist's office. She would leave for the office as soon as Frankie stepped onto the school bus, and she would return home just in time to start making the evening meal. He really didn't mind being home alone. Most afternoons, Frankie would come home to the quiet house and head straight to the television set. He loved to watch *Howdy Doody* each day after school.

However, now he had his tree house. This was his paradise. It was only here that he could be as loud and silly as he desired. He loved to spend hours here, enacting imaginary pirate battles or alien invasions. He also had a treasure trove of special items he kept hidden in the cigar box he'd found discarded in their trash can.

Frankie hopped down the ladder and called out, "Coming, Mom," so she wouldn't be worried. He scampered across the field toward the glow of lights from the windows of his home.

\*\*\*\*\*\*\*

The tree house project had begun a few months earlier. One day when Frankie was walking home from school, he saw a construction crew dump a pile of unwanted two-by-fours, nails, and wires in the vacant lot by his house. The idea of a tree house exploded in his brain, and he ran as fast as he could the rest of the block—until he stumbled into Mr. Druthers's open garage.

Mr. D., as Frankie endearingly called him, was a project man. Since his wife had passed a few years earlier, Mr. D. spent a lot of his time tinkering in his garage. He was in his late fifties. His usual attire was bib overalls and a white T-shirt. Mr. D. wore tan work boots that were often unlaced. When Frankie asked Mr. D. why he never tied his shoes, he laughed and said, "When you get my age, son, bending over isn't as easy as it used to be."

Unlike Frankie's father, who had a full head of wild, unkempt hair, Mr. D. was bald, and his head often glistened with sweat. Unlike the scowl imprinted on his grumpy, tired father's face, Mr. D. always wore a warm smile, which seemed to invite a hello from any passerby. His periwinkle eyes twinkled with mischief, and that is what Frankie loved most about him. Mr. D.'s favorite hobby was building birdhouses for his backyard garden. Several times in the past few months, he had even invited Frankie over to help him construct these projects.

Frankie's own father was rarely present because he worked twenty-four/seven. Other than to sleep or grab a late dinner, Frankie rarely caught sight of his father. Hanging out with Mr. D. gave Frankie some much-loved "man time." He delighted in spending his free time with Mr. D., and today was no exception.

Gasping for breath, Frankie sped into the open garage. Mr. D. was hunched over his latest birdhouse masterpiece. Hearing gasps, Mr. D. stopped hammering and looked over his shoulder. "Frankie, my boy. What can I do you for?" he asked tenderly.

"I got myself a great idea, Mr. D." Frankie continued to gasp for air as the words tumbled out of his mouth. "You know that open lot by our houses?"

Mr. D. nodded in acknowledgment.

"Well, a construction crew just dumped some junk back there by the big oak tree, and I was thinking it would be a perfect place to build a tree house!"

Mr. Druthers stood up and brushed off the sawdust that clung to his bib overalls. He carried over his hammer and handed it to Frankie. "I think you might be needing this, huh?" he asked, with a twinkle of mischief in his eyes.

Frankie grabbed the hammer and took it in his right hand. Then, with delight, he grabbed Mr. D.'s soft, leathery, wrinkled hand with his left. "Come on! Follow me. You've got to see this!" Frankie began to tug on Mr. Druthers. They headed out of the garage and toward the vacant lot.

The vacant lot was the only space left unoccupied on their block. Waist-high weeds covered the space, and a lone oak tree stood at the far end of the space. The neighborhood children loved to come there to fly kites, play ball, or play hide-and-seek. Frankie was the youngest child on the block, and because of that, the other kids treated him like an outcast. The older children called him Frankie the Pest and never let him join in on any of their games. If it weren't for his buddy, Mr. D., Frankie's life would be miserable.

Frankie ran ahead of Mr. D., and when he stood in front of the pile of dumped materials, he looked like a pirate proudly displaying his bounty. He waved his arm at the pile of supplies and said, "Ta da!"

"What do we have here?" Mr. D. asked, more to himself than to Frankie. "Now, I know I've told you a time or two that I used to build houses, right, Frankie?"

"Uh-huh," Frankie said with a nod. "So, what do you think?" he asked Mr. D. excitedly.

"Funny you should ask. Just the other day, I was thinking about how much I miss those bigger projects. My little birdhouses just seem too small these days. What would you say if instead of a measly old birdhouse, you and I build us a tree house?"

Frankie searched the man's face carefully. "You're not just joshing me, are you, Mr. D.? I'm really serious about this."

Mr. D. patted Frankie on the shoulder and said, "So am I, my boy. How about we get started today?"

"You mean it? For real?" Frankie was now jumping up and down.

"Let's head back to my shop and get some plans going. Sound good?"

"You bet!" Frankie squealed with delight. He and Mr. Druthers trotted back to the garage to start on their latest and greatest project.

Mr. D. pulled out a notebook from a drawer on his workbench. He then took a seat on his stool and said to Frankie, "Come on over here, and tell me what you think this tree house should look like."

Frankie quickly pulled up beside Mr. D. and eagerly began to rattle off all he had envisioned. "Well, for starters, I'd like a rope ladder to hang from a trapdoor. Then I could yank it up whenever I was in the tree house. That way I wouldn't have anyone else pestering me when I was up playing." Frankie thought about all the bullies in the neighborhood, and he didn't want to be bothered by anyone.

"Check," Mr. D. replied. "I think that's a great idea. Consider it done. Next?"

"Well," said Frankie, "I was thinkin' a peephole in a doorway would be nice so I could keep an eye on anyone who might be trying to sneak up on me."

"Interesting idea," Mr. D. commented. "How would you feel about a cut-out window on a trapdoor on the floor of your tree house? Would that work for you?"

"That's a great idea, Mr. D. I love it!" Frankie squealed with excitement. A wide smile spread across his face.

"I was thinkin' I might like to have a roof or something covering me in case it started to rain."

"How about if we drape a tarp over top of your fort and then secure it with some nails? I think that would keep out the rain."

"Sounds good to me, Mr. D."

With each description, Mr. D. sketched. When Frankie's list was complete, his voice became silent. He sat in wide-eyed anticipation. He could hardly wait for Mr. D. to make the last stroke with his pencil. Finally, Mr. D. turned over the pad for Frankie's inspection.

'*Wow!* That's it! That's exactly what I'm talking about, Mr. D.!" Frankie jumped up and gave the man a bear hug. "Can we really do it?" he asked as he looked up tentatively for his reply.

"I believe we can, my boy. All we need is the right equipment."

Then Mr. D. began a list of supplies they would need for their new project. Ten minutes later, the two piled into the black Chevy pickup and headed to the local lumberyard.

Frankie marveled at Mr. D.'s precision and wisdom as he inspected each item before placing it into their cart. After spending around twenty minutes strolling up and down the aisles, they headed toward the checkout counter. Suddenly, Frankie's mood fell. It was as if someone had flipped the off switch on his once beaming face. Frankie's shoulders slumped, and his eyes bore a hole into the floor.

"Is something eating you, Frankie?" Mr. D. asked gently.

With tears brimming on his lower eyelids, Frankie timidly met Mr. D.'s gaze and whispered, "I ain't got no money to pay for all this stuff."

Tenderly, and with a sweet smile on his face, Mr. D. gazed into Frankie's eyes. "I see," he responded. "Well, here's a proposition for you: how about if I be the contractor of this here construction project?"

"What's a contractor?" Frankie asked curiously.

"It means I'm the boss. I get to buy the material and hire my help. And I'd like to start by hiring you." Mr. D. stuck his hand out in front of the little boy. "All I need from you is a shake that says you'll give me your word to show up, work hard, and be on time."

Frankie shot his entire arm straight out and proudly said, "You bet, Mr. D. I'm your man! You got a deal!" A smile spread across the little boy's face, exposing his two missing front teeth.

This was the beginning of a very special partnership.

*******

Little Frankie was good on his word. From the moment he woke up, he had his mind set on nothing else but their tree house project. On the weekends, he would jump out of bed, throw on his bib overalls and tennis shoes, gulp a quick bowl of cereal, and then run across the street to Mr. D.'s garage. On school days, he would run as fast as he could from the bus stop to the garage.

Today was no exception. It was Saturday morning, and Frankie's mother was sitting at the kitchen table, drinking a cup of coffee. As usual, his dad was already out the door, driving his latest load of cattle to Omaha. His mother sipped on her cup of coffee while she glanced over the morning newspaper. Her hair was still up in rollers underneath her hairnet; her pale pink, terry cloth robe hung loosely over her thin frame. A lit cigarette was held in her delicate fingers, which were adorned by a bright red polish. To Frankie, his mom was the prettiest woman on the block. She always wore a skirt and pumps to work, and she prided herself on her well-manicured hands. She was a petite woman.

She reminded Frankie of his grandma's fine china, which was used only for special holiday dinners. His mom was also delicate and beautiful.

"Morning, Mom." Frankie kissed his mother on the cheek as he passed her chair on his way into the kitchen. He had managed to buckle only one strap of his bib overalls, so they hung cockeyed on his skinny frame. His bare feet squeaked as he walked across the newly mopped linoleum floor.

"You sure are up awful early for a Saturday morning, aren't you?" she asked as she peered around the edge of her morning paper.

"Me and Mr. D. are working on a new project." Frankie beamed a toothless smile as he spoke. "He's helping me build a tree house in the vacant lot behind the house."

"Well, don't be stirring up any trouble, you hear me?" she replied tersely. Then she took a drag off her cigarette. As she exhaled, the smoke billowed over her head like a dark rain cloud.

"Aw, Mom, you know I never get into trouble when I'm with Mr. D.," he replied, but his mother already had the newspaper back up, and his comment went ignored.

As usual, Frankie felt invisible. He quickly replaced the cereal box, grabbed the milk jug sitting on the counter, and took a big gulp from it.

"Frankie, how many times do I have to tell you to pour that milk in a glass?" his mother scolded.

"Sorry, Mom," Frankie sullenly replied. He quietly headed toward the front door, his shoulders slouched in defeat. *It seems like I can never do anything right around here,* he thought.

His mom sure had a way to be the lead in his balloon. Just a few minutes before, he had jumped out of bed, all excited to work with Mr. D. And now, his mom seemed to burst his bubble.

He quietly closed the front door, as not to get more unwanted attention from his mother, and slowly began to cross the street.

Mr. D.'s garage door was open, and Frankie saw he was already bent over and hammering a board. Suddenly, his excitement returned. He trotted across the street, happily leaving his sorrow behind on his side of the street.

"I'm here, Mr. D. Ready to get to work!" He panted as he jogged into the garage.

Mr. D. stopped hammering. He stood up and stretched his aching back. "Well, my boy, are you ready to tackle our project?" he asked with a grin. "What an efficient worker you are, my boy. That's what I love about you, Frankie—your commitment. You are a fine young man that is true to his word, that's for sure."

Frankie smiled from ear to ear as he received the compliment from Mr. D. How different he was compared to Frankie's parents. All they ever did was let him know what he was doing wrong. They yelled at him for being too loud. They ignored him when he asked them questions or tried to share things about his day. On the other hand, Mr. D. was always encouraging. He was patient and kind. He seemed to enjoy the time he spent with Frankie; his parents seemed to treat him as if he were a nuisance. Spending time with Mr. D. made Frankie feel special.

"You bet, I'm ready to get started, Mr. D." Frankie beamed, and he reached up and took hold of the man's wrinkled and calloused hand. Then the two headed across the backyard, chattering away like squirrels about all they wanted to accomplish. Side by side, they walked to the mighty oak in the vacant lot.

On their first day of the project, Mr. D. had drawn up a blueprint. He showed Frankie how it would serve as their map. He bent over and picked up some two-by-fours and began laying them out on the ground. Then he grabbed his hammer and a nail. He demonstrated to Frankie exactly how and where to connect the pieces so they would be secure. For the next several hours, they took turns hammering nails or retrieving the necessary supplies. The morning flew by.

Several hours later, Mr. D. stood to stretch his throbbing lower back. "Let's take a break, partner," he said. Sweat poured off Frankie's nose, and drops like rain plopped onto the board he was hammering. It was a hot and humid September day.

"I'm tired and ready for a break, too," Frankie replied. His red, sweaty face revealed his exhaustion.

Together, they walked tiredly back to Mr. D.'s house. Frankie headed straight to the restroom to wash up, while Mr. D. set out to make a couple of ham sandwiches. Frankie appeared in the kitchen just as Mr. D. poured some fresh lemonade into glasses filled with ice cubes. He passed Frankie the glass, and the boy gulped the cold drink thirstily. The ice tinkled in the empty glass as Frankie handed it back for a refill.

"Wow, does that ever hit the spot." Frankie sighed with delight.

"There's nothing better on a hot day," Mr. D. agreed. He smiled at the young boy as he eagerly refilled the empty glass. Then he grabbed their sandwiches and placed them on napkins laid out on the kitchen table.

Frankie pulled out a chair for his friend. Mr. D. said, "I sure like your manners, son." Then he took a seat.

"You taught me that, remember?" Frankie replied.

"Well then, I must say, you are a good learner." Mr. D. chuckled.

Frankie plopped into the chair next to him. He waited patiently while Mr. D. bowed his head and offered up a quick prayer. Frankie's family never said any prayers, but he respected Mr. D. and waited quietly as the old man bowed his head and gave thanks to the God he loved. When Mr. D. said, "Amen," Frankie grabbed his sandwich and took a big bite.

"How long do you think it is going to take us to finish?" Frankie asked, with his mouth full of bread and ham.

"If we keep up this pace, I'm sure it will be ready in about a couple of months."

Frankie looked forlorn. "A couple of months? That's forever! What if it snows before we finish?" he asked dejectedly.

"In order to do it well, it takes time, Frankie. A good life lesson to remember is this: things that are important to us are worth the wait," Mr. D. said.

Frankie respected Mr. D. and knew he had never steered him wrong. He shrugged his shoulders as if to say, *Okay, I accept this.*

They both ate their sandwiches while they chatted excitedly about all they had accomplished that day. When there was nothing but crumbs left on their napkins, Mr. D. headed toward the sink with the empty glasses.

"Well then, we'd better not spend anymore time in here." Frankie tugged at Mr. D.'s hand and began to pull him toward the door.

"What a slave driver you are," Mr. D. teased. Then he followed the little boy through the backyard and over to the vacant lot.

By the end of the afternoon, they had not only assembled the frame to the fort but had also hoisted it up into the outstretched branches of the mighty oak, about five feet high, using a rope as a pulley.

Frankie stared up at the skeletal outline of his future fort. "Wow, Mr. D. She's a real beauty!" he said with pride.

"We've only just begun, my boy. But I'd say we're off to a good start."

Tired and sweaty, they stood and restacked their supplies. Then they headed toward home. Day number one of their new project had come to an end.

About six weeks later—after much sweat, aching muscles, and hard work—they stood craning their necks as they gazed at their finished masterpiece. The smell of fresh paint loomed in the fall breeze; silver nails glistened in the sunshine. "Frank's Place" was written in large capital letters in white paint and stretched across the side of the 5′ × 8′ wooden fort. A retractable ladder dangled in the breeze from the open hatch on the floor, which also served as the entrance. A window cut out of the side of the fort was covered with heavy plastic and served as a lookout hole. A blue tarp covered the top of the fort and was secured by heavy-duty staples. It rustled quietly in the breeze.

"We did it!" Frankie exclaimed, awe in his voice.

"We sure did," Mr. D. stated proudly. "Well, what are ya waiting for? Get on up there."

Frankie hopped onto the rope ladder and scampered up without another minute wasted. He disappeared through the open flap of the door. Then he peeked out of the window. He waved enthusiastically at Mr. D., and Mr. D. smiled and waved back.

"Thanks, Mr. D., you're the best! I couldn't have done this without you," Frankie hollered through the floor door.

\*\*\*\*\*\*\*

From that day on, Frankie's free time was spent in his tree house. He spent hours shooting invading pirates, reading his comic books, or sorting his collection of prized possessions. Mr. D. had a talk with the neighborhood children and told them to stay away from Frankie's fort, "Or else." The kids respected Mr. D., so they left the fort alone.

Sometimes at night, Frankie would climb the ladder and lie on his back, gazing up at the stars. On one of those nights, as Frankie lay staring up at the beautiful night sky filled with twinkling stars, he began to think about God. That week he'd gone to vacation Bible school with a friend. He'd enjoyed listening to the stories the kind teacher, Mrs. McGregor, had told them. She was a plump woman, who reminded Frank of his own grandma. She had gray hair and glasses. She always wore a colorful dress and an apron. Something about her smelled like fresh-baked cookies. Her apron was always filled with hard candy that she would generously give to any boy or girl who could correctly recite the Bible verse for the day. She had taught the class about how God created everything. As Frankie stared up at the vast night sky, he remembered the Creation story: how God had placed each star in the sky. Mrs. McGregor had told the children God even created them and knew every hair on their head. She told them about how God was their Father and how much he loved them.

Frankie had never ever heard his own father say, "I love you." He always wanted to hear those words from his dad. Somehow, not hearing them made Frankie wonder if his dad even loved him at all.

As he gazed up at the vast universe twinkling in the summer night sky, it felt as if something in his heart warmed. As Frankie thought more about God and the possibility God knew him and might even love him, Frankie smiled. All of a sudden, Mr. D.'s face came to Frankie's mind. He knew without a doubt that Mr. D. cared deeply for him. He was always kind and patient, and he made Frankie feel special.

Frankie sighed with deep contentment. He inhaled the smells of the crisp night air: fresh-cut grass and wildflowers from the lot below. That night, little Frankie felt like maybe—just maybe— God was smiling back at him.

*******

Smells from the cafeteria brought Frank back to reality. The aroma slapped Frank back into the present time like a cold glass of water. He looked up at the clock on the wall of his room. It read 5:45.

"Time for dinner," Frank mumbled to no one but himself. As usual, he was alone in his room at the assisted living facility. Once again, he was faced with the cold reality of life. The once happy-go-lucky little boy was now a grumpy and lonely old man.

Chapter 2

# MATCHBOX DERBY

Frank grabbed his walker, and with great effort and several grunts, he raised himself to a standing position. Slowly, he shuffled out of his room and headed down the hall, following the scent of the cooked food.

He could hear the clattering of trays, plates, and glasses tinkling with ice. He could hear the hum of voices engaged in friendly banter. Frank despised all of this. If it weren't for his love of food and the rumble from his gut, reminding him of his hunger, he'd be content to stay put in his room.

Since he'd moved into The Haven, Frank had felt like an outcast. Most of the residents had been there quite longer than Frank. He was the new kid on the block, since he'd moved in just three months ago.

Frank was no stranger to living as an outcast. He believed making friends was a huge waste of time. It took too much effort and usually ended up with some sort of pain and anguish. He needed no more of that; he'd been dealt enough pain to last a lifetime.

As usual, Frank shuffled over to the table in the most isolated area of the cafeteria. He plopped down his tray of food and began to devour its contents ravenously. He always started with the item he liked the most. Tonight, it was mashed potatoes with beef gravy. The mixture of the smooth potatoes and salty gravy almost brought a smile to his normally scowling face. Never lifting his gaze from the tray of food on his table, he next attacked the roast beef covered in gravy. Although it was a bit tougher than usual, it sure beat the boxed meal from his freezer. He cut it into large slices and had it gone in no time. He eyed the pile of green peas but pushed them to the corner of his tray with his fork. He wasn't in the mood for anything healthy tonight. Instead, he dropped the fork and grabbed his spoon. He quickly dove the metal spoon into the cup of chocolate pudding. The chocolate tickled his taste buds, and the cool thickness oozed over his tongue, tickling his taste buds with delight. He leaned back into the dining room chair and sighed with contentment. *At least the food is good in here,* Frank thought.

Fifteen minutes later, he was safely back in the sanctuary of his own room. He once again collapsed into his favorite chair and stared out at the black of the evening. He loosened the belt on his trousers due to his full stomach. He reached for the remote control for the television set, but then decided he would rather get lost in his memories. He pushed the recliner down and got comfortable. Once again, Frank closed his eyes to escape to a happier time.

*******

"On your mark, get set, *go!*" Ten-year-old Frankie's heart was thumping with adrenaline. He nervously lifted his hand off his Matchbox derby car immediately at the pop of the starter's pistol.

That fall, he and Mr. D. had undertaken another project: Matchbox derby race-cars. Their latest entry was a sleek, royal blue racer with silver stripes. The number 15—Frankie's lucky number—was emblazoned on the center of the hood. He loved that number, because his Nebraska Cornhusker football hero, Bobby Dempsey, wore it on his jersey.

Frankie had seen the poster advertising the Matchbox derby event one day at school. The cafeteria had a large bulletin board that displayed local events. This one caught his eye, and he wasted no time in making a beeline straight to Mr. D.'s house after school.

"Hey, Mr. D., I've been thinking about a new project for us," Frankie suggested as Mr. D. offered him a cold bottle of Coke from his icebox. "Would you be willing to help me build a Matchbox car? There's going to be a race at the Civic Center next month, and the winner gets a shiny trophy." Frankie offered his best begging eyes as he gazed with excitement to his friend.

"A Matchbox race car, huh?" Mr. D. stroked his stubbly chin hair as he peered at Frank. "Hmm ..."

"Come on, Mr. D.," Frankie begged. "I know you. You can build anything with wood, and I really think this would be fun. Besides, what else do you have to do with your time?" Frankie walked over and gave Mr. D. a playful punch on the arm.

"Humph," snorted the man. "You're right, Frankie. Not much going on around here these days. Building a sleek racing machine would be a challenge, indeed. I do believe I'm up for some new excitement. You got a deal."

"Who-hoo!" Frankie let out a war cry. He then handed Mr. D. his hand-scribbled note listing the race requirements. Mr. D. eyeballed the list and, once again, pulled out his notepad and began to draw. Right in front of Frankie's eyes, he drew an amazing machine. It was sleek and looked swift. "If that runs as quick as it looks on paper, nobody will stand a chance against us," Frankie said excitedly.

For the next two weeks, Frankie stopped off at Mr. D.'s house every night after school. They would work until dinner, and Frankie would run home and eat a quick bite with his mother. Then, around 6:30, he'd go back across the street and they'd work until 8:30, when Frankie had to head home for bed. Mr. D. showed Frankie how to use a wood shaver and trim a block of wood into a shape. Then he showed him how to sand it. Next, they added an axle with wheels, and last, they painted it a royal blue.

On Saturday morning, the day of the race, Frankie woke up extra early. He crawled out of bed, donned his bib overalls and Chuck Taylor high-tops, and padded quietly into the kitchen. As always, his mother was already up. She'd done her morning chores of baking bread and starting the laundry. The fresh aroma of the dough baking in the oven tickled Frankie's nose. The scent made his hungry stomach growl.

His mother had her hands in the sink, washing the bread pans, when he strode into the kitchen, proudly carrying his finished Matchbox car.

"Mom," he said shyly, "today's the day of the big race. Would you like to go with me and Mr. D. to the Civic Center and watch my car's debut?"

His mother didn't turn around. She just kept staring out the kitchen window into the backyard as her hands mechanically washed the pan. "Look at me, Frankie, do I look like I can go play with you? I'm up to my elbows in work around here. Obviously, your father is never here, and if I don't do it, things don't get done." Her voice was bitter and laced with resentment. Then she laughed bitterly. Frankie slowly and sadly turned away and walked out of the kitchen before his mother could see the tears brimming on his eyelids. He clutched his prized racer in his little hands and slowly walked across the street and over to Mr. D.'s house.

Frankie knocked on the front door. "Come on in, my boy," he heard Mr. D. welcome him in.

Frankie turned the knob and entered. The smell of pancakes immediately greeted his nose. He could hear crackle and pop of frying bacon as he neared the kitchen, where his friend was busy preparing breakfast.

"Thought you might want a little breakfast before we head out," Mr. D. offered.

Frankie walked into the kitchen and slumped down at his usual spot. He put his head on the table and looked forlorn. He always felt so welcome in this house. Mr. D. really made him feel loved, something he rarely felt in his own home.

Mr. D. brought over a plate piled with two large golden pancakes. Three crisp slices of bacon were perched on the side of the plate. Squares of melting butter drizzled their way down the edges of the pancakes.

He patted Frankie on the shoulder and said, "Breakfast for champions, son." Frankie lifted his head, and his mouth began to water as he grabbed the maple syrup waiting on the table. "How about a glass of milk to go with that?" Mr. D. asked.

Frankie nodded as he shoveled the first fork full of pancakes into his mouth. Mr. D. delivered a fresh glass of cold milk and sat down across from the boy. He gazed at their creation. The blue and silver car was parked in the middle of the kitchen table. It looked well made; Mr. D. smiled as he inspected the machine.

"We did good, I believe, my boy. I think you may have a winner there."

Frankie smiled for the first time that morning as he gazed first at his car and then at his friend. "Thanks, Mr. D. I couldn't have done it without you."

The race was set to start at 9 a.m. sharp, so the two piled into Mr. D.'s truck and headed to the Civic Center. As they pulled out of the driveway, Frankie sadly looked across the street toward his house. The door and curtains were closed; just like the hearts of his mom and dad.

Sensing the sorrow in the young lad, Mr. D. said, "I'll bet you a Coke that you come home with a new trophy."

Frankie turned toward his friend and said, "You're on." Then they drove down the dirt road, dust flying as they headed toward town. When they arrived at the Civic Center, the cars were already parking a block away. Several young boys and their fathers were walking toward the auditorium, carrying their prized racers.

"Step on it, Mr. D., it looks like we already got a lot of competition. I don't want to be late, you know."

"No worries, son. We've got lots of time. It's only 8:30." But he quickly found the first available opening and pulled his truck to a stop. Frankie almost jumped out of the door before the truck came to a complete stop.

"Are your pants on fire, Frankie?" Mr. D. hollered through the open window. "Wait for me!" Then he, too, jumped out of the truck and jogged around to catch up to Frankie.

As they entered the auditorium, a line of four deep waited to sign in. Frankie recognized a few boys from his school. They all were with what seemed to be their fathers. Frankie sometimes wished his dad was more a part of his life, but he was used to his old man never being around. He raised his head and shot a quick look up to Mr. D., who was standing in front of him. Boy was he glad Mr. D. was there with him. The ache in his heart diminished as he gazed at his old friend. Together, they signed off on the paperwork, and Mr. D. chipped in the ten cents entry fee. The registrar told them to go inside to the gym. A chart would soon be displayed that would show their race time and track.

Frankie followed Mr. D. into the large gymnasium. It smelled like floor wax and dust. The gym buzzed with excitement as boys and dads chatted. Rumbling rubber tires squeaked on the shiny gym floor as boys tried out their racers on practice runs. The room was abuzz with excitement.

At precisely nine o'clock, a large man with a megaphone walked to the balcony of the gym and spoke loudly. He wore a blue ribbon on his shirt; it had the word "Judge" in large gold letters boldly displayed. He picked up a megaphone and shouted, "All racers must report to the west end of the gymnasium. At that time, you will receive your lane assignment and opponent."

A flurry of activity commenced, with boys running toward the west end of the gym. Dads followed in hot pursuit. Frankie followed the pack like a timid, lost, little lamb. Mr. D. stood on the sidelines and watched closely, like a protective shepherd. Soon, a nice man wearing another judging badge walked over to Frankie. Mr. D. saw the man point him toward a piece of butcher paper filled with names and numbers. Frankie smiled and walked over to the gathering crowd of boys.

There he read his name and his assignment. His first race would be in fifteen minutes on track 5. Quickly, he scampered back over to find Mr. D., who was sitting on a folding chair.

"My first race is on track 5 at 9:30," Frankie reported.

Together, they followed the signs posted around the room, until they came to one that read "Track 5." Frankie did not recognize the name of his opponent. Mr. D. gave Frankie some last minute tips, and then said a quick prayer. "Lord, thank you for this day. May Frankie remember that winning isn't the only thing; having fun is. But if it be your will, dear Lord, help number 15 be as fast as the wind."

Frankie gave Mr. D. a quick hug and then headed over to the starting line, carefully carrying his silver blue car. His opponent was about a foot taller than Frankie and looked to be a couple of years older. Immediately, Frankie was intimidated. However, this boy's racer looked big and clumsy compared to Frankie's masterpiece.

The starter went over the rules one more time and then said, "Boys, place your racers on the starting line." Both boys put their cars on the wooden track.

A crowd of a few other competitors, waiting to race next, and their parents gathered around. The judge fired his popgun, and Frankie lifted his clenched grip from his car. It quickly began to descend down the racetrack. At first, the two cars seemed to be going at the same pace, but as the wooden track began to decline to the finish line, Frankie's silver blue bullet began to pick up speed. He began to jump up and down as his car pulled further and further ahead of his opponents. Frankie held his breath as he watched his handcrafted beauty glide effortlessly down the runway. Mr. D. had shown him how to shave off the wood in order to create an aerodynamic design, and his car was whizzing effortlessly. The other boy's heavy block chugged slowly down the track and rolled to a stop five seconds behind Frankie's winner. It seemed like forever, but in reality, it only took about nine seconds for the blue beauty to cross the finish line in first place.

"I won!" Frankie shouted over the applause of the crowd. He searched the crowd and connected eyes with Mr. D., who was also jumping up and down over on the sideline.

The judge handed Frankie his winner from the track, and he ran over to Mr. D. "One down and three more to go," Frankie said with delight.

His next race would be in about a half hour. Mr. D. took his handkerchief from his back pocket and wiped down the blue boxcar. It glistened even more. The morning flew by as Frankie continued to blow his competition away. Finally, at 11:30, it was time for the final race of the day. It was Frankie's number 15 racer against Mike Hamman, one of the big bullies who lived down the street. Mike took delight in tormenting Frankie, and he was the original source of the nickname Frankie the Pest.

"Well, look who I have here." The boy sneered at Frankie. His fat belly and red freckles made Frankie sick to his stomach. "That trophy is as good as mine," the older boy taunted. Several of Mike's classmates had gathered around him, and they began to snicker and mock Frankie.

Just when Frankie felt the hot sting of tears begin to form behind his eyelids, he felt a strong hand rest upon his shoulder. He gazed up and saw Mr. D. give the boys a rather stern look. All of a sudden, the boastful bullies scurried away like scared cats.

"The bigger they are, the harder they fall, my boy. Don't you ever forget that." Mr. D. smiled assuredly at Frankie.

Frankie took a deep breath. Mr. D. patted him on the back, and they walked toward the starting line. The final race was held on track 1, which was on a platform in the center of the gym. The two racers were the stars on the stage for the final showdown of the day.

Mike Hamman was already waiting at the start. He had his black Matchbox car perched and ready to roll. He rolled his brown eyes as Frankie made his way through the crowd and up to the starting position.

A large man with the megaphone stood on a podium and said, "Now we are down to our last two competitors. Congratulations to Frankie DeMotto and his number 15 racer. He will be competing against Mike Hamman and his black beauty."

The crowd clapped for the two finalists. Frankie looked through the crowd and saw Mr. D., smiling with pride. Even though his hands were sweating and his stomach was flopping with nerves, just sensing Mr. D.'s support calmed Frankie. The judge continued, "Boys, it's time for the final race of the day. Place your cars on their marks."

Frankie's hand was shaking as if the earth was quaking underneath his feet. "Why bother," Mike muttered under his breath, just loud enough for Frankie to hear. "You're such a loser. Do you really think you stand a chance?"

Frankie didn't take his eyes off his silver blue champion. His heart pounded, and he felt like it might just leap right out of his chest, but he looked at his car with a calm confidence. Just then, the pistol popped, and Frankie instinctively pulled his grip off his car. He held his breath as he watched the car careen down the track toward the finish line.

The cars started neck and neck. Mike's car was sleek and fast, too. Unlike the other races, this one was as even as could be. First, the blue would lunge ahead, but then the black car would gain speed and take the lead. Back and forth they went, with neither gaining more than a millimeter of a lead. Frankie could hardly stand to look.

Suddenly, with only about a foot of track remaining, Mike's black beauty lost control and flipped off the wooden track. It sailed over the edge and landed on the ground with a thud. Mike bolted toward his dream machine. In shock, he just stood over his wrecked vehicle and watched Frankie's car roll on. Just like that, the race was over. Frankie's number 15 rolled untouched across the finish line as the champion.

Mr. D. ran over and picked Frankie up in his arms. "We did it!" Frankie cheered. "We won!"

The judge proudly presented Frankie with the shiny gold trophy. It was the first time Frankie had ever won anything. The trophy sparkled as the glowing lights of the gymnasium radiated upon it. The crowd clapped their approval as Frankie held the trophy over his head. A smile spread from ear to ear. Mr. D. beamed with joy.

Afterward, Mr. D. drove Frankie home. They placed the gold trophy on the dash of the truck. Both men proudly smiled as they eyed their prized possession.

"Thanks, Mr. D. I couldn't have done this without you." Frankie shyly reached over and patted the man's leg.

"My pleasure, Frankie. My pleasure," Mr. D. replied as he gave Frankie a wink with his right eye. "She sure is a beauty." He handed Frankie the sparkling cup as he parked the truck. "I'll be seeing you tomorrow to mow my yard. Right?"

"You can always count on me, Mr. D.," said Frankie as he exited the pickup. He skipped home, carrying his newly won trophy above his head.

As he skipped, he began to think about this special day. He realized his own parents had rarely been a part of his life, yet Mr. Druthers had always been his faithful companion. Mr. D. was available to provide Frankie a ride where needed, give help on a hard homework assignment, or just hang out and play a card game. Over the past few years, the two had become good buddies. In fact, Frankie spent most of his waking hours at Mr. D.'s house. His parents both worked all the time, and Mr. D. had offered to keep an eye on the boy while they were gone. It was a win-win situation for all of them. Frankie loved spending time with the wise older man, and Mr. Druthers enjoyed the company, too.

Frankie opened the front door. He could hear the radio playing in the kitchen. He gingerly walked in, holding his trophy out in front of him. His mother was sitting at the table, drinking a Coke and reading a magazine. As usual, his father was nowhere in sight. She caught sight of her son and his prize. "Well, well. What do you have there?" she asked.

"My car won, Mom," was all Frankie said. He really wasn't sure how she would react.

His mom stood and walked over to her son. "That's a pretty nice looking trophy you have, Frankie. You must have done good." She patted him on the head and walked out of the room. Frankie just stood there, amazed at her words. It was rare that she ever even acknowledged him. He strode over to the kitchen table and proudly set his trophy right smack in the center. He took a few steps back and gazed in awe at his new trophy.

The next day was Sunday, the only day his mom and dad slept in. He usually had the living room all to himself until about 8:30. As he turned on the television set, a man with solid white hair and a suit popped onto the screen. Frankie paused and listened as the man said, "God promises to meet all our needs." Several people in the crowd nodded.

Frankie's family never attended church. The only time he ever went to church was if a friend would invite him to Sunday school or vacation Bible school. Of course, Mr. D. talked about God and even prayed in front of Frankie. He liked to hear the stories from the Bible. He sometimes caught himself thinking about God, and today was no exception.

As Frankie continued to listen to the gentleman's smooth Southern drawl on the television, the man began to talk about God's love and provision. All of a sudden, something inside of Frankie's heart felt warm and good. Somehow, Frankie DeMotto knew deep within his soul that this man was speaking the truth. God had certainly provided Frankie a lot of things—many of which came through his good buddy, Mr. Druthers. As the man continued speaking, Mr. D.'s kind face came into Frankie's mind. He got up and turned off the television. As he sat back down in the quiet of the living room, Frankie whispered, "Thank you, God, for bringing me Mr. D." And with that, he lurched off the couch and headed to grab a bowl of cereal from the kitchen.

His new trophy sat perched atop the kitchen counter, right where the whole family could see it. A large smile rested upon

Frankie's face. For once in his life, Frankie felt important. Heck, he even felt loved!

*******

"Humph!" Frank scowled at his own reflection in the patio door. "There's no time for such stupid thoughts."

He slowly pulled himself out of his chair and staggered toward his bedroom. Another day was over. A single tear slid down his face as he hobbled into the restroom to brush his teeth. Alone again.

# Chapter 3

# FRIDAY NIGHT LIGHTS

Frank crawled into bed. He glanced over his shoulder at the picture frame sitting on his nightstand. The photograph was taken of Frank and his bride as they exited the church on their wedding day, over fifty years ago. He reached over to the end table and lovingly held the picture close to his eyes. His wife's blond hair was flying in the breeze as they laughed and ran out of the doors of the church. Her beautiful smile radiated the loving spirit that once lived inside her; that was what had captured Frank's heart. He eyed himself in the picture. A handsome black tuxedo that fit his athletic youthful body like a glove adorned his slim figure.

Suddenly, he looked up and caught a glimpse of himself in the mirror of his dresser across from the bed. *What happened to me?* he wondered as he examined his reflection. Staring back at the picture, he saw a happy, fit, thin, young man. As he lifted his eyes once again to the mirror, the wrinkled, unkempt, unshaven, overweight person gazed back mockingly.

He gently replaced the picture frame back on the nightstand. "Good night, my love," he whispered to the frame. Those words had been ending his days since that wedding night. He rolled onto his side, so his back faced the table. *Oh how I miss you, my love. You've been gone way too long.*

Once again, he willed himself to close his eyes and find relief from this hellish reality. Only in his dream world of memories did he find peace, joy, and comfort. He sighed heavily and whispered, "Please let sleep come quickly." The only sound in the room was the whirling sound of the ceiling fan to give him a reply.

*******

"Getting ready to return the kickoff is Stanton's number 15—Frankie DeMotto," the PA announcer spoke over the grandstand. It echoed in the crisp autumn air and ricocheted off the cars parked in the lot outside the stadium.

Frankie, now sixteen, could hear the chant of the cheerleaders and the roar of the crowd as the opposing team kicked the football. His eyes adjusted to the night sky and the glare of the field's lights. He caught a glimpse of the football, spinning end over end, coming directly at him.

Frankie headed straight to the ball and snatched it out of the air. He ignored the players running full speed toward him, intent on tackling him. With confidence, he tucked the football under his right elbow and began to head up the field. His eyes burrowed into the red jerseys worn by his teammates as they attempted to set up his alley of escape.

Carefully, he followed the designed play his team had practiced endlessly. At the ten-yard line, an opponent lunged at Frankie's ankles, but like a cat, he sprung over him with ease.

At the fifteen-yard line, Frankie headed toward the opening on the right side of the field. He followed his blockers along the sideline—twenty-yard line; thirty-yard line. The alley began to close as white shirts from the other team began to attack him like hornets.

Swerving to his left, he avoided another tackler and then he saw an opening. With the speed of a gazelle, Frankie shifted into high gear and picked up his knees to avoid another pursuer.

The fifty-yard line was now in view. Only the kicker remained in his path for a score. With the ball securely tucked into his left elbow, Frankie stuck his right arm out to "stiff arm" his opponent and defend himself from this last obstacle. The kicker's feet got tangled up, and he fell with a thud at Frankie's side. Frankie didn't miss a step and proceeded untouched into his end zone. Holding the ball high in the air, he erupted with delight.

"Touchdown, Stanton High!" the PA announcer shouted with excitement.

The crowd, the cheerleaders, and the Stanton sideline full of players and coaches jumped up and down, celebrating the amazing score.

Frankie's heart thumped wildly with adrenaline; he could hear his breath wheeze in and out. Frankie gazed toward the sideline. There, he saw the most beautiful sight: one of the cheerleaders caught his eye. She was jumping up and down wildly. Her red and white pom-poms clapped with delight. Her blond ponytail was bouncing like a kite tail playing in the breeze. She turned and smiled the most beautiful smile as the crowd stood to their feet, roaring their approval. That smile was mesmerizing. Frankie couldn't take his eyes off her.

Just at that moment, a rush of red jerseys bounded toward him, and his teammates pounced upon him in a dog pile. Then one by one, they got up and trotted off together, with Frankie—their champion—leading the way.

*******

Fresh out of the shower, hair still wet and the smell of soap clinging to him, Frankie stepped into the hallway. It was customary for parents to gather in the hallway following the game. Here, they would replay the game and chat. It was a great way for them to bond with each other and be the first to greet their sons. As usual, Frankie's parents were nowhere to be seen.

But good ol' Mr. Druthers was waiting for him. Win or lose, Mr. D. was always there.

"What a run! What a game!" Mr. D. squealed in delight. "Congratulations, Frankie. You were amazing!" He lovingly patted him on the back.

Several of the other players' parents came over and congratulated Frankie on his stellar game. Shyly, he received their praises, but he always remembered what Mr. D. had taught him: *Frankie, the sign of a great player is that he can win with grace and lose with dignity. Always remember it is the character of the man people remember the most; not the ability he may have on the field. Accept criticism lightly, and do the same with praise. Do not let criticism defeat you, nor the praises inflate your ego. Simply say, "Thank you," when a compliment is given. That's what it's all about, son. Never forget that.*

Frankie had taken Mr. D.'s words to heart, and he remained a man of humility. He earned a reputation at school for being a hard worker and great team player; his peers and adults around him admired Frankie. In spite of all his success as a star football player for Stanton High, Frankie remained shy. It saddened him that his own parents never attended his games. Once again, work ruled their time. They were never present at any of his school activities. And once again, Frankie was so grateful he had his friend, Mr. D., by his side.

It was tradition for Mr. D. and Frankie to stop for burgers after every game. Millie's Diner had the best fast food in town, and this was their regular Friday night pit stop.

Tonight, as they sat in their regular booth, reliving the excitement of the game, Frankie's eye caught sight of a blond ponytail bobbing in a booth across the room.

He began to choke on his greasy goodness as the ponytail turned, and the cute cheerleader with the beautiful smile stared straight at him. Frankie blushed and grabbed his soda to gulp down the lump of beef caught somewhere between his throat and his stomach.

The booth of girls began to giggle. Mr. D.—who rarely missed anything—asked, "Not bad, Frankie. What's her name?" He nodded toward the booth of giggling girls.

Frankie was still regaining his composure from choking, so he simply shrugged his shoulders and then looked intently down at his basket of onion rings.

"Frankie, have I ever steered you wrong?" Mr. D. continued. "If I were you, my boy, I'd certainly find out the girl's name before we leave this place." Then, with a wink, Mr. D. stood and left to pay for their meal at the cash register.

As if on cue from the stage director, the blond cheerleader and her group of friends approached Frankie's booth. Their red, pleated cheer skirts flowed as they walked. With each step, their high ponytails bobbed up and down, like a bobber on a fishing line. Frankie felt like a deer in the headlights of a car. He couldn't move. He just sat frozen as the four girls approached his booth.

"Great game," they said in unison, followed by girlish giggles.

"Thanks," Frankie responded, and he shyly looked down at the empty basket that once contained his food. He'd never been this close or alone with the opposite sex, especially not pretty cheerleaders! He felt like a fish out of water.

"My name is Betsy," the prettiest blond said. "All my friends call me Betts." Each girl then introduced herself, but Frankie's mind was only saying the name Betsy over and over.

After the fourth cheerleader made her introduction, Frankie gulped and replied awkwardly, "Hi, I'm Frank, but everybody calls me Frankie."

"Yeah, we know," they said, again almost in unison. And once again, they all giggled.

Betsey stated, "We cheer for you every Friday night, remember? I even looked up number 15 on the roster to find out your name after the first game of this season. You are quite the player, and I wanted to find out your name."

Frankie blushed. The heat started at his neck, and he could feel it rising rapidly to his face. He felt so warm that he thought he'd start to drop sweat balls onto the booth's table.

Suddenly, Mr. D. appeared at his side. He was like a lifeguard rescuing a drowning victim. "What do you think, Frankie? You done eating that burger, or are you just going to stare it to death?"

Betsy politely spoke to Mr. D. " Hello. We just wanted to stop and say congrats to Frankie on his great game."

"No problem." Mr. D. smiled at the confident young gal.

She looked warmly down at Frankie. He was still blushing and staring at his table. Then she said, "See you Monday at school." Once again, as if on cue, the four girls turned on their white tennis shoes and, with a twirl of their pleated skirts, Betsy Bailey and company departed.

Frankie's eyes followed her every step of the way. He could feel his heart thud, like it might jump right out of his shirt. Mr. Druthers just smiled and shook his head as he watched the smitten boy.

Once outside the diner, Mr. D. finally broke the awkward silence. "So?" he teased.

"So what, exactly?"

"So what do you think of the weather? " Mr. D. joked. "Did you get her name or not?"

"Her name is Betsy. She just congratulated me on my game. That's it. End of story. No big deal!" Even as he spoke her name, Frankie felt his stomach flip.

"Oh really? End of story? Are you crazy? Son, this could be the beginning of a great story." Mr. Druthers gave Frankie a punch on his left shoulder. "Don't blow this one, kid. Girls like her drop by once in a blue moon. Now remember, I never steer you wrong, my boy."

They drove home, laughing and joking about how Frankie was fumbling for words in the presence of the young ladies. "Looks to me like our next project needs to be getting you a date," Mr. D. teased as he pulled his pickup to a stop in his driveway.

Again, Frankie could feel himself blush in embarrassment. "Knock it off, Mr. D.," he replied. "Besides, I think things have changed a little bit since the last time you went out on a date."

"That may be true, my boy, but one thing will always stay the same. And that's called manners and how to treat a lady properly and behave as a gentleman."

Suddenly, Frankie was all ears. He knew his own father would not be having this conversation with him, so Frankie turned in the seat of the truck and looked intently at Mr. Druthers. It was obvious Frankie needed some help when it came to girls. "What would you suggest?" Frankie asked sincerely.

"Rule number 1: treat a girl with respect at all times. That means open every door, let her walk in first, and listen with open ears."

"Okay," Frankie commented. "What else?"

"Rule number 2: never, and I mean never, let your hormones lead the way."

Frankie looked down at the seat uncomfortably. No one had ever talked to him about being intimate with a girl, and he wasn't sure he wanted to have this conversation at all.

Sensing his discomfort, Mr. D. continued, undaunted. "Don't be embarrassed, son. You got to know the facts, so you don't end up hurting yourself or some girl's heart along the way."

Frankie nodded to give Mr. D. the signal to continue.

"Rule number 3: be her friend. Treat her like a friend. Don't get caught up in the whole boy–girl drama. Just be yourself, and be a friend."

Other than Mr. D., Frankie had never had any long-term friends. When he was a child, Frankie was bullied by the boys in the neighborhood, and he became a loner at school. Now that he was in high school and a good athlete, he was respected. His teammates had become his friends.. But since Frankie was so shy, he never accepted an invitation to join the guys for social fun.

Frankie sat, absorbing the information like a sponge soaking up water. Then he looked Mr. D. in the face and said, "I appreciate your input, Mr. D. It sounds to me like you're saying just treat her the way I treat you."

"That would be a great start." Mr. D. chuckled in response.

Frankie reached for the door handle and got out of the truck. He turned and said over his shoulder, "I appreciate your talk and your support, Mr. D. You are the greatest." He smiled as he closed the truck's door.

As he turned to walk across the street in the dark, he began to think about the conversation they had just shared in the pickup. He was glad Mr. D. was so honest and helpful. His own parents rarely even asked him about his life. Sometimes, Frankie felt like they didn't even knew he existed. They were both so caught up in their own jobs and lives they never paid attention to his. His dad was still on the road, driving his deliveries five days out at a time. Neither he nor his mom ever had time with him. When his father was finally home, all he wanted to do was sit mindlessly in front of the television set and drink beer. The more he drank, the meaner and grumpier he got. Frankie had learned early to be invisible around him. He knew that if he were out of sight, he would be out of his dad's mind; it was a good rule to live by as far as his father was concerned.

His mother looked haggard and tired all the time. When she wasn't working at the dentist's office, she had chores around the house. It was obvious his father hardly ever chipped in to help. Frankie did his share of the work by mowing the yard, running to get groceries, and keeping up with the laundry. He didn't have a real relationship with either one of them, but by now, he had accepted that was the way it was. He felt more like their slave than their son.

Frankie entered the front door, and his mom was sitting in a chair in front of the television. She looked her usual tired self. Deep, dark shadows were under her eyes. Her once soft hands looked leathery and dry from doing the chores. It broke Frankie's heart to see his once beautiful mother aging so rapidly.

"So, how'd the game turn out?" she asked.

"We won," Frankie replied. "I even ran one back for a touchdown." He strolled over and sat on the couch.

"That's great, honey," his mom offered. Then she turned her head back to her television program.

Frankie stood, dejected, and walked down the hallway to his room. The lights were off in the back of the house, since his dad was still on one of his trips. He brushed his teeth, changed into his sleeping shorts, and tiredly crawled into his bed.

*I sure wish my parents would come watch a game*, he thought. His parents had never even been to one game. Dad was always off on his latest delivery trip, and mom was either busy at the office or keeping up their home. *I wish my parents took more interest in football. Heck, I wish they took more interest in me.*

Frankie wanted to show them his success. Not only that, but he also wanted to feel loved. *Oh well, at least I have Mr. D.* He exhaled deeply. Then he closed his eyes and drifted off to sleep. That night he dreamed of cheering crowds, bright lights, and a bouncing blond ponytail. Overlooking it all was a big blue moon.

# Chapter 4

# OLIVER HADLEY

Frank hobbled into his small bathroom. It was the beginning of a new day. He splashed some cool water on his face to help bring him to life. He stared at his reflection. Gray stubble formed a film around his face as whiskers poked out like a cactus. Dark circles formed under his eyes from lack of rest, and his skin was ashen from lack of fresh air and sunshine. "Ugh," he groaned. Just the sight of himself started him off in a foul mood.

His mind returned to the dream of Friday night lights and being a star athlete. "How did I ever let myself go and get to this sorry state?" he mumbled to his face in the mirror. He bent back over the sink and splashed more cool water on his face. Then he stood and once again spoke to his reflection. "Snap out of it! There's no time to be feeling sorry for yourself."

He decided to freshen up not only his attitude but also his appearance. He grabbed his shaving cream from the medicine cabinet shelf and began by shaving off his stubble. He then got into the shower and washed himself off. It had been several days since he had showered, and the hot water felt refreshing. It was as if the fresh water was also refreshing his soul.

After soaking in the steamy water for about ten minutes, Frank toweled off and then slowly hobbled over to his dresser. He put on fresh underclothes and grabbed a clean, short-sleeve shirt and a pair of brown pants. He finished by slipping on a pair of tennis shoes. He reviewed himself in the mirror over his dresser.

"Much better," he assessed. "Maybe there is something to that saying, 'You look as good as you feel,'" Frank surmised. "Well, I guess I do feel a bit better now that I've cleaned up." He felt more presentable—physically and emotionally. He grabbed his walker and headed down the hall to the cafeteria. Today, he even admitted he felt a bit lighter on the inside. *Maybe going down memory lane was a good idea,* he thought as he walked.

The aroma of freshly brewed coffee mixed with cooked bacon tickled his nose. His stomach responded with a growl, and he picked up his pace toward the kitchen. With every step, his body ached. This was another thing he daily despised: his dilapidated body. These days, it seemed every joint ached. He felt as creaky as the Tin Man in *The Wonderful Wizard of Oz.* Even thinking about his aches resulted in a headache. By the time he stumbled into the kitchen, his usual scowl was once again plastered on his clean-shaven face.

"Good morning, Frank." One of the servers greeted him with a smile.

"What's good about it?" Frank rudely replied.

She just continued to smile her warmth toward his cold, stone face and handed him a tray.

Frank slid down the serving line, filling his plate with scrambled eggs, wheat toast, and three slices of crisp bacon. He finished off by selecting a glass of orange juice and a cup of coffee. A young man who helped the residents in the cafeteria carried Frank's tray into the sitting area.

In his first months at the residence, Frank had gained the reputation of being a very grumpy old man. The staff had daily bets to see if they could be the one to bring a smile to the old man's sour face. So far, only one person had ever won the pool. His name was Robbie O'Connor.

"Your regular table, Frank?" Robbie asked as he grabbed the old man's tray. Robbie—the "waiter" as Frank called him endearingly—was a high school student who worked part time at The Haven to earn money for college. At age seventeen, the red-headed Irish Catholic boy had a servant's heart. Robbie stood there with a crooked grin on his face as if determined not to move until Frank answered. Frank secretly liked having this goofy redheaded kid help him with his tray. He could tell the kid had a good heart. He was about the only person in this god-forsaken place Frank actually could tolerate.

"You got that correct," Frank responded gruffly as he followed Robbie toward the isolated table for two in the corner of the room. As they approached the table, Frank suddenly realized "his" table was occupied.

"Wait a minute, son." Frank stopped dead in his tracks. "Is that somebody sitting at *my* table?" Frank asked grumpily.

"Yes, Mr. DeMotto." Robbie paused and turned to face Frank. " It's a new resident. He just moved in yesterday. His name is Mr. Hadley."

Before Frank could protest, Robbie turned and kept walking toward the table. He set Frank's tray of food in his usual spot. However, today there was a new twist: this time, his tray sat opposite that of a bald man with silver gray hair on the lower half of his head. This "intruder" was intently reading a newspaper. Frank made a quick observation of him as he continued to hobble slowly to his seat. The stranger was frail, and his bony shoulders stuck out of a tank top. He wore khaki shorts and white tennis shoes. His legs looked well toned, as if he did some type of exercise. His shiny baldhead was covered with sunspots. Frank surmised he must be an outdoor type of guy. Lastly, Frank noticed this man wore spectacles on the edge of his nose to help him read the paper. The thing that caught Frank's eyes the most, however, was the man's mouth. It was turned up in a big smile exposing not only his dentures but, Frank sensed, a kind heart as well.

Frank didn't want any company. He wasn't in the mood for small talk; he felt it was a big waste of time. Even though this gentleman seemed harmless, making small talk just took too much effort, and Frank was not up for it. He frantically scanned the room one last time in search of a vacant table, but it was to no avail.

Robbie could tell Frank was not happy about meeting someone new, so he took the initiative. As he laid down Frank's full tray of food, he spoke to the new resident. "Good morning, Mr. Hadley. I'd like you to meet one of my favorite residents. This is Mr. DeMotto." Robbie grinned warmly as he spoke. His brown eyes twinkled with delight.

Frank now had to make a choice: either sit down with this new person or make a quick exit. The latter would mean he would return hungry to his room. As if his stomach could read his mind, it let out a loud rumble as if it was voting, *Feed me!*

Hesitantly, Frank sidled his walker next to the table and plopped into the open chair in front of his tray. Robbie sensed it was if the old man had surrendered.

"Thanks Robbie," he said to the boy rather sarcastically.

"My pleasure, Mr. DeMotto," Robbie replied with a grin. He turned to go back to the kitchen to help other residents with their trays.

The "intruder" noticed Frank, so he set down his newspaper. With a smile upon his face, he extended his hand and said, "Good morning to you, my breakfast companion. My name is Oliver Hadley. I just moved into this wonderful establishment yesterday."

Oliver's voice was warm and friendly. His blue eyes sparkled with the glee of a merry heart.

Frank, with his crabby, down-turned mouth, ignored Oliver's greeting and simply responded, "Humph!" His eyes never left his tray as he focused on his plate of food in front of him. Without another word, he ravenously began to devour its contents. *The faster I eat, the sooner I can escape,* Frank surmised.

Not allowing Frank's fowl mood to be contagious, Oliver chuckled and returned to reading the sports section of the newspaper. He decided to try another angle to lure Frank into a conversation. "How about them Yankees? Looks like they might win themselves another pennant."

Frank took a loud slurp of his orange juice and then grumpily mumbled, "I hate baseball. Baseball's for wusses."

Once again, Oliver chuckled. Still not deterred, he responded, "I'm really not much of a baseball fan myself. Those darn players make too much money for simply standing around in the dirt. 'Dirty money' is what I call it." He let out a belly laugh that came from deep within his happy heart. Several other diners in close proximity began to smile, because his laugh was so contagious.

Oliver grabbed his napkin and began to wipe his mouth, because a few toast crumbs had escaped his mouth when he laughed.

Frank lifted his eyes, and for the first time since taking his seat, he made eye contact with the happy man sitting across from him. He wondered how anyone could be that happy, especially in this place. But the laughter had an amazing effect: it seemed to break the ice between the two men. It was as if the warmth from Oliver's heart began to thaw the ice surrounding Frank.

"Football. Now that a real man's sport." Frank was surprised the words had escaped from his mouth.

Frank now had Oliver's attention. With eyebrows raised, Oliver laid the used napkin on the table and took the bait. "A football man, eh? Who's your team?"

"College or pros?" Frank shot back with a competitive look.

"Let's start with college," Oliver quipped.

"No doubt about that one," Frank responded. "Got to go with the Big Red: Nebraska Cornhuskers. I was born and raised there, so I've got them in my blood—so to speak," Frank said proudly.

"I see," replied Oliver. "I'm a Notre Dame man myself. Born and raised Catholic, so I guess I kind of got them in my blood … so to speak." Once again, Oliver got a kick out of his own comment, and a chuckle erupted.

Frank just stared at the man in disbelief. *How could anyone be so happy this early? He must be on some mighty good medication!*

Oliver regained his composure. "Well, Frank, there you go. We at least have one thing in common. Looks like football will be our bond over breakfast."

*Bond! Did I hear him correctly?* Frank almost choked on his orange juice as he pondered Oliver's words. The thought of sharing a table on a regular basis had never crossed Frank's mind. He had been perfectly content to sit alone in the corner for these past few months. Frank took one last bite of toast and then angrily threw his napkin onto his empty plate. He slid his chair back disgustedly, grabbed his walker, and without another word, headed toward the door as fast as he could hobble.

Oliver looked like he'd been kicked in the stomach. Disappointment was plastered on his once happy face. "Will I be seeing you in the card room this morning?" he asked.

Frank ignored him and just kept walking. *The card room is another waste of my time,* Frank thought as he walked away hastily.

Oliver watched the slumped-shouldered breakfast companion hobble away as if he were trying to escape a fire. *Well, it looks like I've got a new challenge,* Oliver thought. He smiled as he watched Frank disappear from the dining hall. *You can run, but you aren't going to be able to hide forever.* He picked up the newspaper and returned to reading. As he read, he hummed "Amazing Grace."

Robbie O'Connor had been observing the encounter from across the dining hall. He watched Frank make his quick exit and then turned to view Mr. Hadley's response. Robbie smiled and thought, *Now I've got a partner to help me crack the ice of this cold heart. Frank DeMotto, your grumpiness doesn't stand a chance!* Feeling a bit victorious, he returned to the kitchen to help the next person with a tray of food. The challenge to renovate Frank DeMotto's wounded heart had begun!

When Frank arrived back at apartment 105, he plopped into his cozy chair. He was huffing and puffing from the quick exit he had made from the diner escape. "Ahh," he sighed, "peace and quiet." He instinctively grabbed his remote control and turned to Fox News. His mind was now focused on the gloom and doom of world events. His cheerful breakfast companion was soon forgotten.

*******

It was game day at Stanton High School. This meant the football players wore their jerseys to school. As Frankie loped across the parking lot proudly displaying his number 15 Stanton High jersey, he saw number 68, Jimmy Watson, getting out of his car. Jimmy was an offensive lineman on the team. As Frankie strolled closer, Jimmy waved to him. The boys were classmates, yet they hadn't connected off the football field. Jimmy was outgoing and popular, whereas Frankie was a loner. Frankie was quiet, shy, and very much stuck to himself. Yet, there was something mysterious about Frankie that piqued Jimmy's interest. The two boys contrasted not only in personality but also in physique. Frankie was tall, slim, and wiry; Jimmy was as wide as he was tall: 5'8" and 220 pounds of solid muscle. He wasn't very fast, but he was as strong as a bull and known to open huge holes Frankie could glide through. Jimmy was also the head football coach's son. This would usually be a stigma for a boy in high school. However, all the kids at school liked Jimmy. He was such a happy guy and seemed to make friends quickly due to his easygoing manner. Everywhere he went, people greeted him, and they always received a smile and a, "Hey," in return.

"Hey, Frankie. What's up?" Jimmy asked as Frankie strode toward his car. "I'm already pumped for the big game tonight. I can't wait to open up some holes so you can score!"

Frankie was a man of few words. He simply smiled and said, "That would be great," and kept walking toward the front entrance of the high school.

Jimmy wasn't daunted by the lack of conversation. He broke into stride and joined Frankie by his side as they walked. Jimmy tried a new angle to open up some conversation: "By the way, my dad and I are going to the Husker game tomorrow in Lincoln. We've got an extra ticket. Would you want to join us?"

Frankie froze in his tracks. He had never been to a Nebraska game in person. In fact, Frankie rarely did anything social outside of his time with Mr. Druthers. He absolutely loved to listen to the Husker games on the radio, but he never imagined attending one. Getting tickets was hard, since every home game was sold out way in advance. Plus, he didn't have the kind of money it took to spend on game tickets. Asking his parents for any extra money was certainly out of the question. He quietly pondered all of this as he stood there. Finally, he spoke, " I'd give my right arm to go with you. The only problem is I work on Saturdays, mowing yards in my neighborhood." *Let alone, I can't afford to pay for a ticket.*

"Well, my dad and I have an extra ticket. It would be our treat, so don't worry about paying for the ticket. You'd be our guest." It was as if Jimmy had read Frankie's mind.

"Let me see if I can make it work. Can I let you know tonight at the game? Maybe I can find someone to stand in for me."

"Sure. No problem," Jimmy replied. "I'd better get to class, or my dad will let me have an earful. I'll see you tonight." Jimmy trotted into the school ahead of Frankie. Frankie noticed several people greet him as he passed by. *Jimmy sure is popular,* Frankie thought.

When the final bell rang at 3:15, Frankie grabbed his books and started the half-mile walk home. Since his family couldn't afford to buy him a car, and both parents worked afterschool hours, Frankie walked most days, unless a teammate or Mr. D. offered him a ride. Today, as he headed home, he noticed a younger neighborhood kid named Danny Smith walking ahead of him. Danny lived a couple of houses down from Frankie. He was a frail kid who wore glasses. *The ultimate nerd,* Frankie thought. He knew Danny usually walked home alone, too. This kid reminded Frankie of himself as a little boy: how the neighbor kids used to pick on him and call him Frankie the Pest. Frankie guessed Danny probably endured some teasing, too. This kid had to be about a fifth-grader. His huge knapsack was full of books and engulfed his frail body. *If a strong wind comes up, the kid will blow over,* Frankie thought as he watched the boy walk.

A thought popped into his mind. *Danny would be a great stand-in to mow my yards this Saturday! He lives in my neighborhood, and I bet he could probably use some cash.* Frankie broke into a jog to catch up to the boy.

"Hey Danny," Frankie called out.

The boy tentatively looked around to see who had called out his name. Frankie thought he looked a bit scared and paranoid, as if he had been bullied in the past. Frankie slowed his pace to a walk and strolled up to the startled young man, who just stood frozen as if in fear.

"Are you t-t-talking to me?" the boy stammered. Fear and worry covered his delicate features on his pale face.

"Yeah. Don't worry, kid, I'm not about to hurt you or anything." Frankie smiled as he spoke tenderly to the scared little boy.

Danny's shoulders and face relaxed. "What do you want?" he asked shyly.

"Would you want to earn some extra money this Saturday? I mow a couple of yards in our neighborhood, and I need someone to stand in for me this weekend. Are you interested?"

Danny's eyes lit up. "You're asking me to help you?" he asked. "What exactly would I have to do?" He shifted his heavy knapsack, and the boys continued on their way.

"Can you rake leaves and mow over at Mr. Druthers and Mrs. Franco tomorrow morning? They will each pay you $1 plus a tip—*if* you do a good job."

"Sounds great!" Danny chirped. "Count me in. By the way," Danny continued, "you sure are having a great season. I come to watch your football games, you know. Good luck tonight!" he said with admiration.

Frankie could tell Danny looked up to him. It made him feel special and sort of like a hero. He ruffled Danny on his Husker ball cap and said, "Thanks, Danny. I appreciate that."

The two walked together the rest of the way home and talked about football. When Frankie came to his house, he peeled off and said, "Don't let me down on the yards tomorrow."

Danny smiled. "You can count on me, Frankie. And by the way, don't you let me down in your game tonight. Run as fast as lightning." Then he waved good-bye as Frankie ascended the steps to his front door. Frankie noticed that Danny now had a spring in his step and a smile on his face.

*I guess I had a positive impact on that kid,* Frankie thought. He smiled as he thought of the loneliness of his own childhood. Maybe he'd make an effort to befriend this nerdy, freckle-faced kid. After all, Mr. D. had sure been around in Frankie's time of loneliness.

Frankie turned the knob of the front door. He dropped his book bag behind the sofa and headed straight to the kitchen where the phone hung on the wall by the fridge. With his Saturday commitment now covered by Danny, Frankie had only one hurdle left: to call his mother. He didn't think she would have a problem with him going, since he rarely asked to do anything socially.

He dialed the number of the dental office where she worked as a receptionist. "Doctors Wattle and Jones. How may I help you?" his mother's familiar voice asked on the other end of the line.

"Hey, Mom. Hope you're having a great day," Frankie said cheerfully.

"Hi, Frankie. My day's not going too bad. How about you?"

Frankie spoke enthusiastically. ""Jimmy Watson invited me to join him and his dad for the Husker game in Lincoln tomorrow. His dad is my football coach. They are really good people. Do you care if I go?"

"Don't you have some yards to mow?" she asked.

"I got Danny Smith, the kid who lives down the street, to cover for me. The ticket's free, so it wouldn't cost me anything." Frankie realized he was holding his breath as he waited for his mother's response.

"Well, I can't see why not. It sounds like a fun time to me. I guess you can go."

Frankie exhaled as she gave her approval. "Thanks, Mom," he chirped excitedly.

"No problem, son. Now, you know I'm not supposed to take personal calls at work. I've got to hang up before I get into any trouble." She quickly hung up the phone, and the buzz on the other end signaled the call had been disconnected. Frankie stared at the receiver, disappointed he didn't get to say good-bye to his mom. Nor had she asked him about the big game tonight. Once again, he felt the ache in his heart at the lack of relationship he had with his family.

"Why don't my parents like me?" he had asked Mr. D. a few years ago, when he'd been over raking leaves for his friend.

Mr. D. responded, "Listen, son. Hurting people hurt people. I don't think your parents don't like you. They just seem to have a hard time showing it. When life gets hard, it can harden peoples' hearts. Maybe their hearts have just been roughed up a bit by these tough times."

Frankie listened intently to Mr. D.'s words. What he spoke felt right to Frankie. After that discussion, it helped Frankie accept his family as they were.

Frankie brought his mind back to the present and quickly grabbed an apple off the counter. Today was game day, so he headed to his room to pack his gym bag. He plopped down on his twin bed and closed his eyes. He began to go through the football plays as he lay on his bed.

## Game Time

It was a team tradition to kneel in silence before every game. It had begun three years ago, when Coach Watson took over as the head coach. It was no secret that Coach Watson was a Christian. He was an active member at the Sunset Valley Baptist Church in town. Plus, he and his wife led the Fellowship of Christian Athletes (FCA) at Stanton High. Their son, Jimmy, was also known as a Christian. He served as a leader for the Stanton High FCA group.

Frankie's family didn't go to church, but he enjoyed these moments of silence before each game. He still remembered hearing about God as a little boy; Mr. D. also prayed in front of Frankie, so he knew a little about God.

During this time of silence, Frankie would ask God to watch over him and his teammates; that God would keep them all safe from injury. He loved this time spent on his knees in the locker room before each game. Somehow, it gave him an amazing sense of peace.

Frankie had gained great respect for Coach Watson. As Mr. D. reminded him all the time, "That Coach Watson is a man of good character."

Coach Watson was a big man. He had played college football back in the late forties. He stood about six feet tall and still weighed over two hundred pounds. His buzz haircut was always "high and tight." Although he looked tough on the exterior, he had the heart of a teddy bear. The thing his players loved most about him was that he was firm but fair. His discipline was consistent and his expectations very clear. There certainly were no shenanigans on the field. One of Coach Watson's greatest strengths was that he could motivate anyone with his words of encouragement. Most important to Frankie was the fact Coach Watson really seemed interested in getting to know his players. He would sometimes tape notes of encouragement to their lockers or stand in the hall and talk sports as his students passed between classes. Since he rarely got any attention from his own parents, this was something Frankie enjoyed the most. As far as Frankie was concerned, Coach Watson was well liked by everyone in Stanton.

Frankie's thoughts were interrupted by the booming voice of his coach. "Huddle up, team. Let's head off to victory!" he commanded, like a general ordering his troops.

With that, the flock of red jerseys rushed together, their cleats clacking like tap shoes. They encircled their coach and joined hands up in the air. Coach continued, "On the count of three, let's shout *victory!* One. Two. Three."

And in unison, the team bellowed, "*Victory!*" With the clicking of their cleats ricocheting off the walls, the team trotted out of the locker room and to the football field. Frankie saw number 68 in front of him and jogged to catch up to Jimmy Watson.

"Hey, Jimmy. I can go with you to the game tomorrow!"

"That's great!" Jimmy replied with a huge smile. "We will pick you up at 11 a.m. sharp. You know my dad. Don't be late!" The boys ran out side by side onto the grassy field, like warriors heading to battle.

## The Jersey

Frankie didn't have to wait for his alarm to wake him up. At seven, he was lying in bed, anticipating the day and his first Nebraska Cornhusker football game. He gingerly crawled out of bed, because he felt some new aches and pains as a result of last night's game. He sauntered quietly into the restroom and turned the shower on to hot. The steamy water worked like magic to loosen his stiff muscles.

By 7:45, he was showered and dressed in a T-shirt and jeans. He ran out to the curb and grabbed the local newspaper. When he sat down at the kitchen table to have a bowl of cereal, he turned straight to the sports section. Frankie smiled as he read the front cover of the sports page. His name appeared in large print: "#15 Frankie DeMotto Leads Stanton to Victory," the headline stated.

Frankie had rushed for 105 yards last night, and his team had beat Morse High 24–7. Frankie was thrilled to be having such a stellar season. The only thing that would've made it better was if his parents showed interest. Mom never followed sports, and she worked long hours. Dad was always traveling on some delivery trip, so he was rarely home. Neither of them had ever been to a game; nor did they ever show interest. In the beginning of his football career, his parents' lack of support really left him feeling rejected. Now the sting wasn't so harsh. He was used to their disinterest. *It is what it is,* Frankie thought. *At least I have Mr. D. as my fan club.* Frankie smiled as he thought of the kind man across the street who had never missed a game. Not even the away games.

Just then, the phone rang. Frankie jumped up to get it before it woke anyone. He wondered who in the world would be calling this early.

"Hey my boy. I saw your light on across the street and figured you were up." Mr. D.'s familiar voice rang out on the other end. "Did you see the paper yet? I sure enjoyed reading your name on the front page. Are you giving any autographs yet?" he teased.

"You'll be the first to receive one," Frankie replied, smiling.

Mr. D. continued. "Hey, you've sure got a great day for the Husker game. I hear it's supposed to be about seventy-two degrees. Perfect, wouldn't you say? And by the way, don't forget to wear your red."

Frankie suddenly realized it was a state tradition to attend the home game at Memorial Stadium decked in red—the school color. Frankie's only red gear was his Stanton High jersey, and it was in the laundry. It reeked of sweat and was covered with mud and grass stains from last night's game. Wearing it was definitely not an option.

There was a long, silent pause on the phone. Finally, Mr. Druthers said, "Meet me out front." Then he quickly hung up the phone.

Frankie heard the sudden click, followed by a buzz as the phone went dead. *What the heck is that all about?* Frankie pondered. Curious, he placed the phone back on its cradle and headed outside.

Mr. D. was already halfway to their front yard. "Good morning, Mr. D. What's up?" Frankie asked.

"Well, I took some liberty and got you a surprise. It's a little something in honor of your big day today." He thrust forward a paper sack that had "SEARS" written across it.

"What's this?" Frankie asked, and he peeked inside the bag. Frankie sucked in his breath at what he saw. He immediately recognized the contents of the mystery package. Frankie carefully retrieved an official Nebraska Husker red jersey. Number 15 was emblazoned in white on the back, under the name Jordan. Tommy Jordan was the star quarterback at Nebraska, and he wore number 15. He was one of Frankie's favorite Husker players, and fifteen was still his favorite number.

"Holy smokes!" Frankie exclaimed. "It's great, Mr. D.!" he said excitedly. "You're the greatest." He reached over and gave the man such a huge hug it lifted him off the ground.

"Whoa, son. Don't be throwing your back out on me," he teased. "I hope you have a terrific time. You never know. Someday, I may be reading your name on a Husker jersey." And with a wink, Mr. D. retreated to his house.

Frankie ran back to his room and threw on his new red jersey over a white undershirt. It fit perfectly. He felt like a kid opening his dream gift at Christmas. *I really think this feels like it could be an amazing day!*

## The Game

The Watsons' car pulled up at promptly 10:55 a.m. Frankie was already sitting on the front step, anticipating their arrival. He knew Coach Watson was a punctual man, and he didn't want to disappoint him by being even one second late.

He hopped down the steps and bounded over to their car. Jimmy rolled down the front, passenger-side window and said, "Great shirt! You definitely look ready to cheer the home team on to victory."

Frankie crawled into the backseat behind Jimmy. Coach Watson sat behind the wheel, and off they headed to the big game. The drive to Lincoln took about forty-five minutes, but the time flew by as the boys chatted nonstop, reliving the highlights of the game they played the night before.

As they passed other cars, it seemed to Frankie most of the people were also donned in red. NU bumper stickers reading "Go Big Red!" were attached to windows. People honked and gave the thumbs-up sign as they passed. Frankie was pumped even before the stadium came into view. The atmosphere on game day was already electric with excitement.

Around 12:15, Coach Watson pulled the car into a packed parking lot at the north side of Memorial Stadium. The tailgaters had arrived hours before kick-off to celebrate. The smell of brats cooking on the grill and fresh popcorn filled the air as Frankie stepped out of the car. He could see nothing but a mob of red in every direction he looked. It was mesmerizing.

Coach Watson spoke up, "Follow me boys," and they began walking through the maze of grills, chairs, ticket scalpers, and fans. As they walked, Frankie could hear the cadence of drums. He caught sight of the marching band, parading through the street. The two boys followed Coach Watson to the north gate entrance. In single file, they lined up and handed the man their ticket. They slowly proceeded into the stadium and followed the markers to their seats.

When they entered the stadium, Frankie's mouth fell open. It was massive. The brightly lit scoreboard loomed above the stadium. It was more impressive in person than he ever imagined. In about a half hour, the place would be packed with over thirty thousand screaming, red-clad fans. The emerald green of the turf was painted with crisp white lines and numbers. Players from both teams warmed up on the field. Awestruck, Frankie stopped dead in his tracks.

"Some sight, huh?" Coach Watson asked. All Frankie could do was nod. No words could adequately express how he felt at that moment.

The surge of the crowd pressed them forward, and Frankie continued to follow Coach Watson until they came to their designated seats. They were seated in the north end zone, in the center of the goal posts, about forty-five rows up. It was a perfect view!

Just as Mr. Druthers had predicted, it was a perfect game day. To top it off, Nebraska prevailed over Iowa State, 32–14.

On the way home, Coach Watson chatted with the boys about various plays of the game. The slow trek due to bumper-to-bumper traffic flew by because of their camaraderie. As Coach pulled into Frankie's driveway, his wristwatch read 7:45 p.m. It had been a full and very fun day.

Frankie stepped out of the car and stopped at Coach's open window. He thrust out his hand (just like Mr. Druthers had taught him) and said, "Thanks so much for this great day. I really appreciate it."

Coach Watson exchanged his handshake and looked Frankie in the eye. "Listen, son. I truly believe that if you keep up your hard work, both on and off the field, I may be coming to Lincoln to watch you play in a couple of years."

"Really?" Frankie responded in wonder.

With a nod, Coach rolled up his window, Jimmy gave him a thumbs-up, and they backed out of the driveway.

That night, Frankie wore his red number 15 jersey to bed. He dreamed his name was on the back and that the Memorial Stadium crowd chanted in unison, "Frankie! Frankie! Frankie!"

Chapter 5

# BORN AGAIN

Frank was startled when the phone rang, breaking the silence in apartment 105. *Who'd be calling me,* he pondered. Slowly, he reached over and grabbed the ringing phone sitting on the table next to his chair. "Hello?" Frank spoke gruffly into the receiver.

"So, cards or what?" a man's voice asked.

"Who is this?" Frank asked, even more irritated.

"Your breakfast buddy from this morning. Remember me? Oliver Hadley's the name. We are looking for a fourth player to join us in a game of bridge. Marsha, the recreation coordinator, thought you might be a good candidate."

"I'm not!" Frank shouted into the phone and then slammed the receiver onto its cradle. *What the heck does this guy want from me?* Frank thought. *Everybody always wants something. Nothing comes without some price. Besides, I hate playing cards.*

Frank grabbed his remote control and turned on the television. *I'd rather be here by myself any day.* He kicked back his recliner and positioned himself to take an afternoon nap.

*******

After their adventure to Lincoln, Jimmy Watson and Frankie DeMotto became inseparable. Numbers 68 and 15 became know as Stanton High's "Mutt and Jeff." They were soon best buddies both on and off the football field.

Frankie enjoyed hanging out at the Watsons' home. He and Jimmy enjoyed playing catch in the front yard or a game of one-on-one basketball in the driveway. Sports were the boys' common link. On most weekends, Frankie spent his free time over at Jimmy's house. It was here he felt the loving environment of a Christian family. Frankie soaked this atmosphere up like a dry sponge in water. *I sure wish my own family could be like the Watsons. Their home is so full of life, laughter, and love.*

Tonight was a new adventure for the pair. Jimmy had invited Frankie to an FCA event. All of the Watsons were actively involved with FCA. Coach and his wife, Mary, led the Stanton High group. Jimmy served as a leader. Frankie had agreed to go, but only after Jimmy had assured him several times it would be a great time. Besides, he told him nobody would care if Frankie didn't go to church regularly. "There's no secret handshake or anything," Jimmy assured him with a teasing grin.

The Watson's car pulled up in the DeMotto driveway and honked. Frankie bounded down the steps and opened the backseat door. For the first time, he felt awkward with this family. Coach Watson could sense Frankie's tension, so he broke the ice. "I'm sure glad you could make it, Frankie. I've been hoping you'd join us at FCA one of these nights."

Mary Watson sat in the front passenger seat. She was a pretty brunette. Her slim figure was the opposite of her burly husband and son. She had a delicate physique, yet she ran her family like an admiral in charge of a ship. Both of the Watson men respected her greatly. Mary peeked over her shoulder and smiled reassuringly at Frankie.

"You'll be fine," she assured him. "The event is going to draw a lot of people tonight, Frankie. You won't be the only newcomer. I promise."

Jimmy chimed in next. "Don't sweat it, Frankie. You can be my sidekick. We can be like the Lone Ranger and Tonto," he teased. "Just like on the field, I've got you covered." He smiled his contagious grin.

Frankie trusted these people and knew they would never do anything to harm him. With a deep sigh, he relaxed and settled into the backseat of the car.

All four enjoyed the banter of small talk for the next ten minutes as they drove to the Civic Center. When they arrived, the parking lot was already three-fourths full. "Wow! What a great crowd," Mary exclaimed. "Getting Tommy Jordan to come speak tonight is really packing them in."

"Tommy Jordan?" Frankie piped up from the back seat. "*The* Tommy Jordan—number 15?" he asked excitedly.

"The one and only," beamed Jimmy. "I didn't want to ruin the surprise. That's why I asked you to come tonight. I know you are a big fan of his." Then he slugged Frankie playfully on the arm.

Coach Watson parked the car, and everyone scampered out excitedly. A continual stream of vehicles filed in, trying to secure a parking spot. It looked as if the auditorium was going to be filled to capacity.

"See you after the event," Coach Watson said to Mary, giving her a quick peck on the cheek. He headed to the stage to help with any last minute preparations, since he was the one who had organized the event.

Jimmy, Mary, and Frankie walked into the auditorium. The theater-style seats were beginning to fill up rapidly. The red velvet curtain on the stage was closed, but a podium with a microphone was on the left side. The balcony was brimming with people as the crowd began to pack the auditorium in anticipation of hearing one of their Husker heroes speak.

As they entered the auditorium, Mary handed a man wearing an usher's uniform their three tickets. He glanced at them and quickly escorted Mary, Jimmy, and Frankie to the front row, where a rope with a small sign that stated, "Reserved," was in place. They had been given the best seats in the house, since Coach Watson was the event's organizer. Excitedly, they took their place, leaving one of the seats open so Coach could join them.

Frankie turned and took in the sight. The crowd was buzzing with excitement. The hum of voices sounded like a swarm of locusts on a summer night. Promptly at seven, the lights in the auditorium dimmed. The crowd fell to a hushed silence, while electric anticipation hung in the air. Coach Watson stepped onto the stage and stood behind the podium. He smiled at the crowded auditorium.

"Welcome to our Fellowship of Christian Athlete's event. Tonight, as most of you know, we have a very special guest. Before he comes on stage I'd like to ask one of our Stanton High FCA huddle leaders to open with a prayer."

Betsey Bailey, the incredibly cute cheerleader, stepped out from behind the curtain. Her hair was in its usual ponytail, but she was wearing a red felt skirt, white button-down shirt, and black flats. A red satin ribbon was tied in a tight bow around her ponytail. Her radiant smile made Frankie's heart skip a beat. He couldn't take his eyes off her. She beamed like a heavenly angel as the spotlight radiated upon her.

Betsey stood next to Coach Watson. With a confident, clear voice, she began to speak. "Let us pray." Her voice radiated through the speakers. The crowd fell dead still. "Thank you, Lord, for this night. We come here to celebrate you as our Lord and Savior. We thank you for bringing Tommy Jordan to us safely. Please open his mouth to share what you desire him to say; open our ears to receive your message for us. We love you, Jesus, and thank you for all that you do. Amen."

Several voices from the crowd echoed the word, "Amen," as Betsey walked off the stage, leaving Coach Watson alone at the podium. All of a sudden, the quiet auditorium was rocked into a frenzy of enthusiastic hand clapping as the Nebraska school fight song began blaring through the speakers. Slowly, the red velvet curtains began to open. People rose to their feet and applauded wildly. As the lights hit center stage and the music faded, Frankie could see two black men sitting on stools.

Coach Watson lifted his hands in an attempt to quiet the raucous crowd. One by one, people returned to their seats. He spoke into the microphone. "It is my pleasure to present the UNL running backs coach Jamar Jones. And with him is our current starting quarterback: number 15—Tommy Jordan!"

The music cranked up again, and everyone jumped up to his or her feet, cheering enthusiastically. Frankie gazed intently at the two men at the center of the stage. Coach Jones was wearing a black Husker sweat suit, with a big N in red above his heart. Tommy Jordan was decked out in his red game jersey and gray sweatpants. They stood and waved to their excited fans.

Slowly, the music faded, and the crowd settled back into their seats. Coach Watson handed the microphone to Coach Jones and slipped offstage.

"Hello, Stanton," Jamar Jones boomed. His baritone voice ricocheted throughout the speakers. Once again, the excited crowd erupted in applause and whistles. "Let's hear it for Jesus," Coach Jones continued. The crowd cheered even louder, and some people got to their feet once again. Frankie had never experienced such an exuberant audience outside of a sporting event. He felt like the room was about to explode with the electric-like energy.

Coach Jones continued. "Many of you are familiar with number 15's moves on the field. But tonight, you are going to hear about one of the greatest moves Tommy Jordan ever made in his life: his move to become a follower of Jesus Christ."

Several people seated behind Frankie shouted, "Hallelujah!" and, "Amen brother!" Others just clapped in approval. Coach Jones looked over at Tommy. "Will you tell us about your personal encounter with Jesus Christ?"

Tommy Jordan smiled a gentle, yet confident smile. "You bet, Coach. It would be my pleasure." Then Coach Jones passed him the microphone and returned to his stool on the center of the stage.

By this time, Coach Watson had made his way down to the front row and nestled in between Jimmy and Mary. Frankie glanced over to his right and wished his own mom and dad could be here for this event.

Tommy Jordan walked toward the edge of the stage. As he moved, Frankie regained his focus. He was mesmerized by the quarterback's stature. Tommy stood 6'2" and weighed about 180 pounds. His body was tight, with well-honed muscles. His massive right hand almost swallowed the microphone he held. He looked so strong and confident as he stepped to the edge of the stage. Frankie couldn't take his eyes off his hero. Tommy paused and looked throughout the crowd. Frankie felt as if their eyes locked for a brief moment. Frankie's heart almost skipped a beat, because he was so close to this icon.

"Let me start at the beginning," Tommy spoke, and a smile spread across his face. "I grew up in Kansas City. My momma had ten kids. I was number eight, and I spent most of my growing up time at my grandmamma's house. At the age of ten, I was starting to get into lots of trouble. I was skipping school, vandalizing the neighborhood: just a bunch of no good stuff. By the time I entered junior high, I was failing most of my classes." He paused and cleared his throat. Coach Jones handed him a glass of water, and Tommy took a sip.

He placed the glass on his empty stool and continued. "One day I was goofing around in the front of the school. Me and a couple of my friends were playing football as we waited for the bus. A teacher named Ben Wright was on duty, and he approached me when the bus pulled up."

"'Hey, you are quick. Looks to me you like to play football.'" Ben said to me.

"'You bet I do.' I replied. But I was suspicious of him. Usually when teachers spoke to me, it was because I was in trouble for something."

"'What team do you play on?'" Ben asked me.

"'I don't play on a team mister. I live with my grandmamma, and we ain't got no money to play ball,' I replied, thinking maybe now he would walk away and let me get on the bus."

"'Well, would you want to play if you could?' Ben was being persistent and not letting up."

"I cocked my head and replied, 'Heck ya! But right now I gotta get on this bus, or my grandmamma will have my hide.' He quickly told me his church sponsored local football teams and even offered busing. The only catch was I had to have passing grades in order to play."

"After his spiel, he asked, 'So what do you think? Are you interested?'"

"The lady driving the school bus honked the horn, and I just shrugged my shoulders and ran to the door. Ben told me to go home and talk to my grandmamma about it. I got on the bus, took the front seat, and stared at Mr. Wright as the bus pulled away from the school. All I could think about on that whole ride home was the chance I might actually have to play football on a real team. I could hardly wait to get home and talk to my grand mamma."

"The next day at school, I sped straight into Mr. Wright's classroom. I asked him how I could sign up. From that day on, he became my tutor and helped me get my grades up. Before long, I was running up and down the youth football fields, having the time of my life. At the end of the season, Mr. Wright invited my team to attend his church service. We felt obligated to go, since they had been so nice to sponsor us."

"That Sunday, ten members of our team, plus some of our family members, waited at the ball field, dressed in our Sunday finest. Mr. Wright pulled up in the bus, and we piled in a little bit tentatively. See, we were pretty much the only black faces going to be in attendance at that church. Mr. Wright could tell we were uncomfortable, and he assured us by saying, 'Please folks, just relax. You are with me. I promise, nothing is going to happen to you.'"

"When we pulled into the parking lot of the church a big banner on a white bedsheet was hanging out of a second-story window. On it was painted—in big red letters—'Welcome to the Panthers Football Team.' When we saw the banner, the whole bus broke out in a loud cheer."

"Ben parked right in front of the main door. As we descended, one by one, a crowd of white people, all dressed up in their suits and pretty dresses, lined the path to the door. Every one of them smiled and welcomed us. They even started clapping as we walked by. Some of the white folks even reached out and patted us friendly-like on the back. We felt like celebrities or sports stars. Each of us felt like VIPs walking on the red carpet."

"Mr. Wright led our pack of misfits right up to the front and center of the church. The wooden pews were divided into four sections. The front of the church held a choir loft for around twenty-five people. A large wooden cross was suspended from the ceiling, and the altar with shiny, gold offering plates were displayed in the center of the sanctuary. A podium, where the preacher stood, was on the left side."

"The congregation continued to come in and find their seats. I just sat and took in the whole scene. It was the first time I'd been inside a church. The stained-glass windows were my favorite, and I stared at the bright colors as the light from the bright morning streamed through. It was so beautiful it almost took my breath away."

"Mr. Wright and my grandmamma sat next to me. We were in about the third row from the front. The pastor stood behind his podium. He wore a white robe and a satin sash that was scarlet. It hung around his neck, and the fringe of the sash descended halfway down his robe. I thought he looked mighty important up there."

"I couldn't take my eyes of the preacher. Throughout his message, I felt like he was talking right straight at me. It was like nobody else was in the building. Now I know it was God getting my attention through this man."

"The pastor was talking about how much Jesus loves each of us. He said that God even knows us by name. He talked about how He has a plan for us. At the end of his message, he told us that the Bible is sort of like God's playbook for our lives. He said we wouldn't be able to run the race of life victoriously unless we learned the plays and listened to the coach, who was God."

Tommy paused and walked over to his stool. He took another sip of water, and during this whole time, it was as quiet as a mouse. You could've heard a pin drop in the auditorium.

Tommy continued, "I sat on that pew with my heart pounding out of my chest. With each word the pastor spoke, it was if something inside of me had been lit up. I felt so alive for the first time ever. Then the pastor said if there were any people who wanted to come to the front and give their life over to Jesus Christ, now was the time. I can remember it like it was yesterday. I jumped right up, as if someone had lit a firecracker under my seat. I stepped over Mr. Wright and almost ran to the front of the church. The pastor just looked at me with a warm, sweet smile and held out his hand to me. I took it, and something inside of me felt loved and safe. It was as if I'd found a new home."

"About twelve other people joined me down front. Some were on my team. One was a white-haired old man, and most were girls in their teens. I didn't care if I was a black kid; somehow, I just felt accepted."

"The pastor continued speaking as we knelt down at the altar. 'Romans 10:9–11, 13 (NIV) says it like this: if you confess with your mouth Jesus is Lord and believe in your heart that God raised him from the dead, you will be saved. For it is with your heart that you believe and are justified. And it is with your mouth that you confess and are saved. As the scripture says, "Anyone who trusts in him will never be put to shame … for everyone who calls on the name of the Lord will be saved."'

"Tears were streaming down my twelve-year-old cheeks as I listened to those verses. 'I believe,' I said through my tears."

"Welcome to the family of God dear Ones," the pastor continued.

"All of a sudden, I felt a pair of hands resting on my shoulders. I opened my eyes and turned around to see my grandmamma standing behind me. Fresh tears were rolling down her round, puffy cheeks. I jumped up, and we stood there at the front of the church and embraced in a bear hug."

"Everyone in the congregation stood and applauded as we made our way back to our seats. I knew that something real had just happened and that my life would never be the same again.

My whole life I had always wanted to belong to a family, and this place truly felt like home."

"From that day on, and for the next five years, my grandmamma and I attended church weekly with Mr. Wright. I even got involved in the church youth group and actively participated in FCA at my high school. I'm proud to say I even graduated with a B+ average. Jesus Christ changed my life forever." A wide grin spread across his face as Tommy Jordan returned to his stool and passed the microphone over to Coach Jones. The crowd rose to their feet, applauding this wonderful testimony.

Coach Jones now stood and spoke. "I believe many of you here tonight already have made the decision to know personally Jesus Christ as your Lord and Savior. That's great! But my question is, what about those of you who haven't? May I be bold enough to ask why you haven't?"

Frankie was riveted to his chair. He felt his heart pounding so hard. It seemed like he didn't have an answer for Coach Jones.

Coach Jones continued. "Jesus knows every one of you in this place tonight. The question is, do you know Him? Isaiah 55:6 (NIV) says it like this: 'Seek the Lord while He may be found; call on Him while He is near.'"

Frankie felt perspiration form under his armpits and on the palms of his hands. He sensed something very near, as if a magnetic field was drawing him. It was unexplainable yet, at the same time, very real.

Coach Jones went on. "Why not change that tonight? Make tonight the night you introduce yourself to your Savior. He already knows you, because He made you. He is calling your name. Come to him. Be willing to trust Him. Seek Him, and you will find Him. Call on His name while He is near."

Frankie was now sitting on the edge of his seat. The room was completely still in this special moment.

Coach Jones spoke gently. "All of you wanting to make that step of faith into God's family repeat this prayer after me: Dear Jesus, I confess that I'm a sinner. I'm sorry for all the bad things I've done in my life. Thank you for dying for me and for nailing my sins on the cross. Lord, please forgive me.

I confess you are my Savior and believe you are my Risen Lord. Come live in me now and forever more. Thank you Lord. In Jesus' name, Amen."

Frankie could hear voices echoing the prayer. His was one of the loudest of all. When he opened his eyes after saying those words with utter sincerity, the first person he saw smiling at him was Betsey Bailey. She had been sitting in the wings on the stage the whole time. Frankie blushed as their eyes interlocked across the room. Frankie's heart had never felt this way. He couldn't put it into words, but he knew it was real. *I wonder if this is what love feels like?*

The lights in the auditorium rose, and Frankie noticed Coach Watson had made his way back onto the stage. Once again, he stood behind the podium and spoke. "I want to thank all of you for coming tonight, and especially a big thank you to our two guests."

The crowd rose to their feet and applauded with delight. People began to find their ways to the nearest exit, talking excitedly as they moved. Frankie noticed smiles seemed to be etched over each person's face. Even he wore a smile.

"Well, what did you think of this?" Jimmy asked Frankie. Mary Watson turned to listen to Frankie's response. A smile was on both of their faces as they waited eagerly.

As usual, Frankie was a man of few words. "I enjoyed it," he said simply. But the smile on his face spoke louder than any words he could speak.

Mary gave him a hug and said, "Welcome to the family, Frankie." And Frankie knew exactly what she meant.

That night, Frankie DeMotto's life was forever changed. Just like his football hero, Tommy Jordan, Frankie was now a believer in Jesus Christ.

# Chapter 6
# CHURCH

Frank flipped through the television channels for the tenth time in ten minutes that morning. *There's never anything good to watch on Sunday morning,* he thought. The only programs seemed to be either news, politics, or, of course, some darn church service. "Bah," Frank grumbled as he hit the off button on his remote control.

Just then, there was a knock on his door. Without lifting his tired old body out of his cozy chair, he hollered at top volume, "Who's there?" His crabby tone usually worked to scare away all unwanted visitors.

"It's me. Oliver Hadley," a gentle voice spoke through the wooden door. "Are you going to be joining me for breakfast?" he asked cheerfully.

Before Frank could respond, Oliver spoke again, "Belgian waffles look pretty tasty this morning."

Then Frank heard the creaking of the hallway floorboards as Oliver made his trek toward the cafeteria. "I suppose Belgian waffles wouldn't hurt. It sure beats being hungry in front of this worthless TV," Frank commented out loud to the empty room. This time, he did raise his creaky body, grabbed his walker, and headed to his door.

*******

Following the Tommy Jordan event, Jimmy and Frankie were joined at the hip. They seemed to be inseparable. Frankie even became involved in the Stanton High FCA and regularly attended Sunset Valley Baptist Church with the Watson family. Mr. Druthers even attended whenever Frankie invited him to join them.

Frankie loved hearing the messages about God's love; the purpose God had for His people; and God's mercy, grace, and compassion. He grew very passionate about his newfound faith. He and Jimmy could often be found reading their Bibles in the school cafeteria. Everyone at Stanton High took notice of the two young men, who were bold and passionate about their faith. Some thought they were too religious, and they made fun of the boys. Others had a deep respect, because their lifestyles seemed to match what they professed. Even Frankie's family couldn't help but notice the change.

"Why do you go to church all the time?" his mother asked Frankie one Sunday morning as Frankie was waiting for the Watsons to pick him up for church. As usual, she was smoking her cigarette as she read the morning paper.

"Because I love Jesus, and going to church helps me know Him better," Frankie replied patiently. He was glad his mom at least noticed something about him.

His dad was already parked in front of the TV, watching a news show. "Seems to me you're becoming a Bible thumper, son. I notice you've got your nose in that book an awful lot these days," he commented gruffly. "I don't want my son turning into some religious nut," he warned as he gave Frankie a stern look.

"Don't worry about me, Dad. By the way, you should try reading it, too," Frankie responded calmly. He held out the Bible toward his dad.

"I don't get it," continued his dad. He rolled his eyes and turned his attention back to the show. He held up his hand. "Don't be pushing your stuff on me. You can do your thing, but don't be expecting me to join the bandwagon."

Frankie sadly turned away from his father's rejection. Then he returned his attention to his mother. She was still seated at the kitchen table and had quietly been observing this dialogue with interest. Frankie stood next to her and laid his Bible on the kitchen table. Then he opened it and pointed to the words on the page. He read out loud, "Romans 3:23 (NIV) says, 'None are righteous, no not one.' Basically, that means that every person is a sinner. We are all in need of Jesus Christ to be put back into a right relationship with God. Sin separates us from God. Nothing any man can do, no matter how good it is, can ever fix that space. Only Jesus can make that right, and He did it by dying for us on the cross.'"

"Preach on, Billy Graham," his father jeered from the living room, and he clapped his hands mockingly.

"Oh shut up, Stan," his mother said defensively. She looked up at Frankie with a meek smile. "Whatever. If this makes you happy, son, that's good." His mother had seemed to age in dog years. Her once youthful appearance was replaced with a haggard look. Her eyes were puffy, and dark black circles were imprinted underneath them. Wrinkles from worrying lined her forehead. Her once beautifully coiffed hair was turning gray, and she rarely went to the salon, since they were always tight on money. She picked up the morning paper and began to read about the latest sales at the department store. It was obvious their conversation was over.

Frankie felt so alone in his family. *Nobody gets this. Nobody gets me.* Frankie walked out the front door, feeling dejected and misunderstood. He sat down on the cement step; his heart felt like a deflated balloon. He was sad that his parents were not interested in attending church with him. He'd asked them to come several times, and each time, they had responded something along the lines of, "That's great for you, but we're not interested."

A car horn honked, and Frankie saw Coach Watson, Mary, and Jimmy pull to the curb. He grabbed his Bible and with slumped shoulders, he strolled over to the car.

Coach Watson noticed his dejected demeanor. "Something eating at you, son?" he asked sincerely as Frankie crawled into the backseat.

"I just wish my parents would come with me to church sometime. I want them to know Jesus," Frankie said with deep concern in his voice. The tears were welling up and about to spill out.

The car became unusually silent. Mary Watson turned and gave Frankie a consoling look. She reached across the backseat and gently laid her hand on Frankie's knee. "Frankie, you're not the Holy Spirit." Her words were soft and comforting. "You can love your parents where they are, and pray for them every day. You don't have the ability to draw them to Jesus. Only He can change their hearts. Just pray, son. Your actions will draw them quicker than any of your words can." She patted his knee, gave him a wink, and then turned around.

Jimmy said, "It must be hard, Frankie. I'm sorry."

Frankie was so grateful this family understood. He always felt like an alien from another planet in his own house. "Thanks," he said to Jimmy. Then Mary Watson passed him her white handkerchief, hand-stitched with a heart. Frankie blew his nose, gave a heavy sigh, and they quietly proceeded to church.

Frankie decided to not let his parents' rejection bring him down. It just gave him that much more urgency to pray for the salvation of their souls. He was grateful for the Watsons' and Mr.

D.'s support of his new faith. *A three-stranded chord is not easily broken*, he thought.

Frankie found peace for the first time that morning as they parked the car in the parking lot of Sunset Valley Baptist Church. Being there always refreshed him.

The organ was playing as they entered the sanctuary. Frankie sat in the pew and closed his eyes. Thoughts of his parents prompted him to say a quiet prayer for them. *Lord, thank you for loving my mom and dad even more than I do. Please draw them to know you.*

That morning, as they sang several hymns about God's grace, it was as if a lightning bolt struck him; Frankie realized the best thing he could do for his parents was to love them—pure and simple. That morning, the pastor's message included the comment that "The best example of a changed life is a changed life." Frankie was determined to "let his light shine" at home, and he prayed it would be his actions, more than just his words, that would draw his parents into a relationship with Jesus Christ. *Nothing is impossible with you, Lord*, Frankie prayed that morning in the pew. He believed this would truly take a miracle.

*******

By the time Frank arrived at his cafeteria table, Oliver had already dug into his plate, piled high with Belgian waffles. The syrup oozed off the edge of the plate in a slow drip, drip, drip and gathered in a pool next to his coffee cup.

"Hey there, Frank," Oliver merrily spoke. "Sorry. I would've waited for you had I known for sure you were joining me."

"Don't worry about it," Frank retorted. Robbie sat Frank's tray on the table. Frank plunked down in his seat, and Robbie gave a sly wink to Oliver. Frank grabbed his fork and began to dig into the mound of fluffy goodness.

"Have a pleasant morning, you two," Robbie said as he headed to help another resident carry her tray.

"I told you, the waffles looked pretty good today, huh?" Oliver commented. He looked intently, his eyebrows raised, waiting for Frank to respond. Frank's mouth was stuffed so full all he could do was nod. "Chapel service starts in twenty minutes. While you're out and about, why don't you join me?" Oliver invited. He wore his usual warm smile, and his eyes sparkled.

Frank nearly choked on his waffles. Bits of waffle spewed out of his mouth and nearly hit Oliver in the face. "Do you mean church?" he squawked. His eyes narrowed as he spoke.

Shocked and surprised, Oliver responded quizzically, "Sure, why not?" He had a feeling he may have just stepped on a land mine and was about to be covered in shrapnel from the explosion.

Without the use of his walker, Frank exploded out of his chair. He pounded his fists loudly on the table. The glasses, silverware, and plates trembled with the assault. Oliver Hadley even jumped in his chair from the loud bang!

"*Never*, and I mean *never*, invite me to that stupid service. Is that understood?" Frank screamed, his voice thick with anger.

The entire cafeteria came to a sudden hush as every head turned and stared in the men's direction. The confrontation had not gone unnoticed. Every eye in the dining hall gawked to see what was going on.

Before Oliver even had time to reply, Frank grabbed his walker and stormed out. He left his food uneaten on his plate and his table companion speechless. Oliver sat with mouth open, but words did not escape.

Frank could feel every eye burn a hole through him as he stormed out of the crowded cafeteria. He raced as fast as he could to get back to his room. He felt like the hallway was tipping, because the fast pace was making him huff and puff. By the time he got his door unlocked, his head was spinning from the anger boiling inside. He slammed the door and plunked exhaustedly into his recliner.

Gasping for breath, he shouted to the empty room, "Listen to me, God, *nothing* and *no one* will ever get me back near you. Just leave me alone!"

# Chapter 7

# THE MOVE

For three days, Frank refused to leave his apartment. He called the nurse on staff and asked if his meals could be delivered to his room. He told her he was feeling under the weather. In reality, Frank was avoiding any contact with Oliver. Since his explosion in the cafeteria on Sunday, Frank's blood pressure had gone haywire. Even the thought of their confrontation made his pulse race.

Finally, on Wednesday, Frank heard a soft rap on his door. Assuming it was one of the staff bringing him his breakfast, he hopped up to answer. Standing on the other side, to his surprise, was Oliver. Oliver looked meek, and his usually smiling face was downturned. His twinkling eyes were soft as he stared at Frank with a serious look on his wrinkled, tan face.

"What now?" Frank sighed. He rolled his eyes and leaned heavily on his walker, as if weak from the battle.

"Frank, I'm really sorry about the other day. I'm sorry if I hit a nerve. Listen, I miss you at our table. It's not the same eating by myself. Won't you come back and join me for breakfast?" Oliver spoke sincerely. He searched Frank's face for a sign of a possible treaty.

Frank just stared at the ground by Oliver's feet. As they stood in awkward silence, Oliver suddenly extended his hand. He was holding a *Husker Illustrated* magazine that previewed the upcoming season of the Nebraska football team. "Consider this a peace offering, okay?" He smiled and thrust it under Frank's nose.

Frank observed the gift being offered. Then he looked into Oliver's eyes. In a weak voice he asked, "Why do you care? Why are you being so nice to me? What's the use of it all?"

Oliver sensed there might be a window opening in Frank's self-protective wall, so he took a step inside the door. "What's wrong with two lonely old codgers—like us—finding someone to help pass the time? Listen, Frank, no strings attached. I'm just a people person, and being alone is not an option for me. It would kill me quicker than any disease. I'm just offering an opportunity for us to become buddies who can talk about sports. That's it. Nothing else."

Frank pondered his comment, while Oliver stood patiently next to him. Oliver lowered the magazine and held it next to his side.

Finally, Frank reached out and took the magazine. He lifted his eyes and said quietly, "Okay, I guess I will give you another try under one condition: we don't ever talk about church or religion again. Is that a deal?" Frank looked at him with very serious eyes.

Oliver stuck out his hand. "That's a deal," he responded, and his smile was back. *There must be some deep hurt in this man,* Oliver speculated. *There must be a reason this man is so angry with God.*

"Thanks for the magazine," Frank said, and his voice brought Oliver back to the present. Frank turned and walked to his recliner. "Want to come in?" he asked in a somewhat friendly tone. It was the nicest tone of voice Oliver had ever heard emanate from his lips.

"How about you join me for some biscuits and gravy?" Oliver countered.

Frank hesitated. He wasn't sure if he wanted to go back into the dining room. He hated being the center of attention, and the last time he was in the dining hall, all eyes had been on him.

It was as if Oliver could read his mind. "Don't you worry about other people, Frank. Most of those folks don't even remember their own names, let alone what may have happened a few days ago."

"I guess I got nothing better to do," Frank replied.

"Well, okay then. Let's head down before the food gets cold." Oliver stuck out his arm as if to say, *You lead the way.* Frank put the magazine on the coffee table, grabbed his walker, and hobbled to the door.

Together, the two men slowly walked to the cafeteria already in a heated discussion about which team should be considered the preseason number-one college football team.

"Hey, Frank. I'm glad to see you back," Robbie said as he spied the two men enter the cafeteria line. "I think Mr. Hadley was about to go into the depression ward if you hadn't shown up today," he teased.

"You got that right, and don't you ever do that to me again, Frank," Oliver quipped.

Frank rolled his eyes and grabbed a food tray. Life as Frank knew it seemed to be getting back to normal.

*******

It was Sunday morning, and the Watsons had just dropped Frankie off from church. He bounded up the front steps and threw open the front door. His mom was sitting alone on the living room couch. Frankie immediately realized something was horribly wrong.

The screen door slammed shut and almost rammed into his rear end, since he had stopped dead in his tracks. His mother stood and walked toward him. She placed her hands on his shoulders and looked into his eyes. He could tell from the redness and puffiness of her eyes she had been crying.

"Mom, what's going on?"

"Your dad has decided to leave us." And she broke down, sobbing uncontrollably.

"What?" Frankie sucked in his breath as he said the word.

"He doesn't want to be married to me anymore," she wailed. Her shoulders were shaking, and tears poured from her eyes. "He's found a girlfriend: some waitress at a truck stop in Kansas City. He wants to start a new life with no 'extra baggage' of a kid and a wife."

"He called us 'baggage'?" Frankie asked incredulously, bitterness spewing like venom out of his mouth.

"He's moving out. He's done with us. Throwing the past nineteen years of my life away like it means nothing." Frankie's mother gasped for air.

"When? When is he leaving?" Frankie asked, bewildered.

"He's staying at the motel on the outskirts of town tonight. He said he'd come by in the morning to grab some of his things."

Frankie stood frozen and wide-eyed, like a zombie. He knew his parents weren't together much, but he never in a million years thought they would get a divorce.

"What are we going to do?" Frankie uttered. His throat was so dry he could barely speak. "Did Dad say he wanted to see me?" But Frankie already knew the answer in his heart.

"He just said he'd be back in the morning to get his stuff. You'll be at school, son." She said it without giving him any eye contact. "I'm sorry Frankie. I don't know what else to say."

Frankie stood dumbfounded. *My own father doesn't even want to tell me good-bye?* The thought overwhelmed him. His knees buckled, and he collapsed into a puddle on the floor. With his head in his hands, he began to sob like a baby.

For the first time in ages, his mother came and tenderly laid her hands on his bobbing shoulders. They stood silently as the tears poured out of their eyes.

After a few minutes, Frankie looked up into his mother's face. "What are we going to do, Mom? I'm sure we can't afford to stay here on your salary."

"I'm not sure yet, Frankie. You're right. I can't afford this mortgage on what I make. I've called my parents and talked with them. By tomorrow I'll know more." With that statement, she looked as limp as a rag doll. She slowly made her way to her bedroom and quietly shut the door behind her. Frankie could hear her sobs escape through the closed wooden door. He stared at the door in shock. Fear and disbelief emanated from his tear-filled eyes. All he could think to do was say a prayer. "Help us, Jesus," he pleaded. Then he slowly walked into his room, closed the door, and he, too, began to cry.

*******

"Topeka!" Frankie screamed incredulously. "Are you kidding me, Mom? I'm almost a senior. I can't move and start over in one year. What about football?" Frankie wailed in desperation.

Frankie's mother just stared down at her hands. Since the initial shock of the news of his father leaving, Frankie had spent every waking minute crying out to God in prayer. He had talked to Jimmy, too, asking his best friend to pray hard for his family during this crisis. His mother had barely eaten or slept. As a result, she had deep, dark bags under her red-rimmed eyes.

Frankie hadn't stayed home from school when his dad had come to get his things. His mother thought it would be better if Frankie were at school when Stan came back. "Really, Frankie, it's best if you don't make a scene. You know your Dad can get pretty ugly sometimes. I wouldn't want you to get hurt or anything."

So, Frankie had reluctantly agreed. There would be no good-bye to the man he had known as Dad for the past seventeen years. *He was hardly around here anyway,* Frankie reasoned. *Good-bye and good riddance,* he thought as he left for school that morning.

When Frankie arrived home from school that afternoon, his mother had showered, and moving boxes lined the kitchen and living room. For the most part, it didn't seem like there was much missing. "So, did the bum show up?" Frankie asked bitterly.

"Frank!" his mother replied sternly. "The man is still your father, and even though he may not deserve it, I don't want you bad-mouthing him. Do you understand?"

Frankie looked sheepish and replied, "Yes, ma'am."

"Now, to answer your question, yes he did show up. I walked over and asked Mr. Druthers to be here with me, just in case your dad showed up in a foul mood."

"So, Mr. D. knows too, huh?" Frankie asked. He shifted his weight uncomfortably at the thought of more and more people knowing their family's dirty laundry.

"Your father took the basics, Frankie, his clothes, some paperwork for the business. There really wasn't much he seemed to want to take with him."

"That figures," Frankie said sarcastically.

"Listen, Frankie, I know this is hard." His mother walked over and gave him a hug. She looked into Frankie's eyes and said, "Your father is a cold man and has basically said we're on our own. I'm not counting on any financial support from him. That's why we need to go back and live with my parents. I can work at their store. They are willing to help us get our feet back on the ground. I really don't know of any other option, Frankie." His mother looked away, because it broke her heart to see her only son so distraught.

Frankie just stood in the middle of the room, his hands at his side. He felt like an orphan with no home and no family. It felt as if he'd been punched in the gut. He could barely breathe.

"I'm going outside," he said to his mother and then he turned his back and headed toward the door. The fresh air hit him with a blast, and he inhaled deeply. He took a seat on the front steps and put his head in his hands. He couldn't help it: he started to cry.

Mr. Druthers was working on his latest project in his garage when he spied the young man slumped over on the stoop. He slowly sauntered over across the street. As silent as a mouse, he came up and stood directly in front of Frankie. Gently he touched his shoulder and whispered, "Hey there, Frankie. I'm really sorry, son, that your dad has up and left you."

Frankie heard the tenderness in Mr. D.'s voice and felt his comforting hand rest on his shoulder. All he could do was weep and try to allow the tidal wave of pain to diminish. The two men embraced. Mr. D.'s ministry of silence was enough. A squirrel scampered across the lawn playfully, and it caused Frankie to glance up. As he lifted his head out of his hands, Mr. D. began to pray: "Lord, thank you that you have a plan for this family. Thank you that you will supply them what they need. You are their Provider. Comfort them, and cover them in your peace."

Mr. D.'s words felt like a soothing blanket; they immediately brought comfort. "Thanks, Mr. D., " Frankie sniffled.

Mr. D. grabbed a handkerchief from his back pocket and handed it to Frankie. "I'm not sure how clean it is, my boy, but it's better than the snot running down your face."

Both men began to chuckle, and the heaviness of the mood seemed to lighten.

"God's faithful, Frankie. Just remember He says that He knows the plans He has for us: to give us a future and a hope. It's in Jeremiah 29:11. You just hang onto that promise. Wait and see.

God is going to show up." Mr. D. patted him on the back, stood, and walked across the street.

Frankie remained on the front steps. He watched the slender man with a bit of a humped back slowly stroll across the street. His bib overalls hung loosely on his body. Mr. D. headed straight for the workbench in his garage and continued sanding his latest creation.

Frankie put his head down on his knees and continued to seek God in prayer. After a couple of minutes, he felt the peace permeating his mind. He stood with resolve in his heart and took a deep breath. He knew he needed to honor his mother, because that was one of the Ten Commandments. He also sensed that God wanted him to trust. *What do I have to lose? I'm going to try it your way, God.* Frankie inhaled deeply and headed back into the house to help his mother with dinner.

*******

When Frankie got home from school the next day, the front door was ajar. *That's odd*, Frankie thought. "Mom, are you home?" he asked with alarm. Slowly, he poked his head into the open front door. He could hear familiar voices coming from the kitchen. His shoulders relaxed, and he threw his knapsack onto the floor. His once normal looking family room was now lined with moving boxes. Furniture had been moved against the walls. The room was in disarray, just as was Frankie's life.

He followed the sound of the voices and headed into the kitchen. When he entered the doorway, the voices immediately stopped. Mr. Druthers and his mom were sitting at the kitchen table, opposite each other. A piece of paper lay in front of Mr. D., and a pile of used tissues formed a semicircle in front of his mom.

His mother blew her nose loudly into a fresh tissue and then spoke tiredly, "How was your day, son?"

"Okay," he responded suspiciously. "What exactly is going on here?" He glanced first at his mother and then over to Mr. D. His mom looked exhausted. *She looks ten years older.* Her face was puffy from days of endless crying. Her shoulders were hunched over, like she carried the weight of the world upon her back. Her hair was a greasy mess of tangles. Frankie hadn't seen her clean up in days.

On the other hand, Mr. D. sat in his usual laid back manner. He was wearing his overalls and a fresh, white T-shirt. He smelled like Aqua Velva aftershave; Frankie figured he'd just showered before coming over here.

His mother finally broke the awkward silence. She put down her used tissue and looked directly into Frankie's eyes. Slowly, she said, "Well ... Mr. Druthers has a proposition for us. He's offered to let you stay here with him so you can graduate from Stanton High next spring. This way, you'll be able to play football here your senior year."

Frankie let her words sink in. He didn't know how to respond. His forehead creased with a furrowed brow. "Do you mean not move with you to Topeka?" he asked, confused.

"Listen, Frankie, it breaks my heart to think about separating from my only son, but it breaks my heart more to think you are the one who has to pay such a high price for your dad's selfishness. Why should both of our lives be ruined by him?" she said with a hint of bitterness.

Mr. D. chimed in. "I'm not trying to meddle in your business, Frankie. It's just that when your mom first told me about this bad news, all I could do was think about the potential you have for college money if all goes well for you next year on the football field."

"Yeah," interjected Mom. "Let's face it, Frankie. Without some kind of scholarship money, college is going to be out of the question."

Frankie just stood in the kitchen doorway, stunned.

"Listen," Mr. D. went on warmly, "it would cost you some yard work, a few household chores, keeping up with your grades, and following my house rules. It's all here in the contract." He smiled as he held up the typed sheet of paper lying on the table.

Frankie walked over and sat between the adults. He took the piece of paper from Mr. D. and eyeballed it like a cross-examiner at a trial. In the top margin, the old man had typed in bold letters "HOUSE RULES." Frankie began to read the note:

RULE #1: Frankie must pass all classes with a C average or above.

RULE #2: Frankie will help with household chores: laundry, cleaning his own space, and dishes.

RULE #3: Frankie will mow the yard, rake leaves, and take out the trash.

RULE #4: Frankie will attend the church of his choice on Sunday.

RULE #5: No drinking, no smoking, and no girls.

When Frankie read the fifth rule, he paused and looked up with amusement on his face. He knew Mr. D. was teasing him about the last one. "Come on, Mr. D., are you serious?"

"Just in case, young man. I want to have all our ducks in a row." He winked. "Well, what do you say?" Mr. D. inquired.

Frankie was dumbfounded. "Mom?" was all he could muster. He looked across the table at her face longingly, as if he were trying to read her mind and her heart.

"I've thought about this long and hard, ever since Mr. Druthers shared his idea. His proposition sounds like a win-win to me," his mother replied softly. "Of course, I'll miss you terribly, son, but I know how much you love it in Stanton. I don't want to ruin your life just because mine has been." She stood and walked over to give her son a hug.

Frankie clung to his mother as if he was hanging on for dear life. Rarely was there any physical contact or display of love in his home. They clung to each other tightly, and both sobbed unapologetically.

"Frankie," his mother's soft voice was almost inaudible through her tears, "I just want to say I'm truly sorry for everything." Her entire body shook uncontrollably.

Frankie hugged his mother even harder and whispered, "It's okay, Mom. I forgive you." He kissed her gently on the cheek. The salty taste of her tears remained on his lips as he pulled away. She laid her head on his chest as if she were a small child. Frankie let his mother sob and quietly prayed for God's peace to soothe her as he gently caressed her back.

After about thirty seconds, Mr. Druthers cleared his throat. "Well, do I have a boarder or what?" His eyebrows were raised in excited anticipation.

Frankie lifted his head from his mother's embrace and gazed lovingly into the kind man's eyes. "Please tell me you don't snore and that you know how to cook," Frankie said with a crooked grin. It was the first time in ages he had smiled. He grabbed a pen that was lying on the kitchen counter and put his name on Mr. D.'s handwritten contract.

"I've always wanted your autograph," teased Mr. D. "I'm framing this, since it will be worth some big bucks once you become a famous football star!" The two men shook hands. Then Frankie jumped out of his chair, rushed over to Mr. D.'s side, and swallowed him up in his arms.

"Thanks, Mr. D.," Frankie whispered into the man's ear. "You have no idea what this means to me."

Mrs. DeMotto gazed serenely across the table at the two men embracing. It was the first time in a long time that she felt peace in her heart. She smiled as a tear of gratitude slid down her cheek. *Maybe things will be all right after all.*

# Chapter 8

# CAMP

Frank lay in bed, staring at the ceiling. The ecru color was as pale as his soul: empty, stale, bland, boring. *What's the point of getting up? I have nowhere to go, nothing to do, no one left who even cares that I exist.* Frank rolled over and closed his eyes. The hum of his fan drowned out the noise of his depressing thoughts.

Suddenly, the buzz of his doorbell broke the silence and caused him to jump with a start. His heart raced, and he held his breath. It reminded him of the days of playing hide-and-seek. He lay motionless, waiting.

Finally, he heard a rap on his door. *Who would be knocking on my door?*

"Hey, Frank," Oliver's familiar voice chimed, "don't let the morning get away from you. I don't want you to skip Miss Celia's famous French toast."

*It must be Sunday.* Miss Celia, the weekend cook, always liked to make special breakfasts on Sunday. She was a large black woman, who was raised in the South. She always was humming a hymn and sharing a favorite scripture verse with the residents every Sunday morning. To the best of his ability, Frank avoided any contact with this woman, because Frank was a proclaimed atheist. He didn't want anything to do with religion and avoided being around anyone who felt otherwise.

"Ugh," Frank sighed, "another stupid Sunday." He couldn't decipher one day from the next. The monotony of sitting and staring was endless. Time meant nothing to him except for the inevitable: death.

He heard Oliver rap once more loudly on his apartment door. "It's your loss, Frank," he heard his friend mumble. Then he heard the rustling of feet. *Oliver must have given up and headed to breakfast without me.* Frank didn't care. He hated Sundays. Once again, he closed his eyes and willed himself to try to remember happier times. His mind drifted back to the spring of his junior year.

*******

Mr. Druthers and Frankie would pile into his pickup and head to church every Sunday. Today was no exception as they crawled into the maroon cab. Ever since Frankie had moved in with the old man, they had made Sunset Valley Baptist their church.

This spring morning, the air was amazingly crisp. It had rained the night before. This morning, the birds chirped merrily, crocuses bloomed, and trees budded new leaves. It was a breathtaking day. Springtime was Frankie's favorite season. He smiled contentedly as they drove to church.

Life was certainly good. Frankie had been living across the street for a little more than a month. Mr. D. had made Frankie feel welcome from day one. The old man had freshly painted the spare bedroom a soft beige color. "I just wanted to freshen the place up for you a bit," he'd commented. He took Frankie shopping at JC Penny so he could pick out a new bedspread, sheets, and pillows. He said, "This is your room, son. I want you make it feel like your home." So Frankie did. He found magazine articles with his favorite college players and taped them on the wall. Tommy Jordan was taped directly above the wooden headboard of the double bed. A nightstand with a lamp sat next to his bed, and Frankie's Bible always rested next to the lamp. His leather journal and a pen also sat atop the stand, plus an alarm clock. A dresser and a closet were the only other items in his room. He enjoyed displaying his football memorabilia around the room; newspaper clippings were tacked to a cork bulletin board; his trophy from the Matchbox derby race perched proudly on the top of the dresser. It wasn't much, but it was his own space, and Frankie loved it.

*So this is what a home is supposed to feel like.* Frankie felt more love in this house in this first month than he'd ever felt in seventeen years across the street. Mr. D. didn't make him feel invisible. They shared meals, laughter, and conversation on a daily basis. Instead of watching television alone, now he and Mr. D. enjoyed the shows together. He was so grateful that Mr. D. had opened his home and his heart.

As the pickup came to a halt in the church parking lot, the Watsons pulled in beside them. Coach Watson tapped on the horn, and Mary waved. Jimmy, Bible in hand, jumped out of the backseat almost before the car was in park. "Hey bud," he chirped as merrily as the birds, "let's go find our favorite spot." Frankie joined Jimmy, and they led the processional into the church.

After the service, Mr. Druthers invited the Watsons to join him and Frankie for lunch. "We're heading over to Millie's for a sandwich. Would you like to join us?" he asked.

"Anytime I don't have to cook, I'm game!" Mary said with a smile.

"Sounds good to me," replied Coach.

"Hey, Dad, can I ride in the truck?" asked Jimmy.

"Sure. First one to get there can put our name in for a table."

Millie's was packed as usual. A hostess took Mr. D.'s name and stated, "Probably going to be around ten minutes," and she added their names onto a sheet of paper half-crossed out.

Coach Watson led the group out to the sidewalk, where they could enjoy the fresh air while they waited for their table to open.

Mr. Druthers noticed that Coach Watson seemed to be wearing a smile similar to that of the Cheshire Cat in *Alice's Adventures in Wonderland*. "What's up, Coach? It looks like you're the cat who ate the canary," Mr. Druthers teased.

"Actually, I've got some exciting news," Coach replied. He looked straight into Frankie's eyes. "Paul Jacobs, a recruiter for the Nebraska football team, called me yesterday."

Frankie's eyebrows shot up. Just the mention of his favorite football team drew his attention.

""Mr. Jacobs asked me if Frankie might be a good candidate for the Big Red football recruiting camp this summer." Coach Watson smiled from ear to ear as he reported the exciting news.

"Are you kidding me?" Frankie asked in a voice a wee bit higher in octave. His eyebrows arched in bewilderment.

"It's the truth, Frankie," Coach replied. He pulled a letter out of his suit pocket and handed it to Mr. Druthers. He took out his spectacles and began to peruse the letter.

"Me? Really?" Frankie asked incredulously as he peeked over Mr. D.'s shoulder, trying to get a glimpse of the contents of the page.

"That's exciting!" Mary chimed in as she clapped her hands in glee.

"Yahoo!" Jimmy squealed. "That's great news!" He pounded his best friend on the back to congratulate him.

Coach Watson continued. "Let's face it, Frankie. You raced over a thousand yards last season as a junior. That caught a lot of people's attention. Plus, you serve as a double threat. You are not only a running back but a great punt returner as well."

"You've got that right," Mr. D. interjected, his head bobbing up and down in acknowledgment as he read. He paused and then looked over at Frankie like a proud papa.

Coach Watson went on. "Paul Jacobs has extended the invitation for you to attend this July. What do you say?" He paused and stared at the pair reading the letter.

Frankie stopped reading and looked anxiously at his coach. "How much is this going to cost?" he asked, nervously. "I don't exactly have a lot of extra money." Frankie swiveled his head between Coach and Mr. D. as he waited for a response.

"That is not an issue," said Mr. Druthers. "The question, Frankie, is do you want to attend this camp?" He looked him square in the eyes.

Without any hesitation, Frankie shouted, "You bet I do!"

"Then consider it done!" said Mr. D., and he clapped his hands as if he were a judge banging his gavel to say, "This case is closed."

A waitress stuck her head out of the diner door and hollered "Table for five available for Druthers."

"Perfect timing," Mary Watson responded, and she held up her hand. She led the way into Millie's.

When they arrived at their table, water glasses were already in place. They scooted into the curved booth, and as they settled in, Jimmy said, "Let's have a toast. To Frankie and his football future. May all your dreams come true."

"To Frankie!" they chimed in unison. They raised their glasses and clinked them in celebration. Frankie had never felt so much love and admiration.

*******

That summer, Frankie mowed neighbors' lawns to earn extra money. He would get up every day at 5:30 and be at the school weight room by 6:00. Coach Watson would be waiting for him with the side door unlocked. Frankie would stumble in, out of breath, while Coach would be bent over his open Bible, a cup of steaming hot coffee sitting on his desk.

Jimmy joined the routine and served as Frankie's lifting partner. Together, the two boys would lift weights, run laps around the track, and toss the football. After a couple of hours, Frankie would jog back to Mr. D.'s, who would have breakfast cooking. They'd sit at the table and share a hot breakfast and conversation. Then Frankie would head out the door, towing the mower. He mowed about every yard in the two-block radius of their neighborhood—nine yards in all. Frankie's days were so packed that by bedtime, he could hardly wait to hit the pillow.

Mr. D. helped Frankie establish a bank account, since he had a steady income. They went to the Exchange Bank of Stanton and deposited Frankie's checks. Frankie learned to divide his money into 10 percent savings, 10 percent tithing to church, and the rest into a checking account. Mr. D. was a frugal man, and Frankie soon learned how to be a wise spender. *Another great piece of wisdom I'm taking away from this man.*

By mid-July, Frankie was in the best shape of his life. The night before he was to depart for the Big Red camp, Frankie spent the night over at the Watsons. As he and Jimmy were playing a game of hoops in their driveway, Jimmy asked, "What's it feel like to be going as a player to Memorial Stadium tomorrow?"

"Like a dream. I still can't believe it's real," Frankie replied.

"You've earned it, Frankie. Don't you ever doubt that!" Jimmy drove the basketball in for a layup.

That night, Frankie could hardly close his eyes. He was so excited about what tomorrow would bring at the football camp he barely got any sleep. At 7:30 a.m., Coach Watson and Jimmy dropped Frankie off at Mr. D.'s. As they pulled away, Jimmy gave Frankie the thumbs-up, and Coach tooted a "good luck" blast on his horn. "Give 'em all you got, Frankie!" Coach encouraged as he drove away.

Frankie had packed his gear the night before, so he ran into his bedroom and grabbed the bulging duffel bag, while Mr. D. waited by the truck. When Frankie bounded down the stoop, Mr. D. handed him a box wrapped in red paper; it had a white bow on the top. A card was taped on the bottom of the package.

"I don't want you opening this until you get to your room in Lincoln. Is that a deal?" Mr. D. said in a serious tone.

"Sure thing, Mr. D. Anything you say." Frankie opened his duffel bag. He carefully laid the package on top of his clothes and closed the bag.

Frankie slung the bag into the bed of the pickup. The two jumped into the cab and started for Lincoln. About an hour later, the truck pulled onto the University of Nebraska campus. The truck slowly rolled down the main drag of the UNL campus. The red brick, two-story buildings sat side by side. They all looked alike—other than a sign on the lawn that stated the name of the residence hall. A large banner hung out of one of the second-story windows: "Welcome football players!"

"I'd say this is the place," Mr. D. quipped as he pulled the pickup into a parking stall. Other athletes and their parents were unloading bags from their vehicles. Frankie didn't recognize any of the other athletes, but he did notice how huge they looked. Large, toned muscles exploded on their arms as boys carried bags toward the residence hall.

"Looks like we're right on time," said Mr. D. "Seems to me those other guys are sizing you up. They see they've got some competition with you stepping on campus." He winked at Frankie.

Frankie smiled a crooked grin at Mr. D. *Thanks for the encouragement.*

Several of the camp's coaches stood at the entrance of the dorm. They were decked out in black sweat suits with a large red

N across the chest. Each coach greeted the parents and players as they entered the building. Wooden tables were set up in the front hallways. They were covered with large packets of paper and organized in alphabetical order. Frankie recognized some current Nebraska football players manning the tables and passing out the information. *How amazing to be in the same building as these players!*

Frankie eyed a sign with a large, black D on it. "Why don't you sit here, while I go over and get checked in?" Frankie pointed to a wooden bench. Mr. D. took Frankie's duffel bag and hobbled over to take a seat.

Frankie joined the line with several other campers. They stood silently as each waited to receive their instructions. *I feel like a little fish in a big pond*, Frankie thought as he sized up other boys in line. Every person there seemed to have huge muscles; they looked like great athletes.

Frankie worked his way to the front of the line and received his packet of information. He turned and walked back to the wooden bench. When Mr. D. saw him approaching, he stood.

"Here." Frankie handed him the packet and bent over and grabbed his knapsack of gear.

Mr. D. quickly scanned the first page. "I see your room assignment, son," he said. "Looks like we need to find a building called Randolph Hall." They headed out of the building and walked across the parking lot. Frankie craned his neck as he searched for the wooden sign signifying Randolph Hall.

"There it is!" Frankie said excitedly, pointing at a building just two down from where they had just exited. They picked up the pace and headed toward Randolph Hall. When they entered the front doors of the dorm, their nostrils were met by the smell of furniture polish. In front of them stood a magnificent stairwell. It glistened with polish as the light shone upon it.

"Wow! This is pretty nice," Frankie admired.

Mr. D. nodded and replied, "We're looking for room 202. My guess is that means your room is on the next floor." Frankie led the way, and they turned to go up the wooden stairs. The duffel bag was growing heavy on his shoulder, and he was ready to drop it. The old, worn stairs creaked with each step they took. As they ascended, Frankie could hear voices of other families discovering their room assignments. He grew more excited with every step.

When they arrived on the second floor, Mr. D. gasped for air. "Slow down, you young thing. I need a minute to catch my breath."

"Sorry," Frankie said sincerely. He put down his bag and caught his breath.

Mr. D. looked once again at the packet and began to read. "Looks like your roommate is named Joey Delgaddo. He's here all the way from New Jersey."

"All the way from Jersey? He must be some kind of player!"

"Frankie, everyone here—including you—are some kind of football player." He patted the boy on the back. "What are we waiting for? Let's go find your room."

"There it is," Frankie stated. He walked toward the open door with the numbers 202 on the frame. Mr. D. followed, huffing and puffing.

When Frankie got to the open doorway, he stopped dead in his tracks, making Mr. D. bump into him. Frankie gawked in amazement. Lying on the twin bed in room 202 was a giant! Joey Delgaddo was massive: 6'4" and 280 pounds. He made the twin bed look like a toddler's. Joey had olive skin and black, curly hair. *With a name like Delgaddo, he sure looks Italian!*

Suddenly aware that someone else was in the room, Joey stood. He dwarfed Frankie and Mr. D. A deep voice with a Jersey accent erupted out of a smiling face. With a hand extended, the young man said, "Hey, welcome to room 202. I'm Joey from Jersey."

Both Mr. D. and Frankie shook his hand. "Nice to meet you," Frankie said. His own hand was swallowed by this young man's mammoth palm.

"Well, boys, it looks like you've got some unpacking to do. Frankie, I'll see you at the end of the week. Knock 'em dead!" He gave Frankie a quick hug and then exited.

Frankie threw his duffel bag on the unoccupied twin bed and began to unload its contents. The gift from Mr. D. was on top, so Frankie extracted it and sat it on the nightstand by his bed. Then he proceeded to unpack his gear.

Joey took a seat on his bed, and they exchanged small talk as Frankie unpacked. When everything was neatly put away, Frankie turned his attention to the unopened gift.

"What do you have there?" Joey asked with interest.

"I'm not sure. I promised I wouldn't open it until I got here," Frankie answered. Joey sat up and leaned on his knees. He was obviously curious about the mystery gift.

Frankie tore off the note with Mr. D.'s handwriting. He read the card to himself:

I thought you'd like to keep track of your adventure. Go get 'em!—Mr. D.

Next to Mr. D.'s handwriting was a different style of penmanship. Frankie recognized his best friend's script. He read on:

Remember, you've earned this! Never doubt! Philippians 4:13 says, "I can do all things with Christ who gives me strength."—Jimmy.

Frankie smiled as he tore off the gift wrap. "This is from my best friends," Frankie told Joey, who stood watching, his eyebrows raised in interest. As Frankie ripped off the red paper, a leather-bound journal was exposed. It was made of black leather and had a large red N sewn in the center of the front cover. He held the gift in his hands and inspected it with gratitude.

"Pretty nifty," Joey commented. "Hey, is that a Bible?"

Frankie had thrown his Bible on the nightstand next to his bed as he had unpacked. Joey eyed Frankie curiously, like a cop about to interrogate a criminal. "Hey, are you a Christian?" he asked.

Still observing his journal, Frankie responded, "You bet," without lifting his eyes.

Joey let out a friendly laugh. This caught Frankie's attention, and he looked up at his large roommate. Joey continued, "I can already tell this is going to be a beautiful friendship." He reached into his own dresser drawer and pulled out a book. He tossed the book across the room. It landed on Frankie's lap with a thud.

Frankie picked up the book and said, smiling, "So you must be a Christian, too?"

"You got that right, DeMotto. Looks like we've be given a Divine appointment—roommates made in heaven!" Both boys laughed at the wonderful grace of God. Joey said, "I think this is the beginning of a beautiful friendship." He slugged his new roomie on the arm.

*******

The week of camp was the most exhausting, thrilling, fun, and demanding week of Frankie's life. The alarm would go off loudly every morning at six. Groggily yet faithfully, Joey and Frankie would turn on the light and start their day by reading a psalm from their Bibles. Each day, they would take turns selecting a scripture verse. Then they would spend a few minutes in prayer, when they would each pray for the coaches at the camp, new friends, and God's protection and provision.

At 6:30, they would head down the hall and hop in the shower. Around 7:00, they would head to the cafeteria to grab a quick breakfast. Position meetings began promptly at 8:00 and ran until lunch.

During each morning session, the position coaches would put the players through a variety of drills. Since Frankie was a running back, they focused on speed, balance, and strength. He learned new ways to explode up the field and ways to carry the ball to avoid fumbling. Frankie was like a sponge, soaking up all the new information. Every athlete at camp was stellar, and they pushed each other to reach new levels of excellence.

Around noon, they would take about an hour lunch break. Then they'd return to the field to work on strength training and skill-work as a whole offensive unit. This was Frankie's favorite part, because he loved to scrimmage. He loved being on the field with Joey, who served as his offensive lineman. Because of his massive physique, Joey could open huge holes. Frankie would ride on his new friend's back and then race up the field, displaying his speed and agility to the coaches. Frankie was having the time of his life.

By the end of the night, every athlete was exhausted from the demanding schedule. Each player would slowly walk—some even limped—into the showers. The day would end with the entire camp eating together in the cafeteria. Most of the time, the meal consisted of beef, potatoes, and vegetables. Frankie had never seen so much food consumed. The offensive and defensive linemen carried two or three plates heaped full of food. Frankie loved to tease Joey about trying to keep it under five thousand calories per meal. Most of the boys' favorite part of dinner was the self-serve ice cream machine. They could top off their meal with a hot fudge sundae covered in nuts. *Now this really is heaven,* Frankie thought as he piled high the ice cream with hot fudge sauce.

Frankie and Joey would always sit together in the cafeteria. They enjoyed discussing their day at camp. "You should've seen Coach McGuire blow some steam when Smith missed his block today," said Joey. "The nerve in his neck was bulging so badly, I thought it was going to pop out!" He snorted as he spoke.

"Sam Smith, from Denver, ran circles around me today," Frankie replied rather dejectedly.

"Don't worry about him, DeMotto. These coaches will be keeping their eyes on every one of us all year. This camp is only the beginning. Keep your head up."

*I'm so glad Joey is so encouraging. He reminds me of a young Mr. D., always helping me look at the glass as half full.* Frankie looked across the table at his new friend and smiled. "Thanks, Joey. I needed to hear that. I tend to be really hard on myself. Maybe tomorrow, if I relax a little, I can perform better."

"Here's my motto, Frankie: Give your best, and give God the rest." A broad grin exposed his tender heart.

"Thanks, Mark Twain," Frankie teased.

After dinner, the boys headed back to their room. Each night, they would collapse with exhaustion onto their tiny beds. But before they closed their eyes, each boy would say a quick prayer. Then Joey would sleepily say, "Good night, DeMotto. Don't let the bedbugs bite." Within minutes, both boys were out cold.

Evening prayer time was Frankie's favorite part of his whole day. Opening his Bible and sharing his heart with his newfound brother in Christ helped him to grow spiritually. He was maturing not only on the football field but also in his new faith. *God, you are so good to me.*

# Chapter 9

# THE FUNERAL

O n Sundays, the cafeteria was unusually quiet at lunch. Most people either had family pick them up for church or for an outing. Therefore, the room was silent as a tomb. Frank and only around seven other residents sat in the massive dining hall. Frank loved Sunday lunch especially for this reason. He also enjoyed Sunday because Miss Celia, the cook, made her special Sunday meals! She cooked specialty menu items all day.

Today as he plodded over to his table, he noticed it was empty. "Where's Mr. Hadley?" he asked Robbie O'Connor.

"I haven't seen him yet, Mr. DeMotto. Maybe chapel service ran long today," he offered. "You know how much he enjoys going to chapel every Sunday."

Frank rolled his eyes. Robbie ignored Frank's rude response and responded with a smile, "Enjoy your meal, Frank. If I see Mr. Hadley, I'll tell him you're here."

Frank plopped down in his seat. Without saying a word to Robbie, he waved his hand as if swishing away an annoying gnat. Robbie shook his head sadly and quietly walked away.

*Ahh … peace and quiet.* Frank picked up the thick Sunday newspaper and sighed in contentment. As he dug into his first bite, he glanced over the first page. *My body may be failing me, but at least my eyes still work well.*

He began to survey the typical "gloom and doom" on the front page. Suddenly, one picture jumped off the page and grabbed his full attention. It was a picture of several high school students, huddled in a circle with their arms wrapped around each other. The headline above the picture read, "Local High School Mourns Loss of Student Killed by a Drunk Driver."

Frank dropped his fork, because his hand began to shake uncontrollably. The clatter of the fork hitting onto the floor caused several diners to turn their heads and look his way. Next, Frank dropped the paper as if it were a red-hot coal. His throat felt constricted, as if he were gasping for air. The room began to close in on him. It felt as though his heart had exploded, and he grabbed his chest. Suddenly, the room went dark, and Frank collapsed onto the floor.

*******

It was the last day of the Husker football camp, and as was customary, it was the day of the award ceremony. Family members and friends had driven to Memorial Stadium not only to pick up their camper but also to attend the event. At this time, the outstanding campers would be recognized. Players and parents alike waited in excited anticipation.

The campers were assembled on the grassy field. Lounging casually, they sat on the freshly cut grass and talked nonstop to their new friends. Now that camp was over, they relaxed. The mood of the day was light and fun; casual conversation, laughter, and reminiscing about the week's activities filled the air.

The boys wore red and white T-shirts that had BIG RED CAMP emblazoned in capital letters across their middle. Gray shorts and tennis shoes completed the campers' attire. It was a hot, July afternoon, and Frankie was grateful they were dressed so casually.

The coaches were seated in folding chairs lined up on a small platform set upon the fifty-yard line of the football field. Parents and friends of the players sat in the bleachers that lined the field. A festive mood emanated over the stadium.

Frankie searched the crowd. Finally, his eyes found Mr. Druthers. He was seated in the front row of one of the stands. Next to him sat a large woman with a head full of curly black hair. As Frankie continued inspecting them, he noticed something familiar about the woman's smile. Suddenly, Frankie smiled as if he was a detective solving the latest mystery. *That has to be Mrs. Delgaddo, Joey's mother.*

As Frankie continued to spy, he noticed that the two adults seemed to be enjoying each other's company This woman was laughing out loud at something Mr. D. had said. "Hey, Joey," Frankie nudged his friend with his elbow.

"Yeah," Joey replied. "What's up?"

Frankie pointed toward Mr. D. "Is that your mom over there? With the black, curly hair and wearing that blue sundress?"

Joey squinted because of the bright sunshine and peered in the direction Frankie was pointing. Finally, he stood up and yelled, "Hey, Mom!" in his booming baritone voice and Jersey drawl.

The woman in the blue sundress immediately recognized her son's voice and quickly jumped to her feet. "Joey!" she squealed in delight. She waved her arms frantically, like a survivor on a desert island trying to attract a rescue plane.

"Yep, I'd say that's your mom," Frankie said with a hint of laughter.

Joey waved back enthusiastically. "We Delgaddos are Italian. What else would you expect, DeMotto? We are not known for our subtlety."

Coach Ramos, the special teams coach, stood behind the microphone on the podium and said, "Welcome to the Big Red

Camp awards ceremony." Everyone settled down, and the buzz of conversation came to a close. Joey took his seat on the field next to his friend.

Coach Ramos continued. "Today, we are going to celebrate the completion of this week's camp. I must say that this camp was filled with many excellent young men who possess great talent." The crowd clapped and cheered in acknowledgment. "Today, we are going to begin by awarding the Teamwork Award. This award is the only one that goes to two people. Throughout the week, coaches watched our athletes on and off the field. This award represents the two young men who displayed an outstanding ability to work with others. Our winners this year bonded like brothers; in fact, they were inseparable. Together, they encouraged each other to excel daily. They were leaders and positive role models to their peers. Their hard work ethic, respect for the coaches, and friendliness toward their fellow campers was exemplary. Today, I'd like to present our Teamwork Award to Joey Delgaddo and Frankie DeMotto. Gentlemen, will you please come forward to receive your awards."

Stunned, Frankie just stared at Joey in shock. Joey jumped to his feet, reached down, and yanked his friend up with a single pull. The spectators laughed at the sight. "Don't be shy, Frankie. You're my wingman." Joey beamed his bright smile at his friend. Together, the two boys made their way to the front. Joey strutted like a proud peacock and Frankie like a shy little lamb.

Mrs. Delgaddo stood and shouted, "Whooo hoo!" Mr. Druthers stood, too, and the crowd joined them by clapping.

By the time Frankie and Joey reached the platform, the rest of the campers were also on their feet and clapping. Frankie smiled sheepishly, and Joey beamed with glee.

"Great job men," Coach Ramos said as he handed each boy a trophy.

Joey held it proudly above his head, like a gladiator exhibiting his victory wreath. In contrast, Frankie received the trophy and held it to his side. Then he humbly shook the coach's hand and said, "Thank you, sir," just like Mr. D. had taught him.

The boys returned to their spot on the field, carrying their trophies proudly. The rest of the awards ceremony lasted about thirty minutes. When the last award was given, the players were excused to meet up with their families. Mr. D. and Mrs. Delgaddo had already made their way onto the field by the time Frankie and Joey had said their good-byes to their new friends.

"Well, I see you found my mom," Joey said to Mr. D.

"When I saw her, I thought you might belong to her, so I went up and introduced myself. I told her Joey Delgaddo was my Frankie's roommate."

Mrs. Delgaddo wrapped her massive arms around her son and kissed him on the cheek. "I told Mr. Druthers that sure enough, you were my boy. From that point on, Mr. Druthers and I have enjoyed each other's company. I really have talked his ear off."

"Imagine that." Joey beamed as he looked down lovingly at his mother.

*I wish my mom and I had a relationship like that,* Frankie thought.

"Well, I'm sorry to break up this merry union, but we have a plane to catch," Mrs. Delgaddo said. "It's time for us to get back to Jersey, son."

Joey unlocked his grip on his mother and strolled over to Frankie. "It's been a pleasure, my friend." He held the trophy above his head. "Couldn't have done this without you," he said. Then he laid the trophy next to his mom and wrapped his arms around Frankie. He picked him up in a bear hug, and Frankie's feet dangled in the air. He felt like a rag doll in the boy's massive grasp.

"Seriously, Joey, you're squeezing me to death," Frankie teased.

"Hope our paths cross again, my friend." Joey extended his hand to Frankie.

As they shook hands, Frankie thought, *Maybe someday we will be teammates.*" God be with you, my friend. Have a great senior year."

Mr. D. and Mrs. Delgaddo bid adieus. The crowd from the field had dispersed, and each camper and his family headed toward their awaiting vehicle. As they walked, Frankie said, "Thanks for coming to get me, Mr. D."

"I wouldn't have missed it for the world, " he smiled reassuringly. He lovingly put his arm on Frankie's shoulder. "I'm so proud of you. You really must have worked hard this week."

Frankie spent the next hour in the car, reliving his camp experience. Mr. D. listened intently as Frankie recounted stories about his new friends and all the things he'd learned. The trip back to Stanton flew by, and before Frankie could believe it, they were pulling up to the house.

"It's sure been too quiet without you here, " Mr. D. said. "I'm really glad to have you back."

"It's good to be home. I can't wait to sleep in my double bed tonight. That twin bed was just way too small."

As soon as the pickup rolled to a stop in the driveway, Frankie exploded out of the truck and ran up the steps. He headed straight for the kitchen and scooped up the telephone. Excitedly, his fingers dialed the number to the Watsons' home. After ten rings, Frankie disappointedly hung up. Just as he did, Mr. D. entered the kitchen, carrying Frankie's duffel bag. "Let me guess," he said. "Trying to call Jimbo?"

"You got it," beamed Frankie. He was still feeling like he was on walking on Cloud 9 because of his fantastic camp experience.

He couldn't wait to share it with his best buddy and his coach. *If it weren't for them, I wouldn't have even gone to that camp!*

"Well, the Watsons are in Branson. They decided to head up to the lake for a quick getaway before the rush of football season crashes upon them," Mr. D. replied.

A look of disappointment quickly flashed upon Frankie's face. "Oh well. I'm glad they got a chance to go fishing." He bent down and grabbed his duffel bag.

Heading out of the kitchen and toward his room, he stopped and called over his shoulder, "By the way, Mr. D., thanks for the journal. Joey and I had some great conversations, and I got to put down several meaningful scriptures. I really appreciate it."

"My pleasure, my boy," Mr. D. responded as he poured himself a glass of iced tea. He looked up and gave Frankie a loving wink.

About twenty minutes later, the phone rang. Frankie exploded out of his room like a sprinter at the start of a race. He yelled, "I got it Mr. D! Maybe it's the Watsons!"

Anticipating his friend's voice on the other end, Frankie picked up the phone and said, "So did you catch any fish yet?"

He was met by silence.

"Hello? Is anybody there?" Frankie asked. Suddenly, his stomach churned. *Something's wrong.*

"Frankie," a somewhat familiar voice replied. But the voice was shaky and thick with emotion. "This is Coach Watson. We've been in a terrible accident. I'm calling from the Springfield Hospital." There was a pause, and Frankie held his breath as he waited for more information.

"We are waiting to hear from a doctor. Jimmy was taken by ambulance from the scene of the wreck. A large semi crossed the median and hit us dead-on. Jimmy was driving the car, and he took the impact." His voice trailed off. Frankie could hear him weeping on the other end of the phone.

Coach took a deep breath and regained his composure. "Please pray for us. I will keep you posted as soon as I hear anything." Then the phone clicked, and the disconnect buzz radiated through the line. Frankie stood frozen in the kitchen, holding the buzzing receiver in his hand.

Mr. D. entered the kitchen and saw the boy holding the phone speechless. Frankie's face was ashen, and a look of shock was plastered upon his once beaming face. "What's the matter, son?" he asked gently.

With trembling hands, Frankie placed the phone back into the cradle. He felt like a giant hand was on his throat, choking the life out of him. He could hardly breathe, let alone speak. He walked over to the kitchen table and collapsed onto the chair. He laid his head on the table and spoke toward the floor, "That was Coach Watson on the phone. They've been in a car wreck. Jimmy's in the emergency room at the Springfield Hospital."

Mr. D. walked over to Frankie and tenderly laid a hand upon his shoulder. Then he began to pray out loud. "Lord. Be with the Watson family. They need you to be their Rock and Refuge in this mighty storm. Be with the doctors as they presently work on Jimmy. Help guide their hands and give them wisdom. Thank you, that you, Lord, are our perfect peace. Through all of this, may we feel you near, providing comfort as we need it, strength as we need it, and above all, peace to trust in your sovereign plan."

As Mr. D. prayed, his words were like a soothing balm over the fear and worry eating away at Frankie's mind. Peace began to wrap around him like a warm blanket. "Thanks Mr. D.," he murmured as he lifted his head.

"Hey, we're in this together, my boy." He patted the boy's shoulder reassuringly.

*******

Around 5:30 p.m. the phone's shrill ring brought Mr. D. scampering across the room. "Hello," he said. "I see … I'm so sorry, Mark. Is there anything we can do?" Mr. D. grabbed the notepad and pen next to the phone and began to write.

Frankie walked into the room. He couldn't clearly hear the voice on the other end of the phone, but he had a good guess it was Coach Watson. He focused on Mr. D.'s body language. It spoke loudly and clearly that whatever was being said was probably bad news.

"Consider it done, Mark. Call me day or night as you need. We are here for you."

Mr. D. put down the phone and slowly turned to meet Frankie's gaze. "Oh, Frankie, I'm so sorry. I don't know exactly what to say or how to say it, so I'll come right out with the truth. Jimmy didn't make it."

"What?" Frankie yelled. "You mean he's dead?" The words reverberated in the quiet house like a shotgun blast.

"I'm so sorry, son."

But Mr. D.'s soothing voice could not penetrate the wall of shock encasing Frankie's mind. Frankie ignored his sympathy and bolted out the door. The front door slammed with a bang.

Mr. D. walked over to the large window in the living room. He watched as Frankie sprinted down the street. He prayed, "Lord, meet this boy's needs. You are close to the brokenhearted. Comfort him, Lord, and help him find peace in the midst of this storm." A tear slid down his wrinkled face as he watched the silhouette of Frankie disappear over the hill.

*******

Frankie ran as fast as his legs would pump. He felt if he ran fast enough, maybe the bad news couldn't catch up to him. Finally, his body was spent in exhaustion. He bent over, and the sweat poured off his entire body. It was a typical hot and humid July evening, and the explosive exercise made him gasp for air.

He huffed and puffed, his body bent over and his hands upon his knees. Suddenly, his mind began to clear. He stood and realized he'd been running straight for the high school. The red locker room door glistened in the setting rays of the sun directly in front of him. Frankie began to sob. Just staring at the school brought back many memories of spending time there with his best friend: Jimmy. The tidal wave of emotions surging through his mind made him bend over again as grief overwhelmed him like a tsunami.

As Frankie thought about the past twelve hours, he was amazed at the roller-coaster events of the day: the super high of coming home from football camp and now to the ultra low of losing his best friend. He stood and yelled at the top of his lungs, "Why, God?"

The only response was the constant buzz of the locusts, humming their summer song.

*******

July 20, 1955, looked like any normal summer morning in Stanton. The sun crept slowly up over the eastern part of town and displayed its dawn splendor of oranges, golds, and pinks. Birds chirped as they welcomed the new day. Frankie lay in bed, listening to the familiar song of the morning glory birds. This usually brought him a sense of delight for a new day. But today, he felt sick. He was nauseated, and his head throbbed. *I feel like I have a bad case of the flu.*

Frankie reached over to grab the water sitting on his nightstand. He took a long, hard drink and then grabbed a tissue. He blew his nose, or at least tried, as his sinuses were clogged from all his crying. *I feel so overwhelmed and exhausted.*

He slowly got up and walked over to his bedroom window. He opened the window to allow some fresh air into his stale room. As the fresh breeze entered, he opened his mouth like a hungry baby bird, hoping the air would revive him. *Will this pain ever go away?* With a heavy sigh, he headed toward the shower.

As he turned from the window, his gaze fell on his red, number 15, Stanton High football jersey, which was lying on top of his dresser. He closed his eyes, wishing it was all just a bad dream. But when he reopened them, it was still there. Today was not game day. It was Jimmy's funeral. Frankie and the entire team would wear their red jerseys and sit together to honor their fallen comrade.

Frankie turned the shower on to cold and stared into the mirror. Dark circles, which seemed hollow and lifeless, encircled his sunken eyes. Jimmy, his best friend, was gone forever. Frankie felt as if part of his own life had died. As he stepped into the icy cold water streaming out of the showerhead, he said, "Help me, God." Then he closed his eyes as the sharp sting of the cold water pounded his skin.

\*\*\*\*\*\*\*

An eerie silence blanketed the entire town as Frankie and Mr. D. drove to the church. Neither spoke. They just sat in their own pain-filled silence. Neither could muster the words to speak. They just drove and stared aimlessly out the front window.

As they pulled into the parking lot, Frankie recognized other teammates and their parents. Slowly and somberly, each person crept toward the front door of the church. No one spoke. Most people looked down at the ground. It felt like each step weighed one thousand pounds. It took all of Frankie's energy to focus on getting into the building. The local mortician, Mr. McFee, was the first person to greet them as they made their way into the foyer of the church. He pointed to a connecting hall off the front corridor. He spoke to Mr. D. "The family is in that room. They'd like you to join them."

Out of the corner of Frankie's eye, he saw the main hallway of the church. It was completely full of floral arrangements, and the aroma of fresh flowers hung in the air. On the far wall, amid all of the beauty, was a stark contrast: a black casket. Inside lay the body of his dead friend.

"Do you want to go over?" Mr. D. asked Frankie as he followed Frankie's gaze to the casket.

Frankie was unsure. He'd never been to a funeral before. He'd never seen a real dead body. He'd only seen them in the movies. He didn't know what to do or what to expect, so he just shrugged.

Mr. D. took the lead and said softly, "Well, I'm going to go pay my last respects. You can come if you want. It's totally up to you." With that, he headed toward the black box.

Frankie couldn't bear the thought of not seeing his friend one last time. So, he quickly caught up to Mr. D., and together, they strode toward the casket. They stopped about two feet away. Frankie stood, gazing at what once was the body of his best friend. Jimmy had been so full of life, but today, his body was so still. It almost seemed plastic. The face was similar to that of his friend, but it was missing the radiant smile his best friend always wore. This Jimmy lay still—too still. Frankie turned away as new tears plopped untouched from his already red-rimmed eyes. *This is not my friend. It is just the shell that had once held his soul.*

Mr. D. took Frankie's elbow and steered him toward the back hall. They came to the room where the family was gathered. Mr. D. gently rapped on the closed door. Coach Watson opened the door. He looked thinner and pale, and his face was taut with emotion. Mary Watson sat in the corner, surrounded by people offering love and support. She looked as frail as a kitten. Frankie thought both of them had aged about ten years since he'd last seen them.

"I'm glad you're here," Coach Watson spoke. "Come on in." He guided them into the room filled with other family members.

Frankie didn't know what to do or say, so he just stood next to Mr. D., awkwardly looking down at the floor. Promptly at ten, Mr. McFee appeared at the door and solemnly said, "It's time."

Everyone in the room stood. Mark and Mary Watson began walking to the door, and other family members followed. When Coach Watson came to Frankie, he said, "Son, I'd like you to sit next to me. Would you be okay with that?"

Frankie couldn't speak, because he had a lump in his throat that felt like a baseball. Instead, he lurched forward and embraced his best friend's dad. Together, the two men stood and cried. Finally, Frankie lifted his head off his coach's shoulder and said, "I'd be honored." Mr. D. handed Frankie a handkerchief, and he quickly wiped his face and blew his nose. Then he fell into place next to Coach Watson. Mr. D. tenderly placed a hand on Frankie's shoulder and fell in line. The funeral procession commenced.

The single-file line of family members entered the sanctuary through a side door. The organ music was playing "Amazing Grace" as they opened the door. Frankie was the third person to enter, behind Jimmy's parents. He could hear people sniff and blow their noses. He could hear coughs, but other than that, it was an eerie, cold silence. He felt like people's eyes were riveted on all of them as they made their way to their seats. *I feel like an animal on display at the zoo.* It felt as if eyes were searing into him like laser beams. Frankie kept his gaze on the floor directly in front of him. Finally, they arrived at their pew. As the last stanza of the song was played, everyone sat down.

Frankie could sense that the church was packed. Even though he hadn't looked up, it just felt full. He glanced over his shoulder.

Seated about three rows behind the family was the entire Stanton High football team. They filled about six rows. The team had decided to sit together to show their support for their fallen friend and coach. Their red jerseys were the same colors as the roses that draped the casket. As Frankie looked, he noticed most of the players had their heads down. Frankie could tell the weight of this was heavy on their hearts as well.

A new song began to play, and Frankie caught a glimpse of the pallbearers, rolling the casket down the center aisle. Frankie again felt like a wad of dough was caught in his throat. Finally, he couldn't hold it back any longer, and he began to cry. He quickly turned his head away from the casket and returned his gaze to his lap. Mr. D. tenderly patted Frankie's leg and handed him a fresh tissue; Frankie dabbed at his tears and nose.

The pastor began the service, but Frankie couldn't concentrate. His only thought was on the pain and agony he felt. He stared straight ahead and sat frozen as he faced the illuminated cross that hung at the center of the sanctuary.

Frankie squinted at the cross, anger brewing behind his eyes. *How could you let this happen God? These are good people. They love and serve you. How could you do this to them? How could you do this to me?* Once again, the hot stream of tears cascaded, untouched, down his face.

Frankie felt the Watsons rise from the pew. He regained his focus and followed their backs; they walked to the pulpit. The pastor stepped back, and Mark and Mary Watson took his place. They stood facing the crowd, holding hands. Mark cleared his throat and spoke into the microphone. "We want to thank each of you for coming today. Mary and I are grateful for the community's outpouring of love and support."

Frankie could hear more sniffling reverberate around the room

Mark Watson continued courageously. "We want to say that we, just like you, don't understand why God called Jimmy home so soon." Mark looked straight into Frankie's eyes as he spoke. Finally, Frankie broke the trance by looking down into his shaking hands. "Throughout the past few days, Mary and I have found our comfort and strength through our faith. Yesterday morning, as I opened my Bible, I was reminded in 2 Corinthians 12:9 (NIV). 'My grace is sufficient for you, for my power is made perfect in weakness.' Losing our son has magnified the weakness in both of us. Yet, these words served as a reminder to me that God is always going to be with me. God's love gives me the strength I need to carry on."

Mark paused and took a deep breath. Then he continued. "Second Corinthians 12:10 (NIV) says, 'When I am weak, then I am strong.' I believe that God's strength will carry us in our weakness." He grabbed a glass of water from under the podium and, with shaking hands, took a sip. Then he went on. "Those of you who knew our son will remember him by two things: his hundred-watt smile and his love for Jesus."

Out of the corner of his eye, Frankie could see several heads were nodding.

"Today, we would like to ask you to honor our son by continuing to live in his legacy of love." With tears flowing freely down his face and his voice choking with emotion, Mark continued, "Smile often, and go make a difference. That is what Jimmy did daily, and that is what he would want each of us to do. But this can only happen if you, like Jimmy, know Jesus Christ personally. Please get to know Him, just as my son did, so that you, too, can live the life Christ died for you to have. " Mark bowed his head, and Mary looked up gently and lovingly. The pastor came over and gently laid his hands upon both parents. Then Mark and Mary made their way down the front steps and back to their seats.

The congregation applauded. When Coach took his seat next to Frankie, he reached out and grabbed his hand. He gave him a squeeze and whispered, "Keep loving Jesus, Frankie. That's what Jimmy would want you to do."

The anger that had been boiling inside his heart dissipated at those words. Frankie took a deep breath and squeezed Mark Watson's hand. Frankie returned his gaze to the cross. At that moment, Frankie realized he was literally at a crossroad. Would he choose to continue to follow Christ or reject his new faith out of anger? After listening to Coach Watson's words, his decision was clear. He knew, without a shadow of doubt, that his best friend would tell him to stay the course and keep following the cross of Christ. Frankie took a deep breath, and as he exhaled, he felt his resentment toward God evaporating into thin air.

The pastor closed in a prayer, and the pallbearers rolled the coffin down the center aisle. The tune of the high school fight song quietly played on the church's sound system. When they had been planning the funeral, Mary had said, "Jimmy was victorious not only on the football field but also for Christ. I want him to go out as a winner. Let's play the school fight song in honor of his victorious life."

The entire congregation stood as the victory song filled the room. Tears flowed from every person as the family followed the casket and exited the building.

Outside the building, bright sunshine met their eyes. Frankie squinted as the men loaded the black coffin into the rear of the hearse. Mary and Mark Watson made their way to the first car in the processional. Frankie stood with Mr. D. and his teammates. They each tried to carry on small talk as they waited for the church to empty.

All of a sudden, Frankie felt someone tug on his arm. He turned and looked straight into the soft blue eyes of Betsey Bailey.

Her voice was soft and gentle. "I'm really sorry, Frankie. I know how close you and Jimmy were. Today, on my way here, as I stepped out of the car, I found this. I thought it was a sign. I want you to have it." She extended her cupped hand and placed something into Frankie's open palm. "Always remember what it says." With a warm smile and not another word, she turned and walked away.

Frankie looked at his palm. Lying there was a bright and shiny penny. The words, "In God We Trust" seemed to glisten in the sunshine.

For the first time in days, Frankie smiled. The heaviness compressing on his heart seemed to lighten. He lifted his eyes to the blazing sun, and it felt as though his best friend was smiling down on him from heaven. At that moment, Frankie realized life would go on, even without his best friend at his side. *This penny really is a sign from heaven. Thank you, God, I really needed it.*

# Chapter 10

# THE Y

Oliver Hadley ran into the dining hall at the instant Frank hit the floor. He yelled, "Help me!" and several of the staff also ran toward Frank's crumpled and apparently lifeless body.

Two of the nurses immediately checked for a pulse. Oliver stood over them and silently prayed, *Lord, please let my friend be okay. Don't let him die.* Oliver focused on Frank's face. His eyes were closed, and he had a furrowed brow. It was if the blood had drained from his face, which was ashen and pale.

"Frank ... Frank, are you with us?" a nurse asked loudly as she wiped a cold cloth over his forehead. The other nurse took out her stethoscope to listen for a heartbeat.

"His vitals check out. I think he's just fainted," she said as she looked up at her comrade.

The nurse continued to dab at Frank's forehead. "Mr. DeMotto, can you hear me?" she asked loudly.

Suddenly, Frank's eyelids flew open. "Where am I?" he mumbled weakly.

Oliver knelt down on one knee, bent over his friend, and said, "Frank, it's me Oliver Hadley. You're at The Haven dining room hall. Remember?" He gently laid his hand on Frank's shoulder. The simple touch made Frank jump with a start. "I didn't mean to startle you, Frank," Oliver spoke gently. "You've sure startled us," Oliver chuckled.

Frank's eyes began to regain focus, and he shook his head as if clearing cobwebs from his mind. The nurses assisted him so he could slowly sit up.

"What happened, Frank?" Oliver asked. Frank just sat on the tile floor in bewilderment. Unmoving and breathing heavily, he just sat and stared straight ahead as if he couldn't hear a word anyone was speaking.

Oliver looked at the nurses and whispered, "Did my friend have a stroke or something?"

"I don't think so, Mr. Hadley. I think we'll call his doctor and get him to check him over thoroughly, just in case." Oliver nodded in acknowledgment. "Frank," the nurse continued, "are you ready to stand up?"

Frank slowly nodded, and the two nurses picked him carefully up. They led him back over to his chair at the table, where Oliver stood guard.

Frank spoke in a constricted voice, "Would you please help me get to my room?"

"Sure thing. " replied the nurse. "We've called for a wheelchair, Frank. I think it would be best if you let us roll you back." Frank nodded and slowly maneuvered himself into the waiting wheelchair.

Oliver grabbed Frank's walker and said, "I'd be happy to walk this back to your room."

"I'd appreciate it," Frank replied. He looked up at Oliver with tired eyes. Without another word, they headed back to room 105. When they arrived at the door, Oliver was surprised when Frank handed him his key.

"Could you help me get in?" Frank asked helplessly.

"No problem." Oliver took the key, placed it in the lock and opened the door.

The nurse rolled Frank straight to his recliner. Frank stood on wobbly legs, hobbled, and collapsed in a heap. He bent over and buried his face into his hands.

The nurse left Frank there for a moment. She went into the kitchen and returned with a fresh, wet cloth. She gently tipped back the recliner and laid the cloth on Frank's head. Oliver stood next to his friend and watched; concern was etched on his face.

"The doctor has been notified to come and check on you today, Frank. Until then, will you be able to keep Frank company?" the nurse asked Oliver.

"I will not leave my post, ma'am." Oliver saluted.

She gently touched Oliver on the arm and whispered, "I think he's going to be fine." She quietly walked out the door.

"Is there anything else I can get for you?" Oliver asked sincerely.

Frank pointed his bony arthritic finger toward the bathroom. He whispered, "Water, please. And a Tylenol."

Oliver jumped to action and was soon back at Frank's side, holding a glass of cold tap water and two Tylenol gel caps. He placed the medicine in Frank's visibly shaking hand and carefully set the glass down on a wooden TV tray next to Frank's chair.

Frank lifted his head, downed the Tylenol, and gulped the entire glass of water. He handed the empty glass to Oliver and weakly said, "Thank you for all your help."

As Oliver stood looking at Frank, his heart was filled with compassion for this man. It was obvious he was in some kind of deep pain. Frank's usual steely gaze had been replaced with a look of agony.

The color was beginning to return to Frank's face. "Do you remember what happened back there?" Oliver asked.

"I just got a little shook up back there."

"Did someone say something to make your blood pressure rise?" Oliver asked. *I remember your explosion the only time I mentioned church to you.*

"Did you happen to see the morning paper?" Frank inquired.

"No, I went straight to the chapel this morning. Why do you ask?"

"Sit down, Oliver. I want to tell you a story."

\*\*\*\*\*\*\*

School was starting in about a month, which meant summer was drawing to a close. The ovenlike heat of August made Frankie sweat the minute he stepped out the door. It had already been a week since they had buried his best friend, and Frankie's world had seemed to come to a crashing halt. He missed his best friend and felt lost. His usual routine of working out at the gym or hanging out with Jimmy no longer occupied his free time. Now, he would mow his yards and just come back to the house. He would either go back to his room and close the door, or sometimes join Mr. D. for a show following dinner.

One night at dinner, Mr. D. slid an envelope across the table. "I thought you maybe could use this," he said.

"What's this?" Frankie asked quizzically. Eyebrows raised, he ripped open the envelope. Inside was a membership card to the Stanton YMCA. He pulled the card out and examined the writing. The name Frankie DeMotto was written on it.

"I figured you didn't want to lose all that muscle right before football started. I thought this might be a way to help you stay in shape." Mr. D. stood and started to clear the dishes off the table.

Frankie just took a deep sigh and then sullenly said, "I haven't thought about football that much."

"I think a good workout is just what the doctor ordered. Why don't you take the truck and go check out the Y. I'll clean up this mess."

Frankie sat and stared at his new membership card. "I guess it wouldn't hurt. It's been a long time since I've lifted any weights. Football does start up in a couple of weeks."

He got up from the table and headed to his bedroom. He stuffed his workout gear into a duffel bag and headed toward the garage door. On the way past the kitchen, he stopped and grabbed his membership card off the table. "Thanks, Mr. D. I really appreciate it."

Mr. D. had his hands in a sink full of suds and smiled. "My pleasure, my boy. Go work up a good sweat." He turned his attention back to his dishes.

Ten minutes later, Frankie pulled the truck into the parking lot of the Y. He walked up to the front desk, where a motherly looking woman wearing a YMCA staff shirt greeted him with a warm smile. "May I help you?"

Frankie dug into his bag and pulled out his membership card. He handed the card to the woman behind the desk.

She glanced at the card. "I see you are a new member. Is this your first time here?"

"Yes, I just joined today."

"Welcome. We like to give our new members a tour of our facility on their first visit. Do you have about ten minutes? We could give you a quick overview."

"Sure, that would be nice."

"Excuse me just a minute." She poked her head into an office connected to the welcome desk. Frankie could hear her speaking to someone behind the door. He couldn't quite decipher the entire conversation, but he did hear her say, "Can you please give one of our new members a tour?"

Out stepped Betsey Bailey. Her hair was up in her usual ponytail. She was wearing a navy blue T-shirt that had the word "staff" in white letters over her heart.

"I'd be happy to, Margie," she replied cheerfully. She rounded the corner and looked up. "Well, Frankie DeMotto," she said with a smile. "Fancy meeting you here."

Frankie was dumbstruck. "Mr. D. got me this. He thought it would be good for me to stay in shape for football." Shyly, he looked down at the newly waxed linoleum floor.

"Well, you've come to the right place," she said. "You'll see we have some weight equipment, a small gymnasium, and a pool. Come on. Follow me, and I'll show you around."

Betsey took the lead. Together, they toured the entire facility. "Well, what do you think? Is this going to help you earn All-State football honors this season?"

"I'm impressed."

"Impressed with the facility or the tour guide?" she teased.

Frankie began to blush. He replied awkwardly, "Thanks for taking me around. I'd better get started on my workout before they close the front doors."

"Listen, Frankie. I work out all the time. If you ever feel like you want some company, let me know. I'm here four days a week."

As usual, Frankie was a man of few words, especially around girls. He smiled, grabbed his duffel bag, and headed to the men's locker room. "See ya around."

"Not if I see you first," she replied.

Frankie entered the locker room. He got a glimpse of his reflection and realized he was smiling.

After getting dressed, he headed straight to the gym. He started out with a slow jog around its perimeter. After a couple of laps, Frankie stood at the end line and turned up his pace. He took off in a dead sprint to the other end line. He continued to sprint back and forth from each line until he had completed ten laps. His T-shirt was drenched in sweat.

With each step, Frankie began to feel as if some of the heaviness of his heart was dissipating. It felt so good to have his heart pumping, his muscles straining, and the sweat pouring. After twenty minutes of this, Frankie was spent. He walked over to the water cooler and downed several cups of water. Then he headed toward the shower. As he changed into his street clothes, he realized this was his first workout since coming home from camp. *This really felt good!* He stuffed his membership card into his wallet and said, "Thank you, God."

When the garage door opened, Mr. D. was reading the newspaper at the kitchen table. Without lifting his head he asked, "So how was the Y?"

"Simply amazing," Frankie replied with delight in his voice.

"Really?" Mr. D. asked with interest. He put down the paper. "Tell me all about it."

Frankie grabbed a glass, filled it with cold water, and sat across from the old man. "First off, do you remember that cute cheerleader who talked to us at Millie's last fall?"

"Blond and beautiful?" Mr. D. teased.

"That's the one. Betsey Bailey is her name. She works at the Y, and she gave me a tour."

"I see," Mr. D. replied with a coy grin and raised eyebrows.

Ignoring Mr. D.'s reaction Frankie went on. "It really felt good to work up a sweat again. Thanks so much, Mr. D., for blessing me with this. I really needed to get back into working out. I didn't realize how much I missed it."

"It's my pleasure, son."

That night, as Frankie crawled into bed, he grabbed his journal. It had been several weeks since he'd written anything. He picked up his pen and wrote: "Today I began to live again! Thank you, God, for Mr. D.'s love for me. He bought me a membership to the Y, and it was just what I needed. He always seems to know exactly what I need. Thank you also for letting me run into Betsey Bailey. She is so sweet and kind, not to mention pretty! That made me smile. She has a way of making my heart beat again and bringing a smile to my face. I feel so blessed by you today. Thank you, God."

Frankie closed the leather journal, laid it on his nightstand, and shut off the lamp. As he lay in bed, he realized his heart didn't ache so much as it beat. He actually felt like a hundred pounds of pressure had been lifted. He closed his eyes and slept peacefully.

After dinner the next night, Frankie grabbed his duffel bag and headed out the door. "I'll be back in an hour or so," he said. "I'm heading to the Y."

When Frankie arrived, Betsey was standing behind the front desk. "Back again so soon?" she asked as she checked him in.

"It felt great to work up a sweat last night," Frankie replied. *She is so easy to talk to.*

"Have a great workout," she said cheerfully, and she handed back his membership card.

This time, Frankie headed straight for the weights. He began by lifting and working out his upper body. Thirty minutes later he focused on his legs. He finished by doing a series of push-ups and sit-ups. By the time he finished, there wasn't a dry spot left on his gray T-shirt. He headed to the shower and cleaned up. As he passed the front desk, Betsey called out, "Maybe I'll see you tomorrow night."

Frankie smiled warmly at her. "Maybe you will."

*******

Frankie now had a new routine. It was only two weeks until practice began for football. He wanted to be in great shape, so each night after dinner, he headed straight for the Y. Frankie enjoyed being greeted by a blond ponytail and a warm smile each night at the desk of the Y.

Tonight, as he finished his workout, he exited the men's locker room and collided with Betsey Bailey. She was carrying a load of folded towels.

"Sorry about that," Frankie said sheepishly. "I didn't see you."

"Not a problem. I'm just getting off work, but I have to put away this last load of towels first."

Frankie's heart was thumping so hard it felt like it might jump out of his chest. He took a deep breath and shyly said, "I was thinking about grabbing a soda at Millie's. Would you want to come along?" He looked down at the ground by her feet.

"Sure," Betsey replied. "Let me call my parents and let them know I'll be a little later than usual. I'm sure they won't mind though."

Frankie's pulse raced as he watched the beautiful girl walk into the ladies locker room. She came back empty-handed and said, "Let me stop at the office and use the phone. You can wait right here." She pointed to a wooden bench against the front hall.

Frankie dropped his duffel bag by his feet and took a seat. *What the heck have I just done? Did I really ask Betsey Bailey to join me for a soda?* Fear and doubt began to circulate in Frankie's mind. *What in the world was I thinking? What am I going to say to her?*

Betsey reemerged from the office. "My curfew's nine o'clock, so we have about an hour. Do you mind if I follow you in my car?"

"Sounds good to me," Frankie replied. He bent over, grabbed his bag, and they walked out the door and into the parking lot.

When they arrived at Millie's, the place was full of teenagers and families out having a summertime treat. Shyly, Frankie walked behind Betsey. Several classmates spotted them as they entered. "Hey, DeMotto!" Mark Smith, a center on the football team, hollered from across the room. Frankie lifted his eyes and waved.

"Hi, Betsey," another girl called. Frankie recognized her as one of the cheerleaders who had been with Betsey the first time they'd met at Millie's.

"Hey Jane," she called back.

A waitress led them to an empty booth on the other side of the room. Betsey bounced into the booth, and Frankie slid in on the opposite side. He had never been this close to a pretty girl, and he felt awkward. Yet, Betsey was so kind and easy to talk to, his nerves soon settled down.

"What can I get for you two?" the waitress asked.

Frankie looked across the table at Betsey. "Any suggestions?"

"How about we split a hot fudge sundae?"

"Sounds great to me," Frankie replied.

The waitress brought over a huge mound of ice cream covered in hot fudge sauce, and it dripped over the side of the dish. Fluffy whipped cream with a cherry topped the treat.

"Now that's a sundae!" Frankie said in awe.

They both laughed as she sat the monstrosity down in between them. She handed each of them a spoon and said, "Enjoy."

"To our senior year," Betsey said, and she raised her spoon to Frankie's. They clanked their spoons and dug in.

After five minutes of eating, the sundae dish sat empty. Frankie and Betsey leaned back in their seats in utter fullness. "I can't believe we ate the whole thing," Frankie moaned.

"What a team we are!" Betsey giggled. "Together we can conquer the world." She beamed her radiant smile across the table.

Frankie's heart leaped into his throat. She was so beautiful, it took his breath away. This thought made him squirm in embarrassment, so he said, "Well, I'd better be going. Mr. D. may be wondering what happened to me."

"Thanks for the sundae," she replied. "It's your fault if I don't fit into my skirt tomorrow," she teased.

They walked out to their cars in the parking lot. As Betsey headed to her car, Frankie called out, "Hey, Betts, thanks for everything."

She turned and looked him square in the eyes. She said warmly, "Frankie DeMotto, it's been my pleasure!" She jumped in her car, tooted a quick "good-bye" honk, and headed toward home.

Frankie watched her glowing red taillights until they disappeared. He climbed into the cab of the truck, and his heart was beating double-time. He looked at himself in the rearview mirror and said, "That's the girl I'm going to marry someday."

With a smile across his face, he put the truck in reverse. He turned up the radio and rolled down the windows. He sang along with the top-40 all the way home.

Mr. D. was watching TV in the living when Frankie bounced in through the door. "Looks like you're in a good mood," Mr. D. quipped.

"We stopped at Millie's for a sundae," Frankie responded. A huge grin spread across his face as he spoke.

"*We?*" And who may that *we* be?" Mr. D teased.

"Betsey Bailey and me," Frankie blushed. "She really is a lot of fun to hang out with."

"Good for you, my boy, "Mr. D. said, and he slapped himself on the leg in delight.

Frankie said good night and headed to his bedroom. He had an early morning of lawns to mow, but he was so full of energy he couldn't settle down to sleep. Once again, he grabbed his journal, and this time he also opened the drawer that contained his Bible.

He opened to Isaiah 61:1, 3 (NIV) and read, "The Lord has sent me to those who grieve … to bestow on them a crown of beauty instead of ashes, the oil of gladness instead of mourning, and a garment of praise instead of a spirit of despair."

As Frankie read those words, Betsey's beaming face came into his mind. He took his pen and wrote in his journal: "Lord, thank you for giving me a new friend. Thank you that Betsey knows you and is helping me have gladness instead of mourning. It feels good to be rid of the heaviness and despair, Lord. Thank you for bringing life back to me again."

Frankie closed the journal and said a prayer out loud: "Lord, forgive me for being mad at you for taking Jimmy away. Help me not to reject you anymore, but to run to you for all my needs. Once again, I've seen your faithfulness in my life with people who love me; plus, you've given me a new friend. Thank you for all the ways you provide for me, Lord. I love you and am so grateful that you love me, too."

As Frankie lay still in his bed, he felt God's peace fall over him like a warm blanket. He heard the still, small voice of the Holy Spirit whisper into his heart, "I will always love you, my child."

Frankie felt safe and secure, and once again, his heart felt so full of love. He closed his eyes as the waves of love washed over him. That night, he dreamed about Jimmy Watson. They were running on a grassy field. On his other side was Betsey Bailey. Suddenly, Jimmy faded into a mist, but his million-watt smile was brighter than ever before.

When Frankie woke up the next morning, he smiled from ear to ear. Somehow, the dream seemed so real. He knew he would always carry Jimmy close to his heart, and that was good. But it was also good to keep living and move forward. It was a new day, and Frankie felt like it was the start of a new friendship. Maybe even the beginning of a new chapter in his life story.

# Chapter 11
# BETSEY

Later that afternoon, Oliver stopped and rapped on the door. As usual, Frank's television was blaring with the Fox News channel. "Who's there?" Frank bellowed.

"It's Oliver. I'm just checking in on my patient. I brought you some coffee."

"The door's open," Frank hollered back through the door.

Oliver turned the knob, and as he entered, Frank poked the off button on his remote. Oliver did a quick overview of Frank's apartment. It was very bare and contained only the essentials: a small sofa that matched the brown suede of Frank's favorite recliner; a small coffee table piled high with old newspapers and *TV Guide* magazines; and a wooden TV tray beside his chair. Only one picture hung on the wall, and it was right next to the door. The picture was of a beautiful blond woman, probably in her early twenties. She had amazing blue eyes that sparkled with life. It made Oliver smile as he gazed at the picture.

"That's my Betts," Frankie said with pride. "She was the love of my life."

Oliver whistled a soft whistle. "I'd say you are one lucky guy. She must have been some catch!"

"Boy, you can sure say that again. She was in every sense of the word a lady." Frank smiled at the picture. "Come on in with that good-smelling coffee, and I'll tell you more about my girl," Frank invited.

Oliver shut the door and strolled over to the sofa. He put the warm coffee on the tray beside Frank's recliner. Smiling, he said, "I'd love to hear about your girl."

*******

It was the first day of school. It felt special, because it was Frankie's senior year. The morning started with Mr. D. waking up extra early and rummaging around in the kitchen, loudly banging pots and pans. Frankie awoke to the noise and groggily made his way from his bedroom to its source.

"What in the world is going on in here?" Frankie asked sleepily.

"Did I wake you up?" Mr. D. asked mischievously. He looked over his shoulder as he bent over the cupboard. "I'm just reorganizing the cookware. You might as well jump in the shower, and I'll start your breakfast."

Frankie wiped the sleep from his eyes and, without a word, headed toward the shower. The warm water soon brought him back to life. He shaved, threw on a new pair of jeans and T-shirt, and then followed the aroma of cooked bacon back to the kitchen.

Mr. D. had made a wonderful breakfast of scrambled eggs, bacon, and wheat toast. His homemade strawberry jam was sitting in the glass jar next to the butter. Frankie strolled to his seat at the table just as Mr. D. handed him a large glass of cold milk.

"First day of school, and you need good energy. The best way to jump-start your day is with a healthy breakfast," Mr. D. chimed in matter-of-factly.

Frankie plopped into his seat, and as he went to grab his fork, he noticed a bulging envelope beside his silverware. His name was scrawled across the front in Mr. D.'s shaky handwriting.

"What's this?" Frankie asked. His eyebrows shot up as he looked at the envelope.

"Just a little something to brighten your first day of your senior year," Mr. D. replied. With a twinkle in his eye, he said, "Well, go ahead and open it. What are you waiting for?"

Frankie tore into the envelope. A set of silver keys fell onto the table. "What are these?"

"Follow me," Mr. D. said. He jumped up from his chair and headed to the large window in the living room.

Frankie quickly followed, and they both stared out of the window. Sitting in the driveway was a 1952 black Chevy pickup. On the side of the door was a huge poster that said, "Happy Senior Year!" Frankie stared wide-eyed. He turned to Mr. D. and asked, "It's mine?"

"You got it." Mr. D. beamed.

"Wow!" Frankie raced out the front door, leaped over the steps, and ran to his new pickup. "She's a real beauty!" he shouted with excitement.

Mr. D. strolled behind. "She's only five years young and has very few miles. I saw an ad in the paper a couple of days ago and figured you could use some wheels. I knew the owner and dropped by to take a look. She's in mint condition and has been taken good care of. What do you think? Will she work for your first truck?"

"Are you kidding me?" Frankie squealed. Then he grabbed Mr. D., picked him up off the ground, and spun him in a circle. "I'm so excited—and surprised. I had no idea."

"That's what made this so fun. Now you know why I wanted to wake you up early. I wasn't just in the mood to organize the cupboards." Both men laughed.

After inspecting the interior of the truck, Frankie and Mr. D. headed back into the house to eat breakfast. "Wow, Mr. D. All I can say is you really have blessed me this time. Thank you sooooo much." Frankie smiled from ear to ear as he gazed across the table at his dear friend.

Mr. D. blew his nose into his napkin and said, "Let's get a picture before you head to school." He strolled over to the desk and grabbed his camera, and they headed to the driveway. Frankie threw his duffel bag with his football gear onto the seat and then stood proudly by the door of his new truck.

He was wearing his red and white Stanton High School letter jacket, even though it was ninety-eight degrees. It was tradition that football jocks wore their letter coats during the season.

"I've got to record all your big events this year," Mr. D. said proudly. "I promised your mom I'd keep her up to date on your season. Might as well start with this photo, don't you think?"

"You bet," replied Frankie with delight.

Mr. D. clicked the camera. He took a couple of shots from different angles of the truck. Finally, Mr. D. said, "I think that covers it. You'd better get a move on so you're not late the first day."

Frankie jumped into his new truck and excitedly turned the key. The engine started right up, and he revved the accelerator just for fun. Frankie rolled down his window and waved good-bye as he headed to school.

As Frankie pulled his pickup into the parking lot adjacent to the locker room, other football players were arriving. Frankie honked as he pulled to a stop. His teammates noticed his new wheels and quickly came over to inspect. "Wow. That's a great new ride," Sam Smith said in awe. "What a great way to start the day!"

Several other classmates began to gather around Frankie's new truck. They greeted each other and congratulated Frankie on his new gift. The first bell rang, and the boys walked in as a group. Each athlete held his head high, as if the crowned princes of their domain. Frankie thought, *This is what it must feel like to be the big man on campus.* As the group of jocks entered the hallway, people parted to clear the way. Many greeted them with hellos or looks of admiration. Frankie found his way to his new locker assignment, and as he was trying to figure out the combination, someone came up from behind and tapped him on the back.

Quickly, he turned, and standing there was Betsey Bailey, wearing a huge smile. "Hey you!" she exclaimed. "Are we on for tonight?"

The entourage of football buddies in unison chimed, "Oooohhhhh!"

Frank could feel the heat rise to his face as he began to blush in embarrassment. "Sure Betsey," he sputtered. "I'll see you at the Y after dinner." Then he turned and punched one of his buddies in the arm as if to say, "Knock it off!"

Frankie could tell this was going to be a special year.

*******

The days flew by, but each one seemed to grow more blissful. From eight until three, he was in classes; football practice was from three to five. A shower and dinner with Mr. D. followed. Then, promptly at seven, he and Betsey would meet for their "date" at the Y. Now that practice was in full swing, Frankie used this time to walk around the track and talk to Betsey. They loved to share what God was doing in their lives and often compared a favorite scripture or devotional story they had read. Those two hours were, by far, Frankie's favorite time of day.

It was now mid-September, and the leaves were beginning to change to the beautiful gold and brown of fall. As they exited the Y and headed to their cars, it was misting. Frankie held his sweatshirt over Betsey's head so she wouldn't get soaked, and he led her to her waiting car.

"You're such a gentleman," Betsey said with appreciation.

As she unlocked her door, Frankie stood close enough to her to rub his body against hers as he held his sweatshirt over her head. The smell of her lilac shampoo tickled his nose. The scent of her perfume excited him; he'd never felt like this before. Frankie feared the fire from inside his body might radiate outward, and Betsey would be able to feel his passionate heat. Shyly, he backed away just as she opened the door. Betsey turned and looked Frankie in the eyes. Tenderly, she said to him, "I'm so glad we're friends." Without another thought, he bent his head toward her, and their lips touched gently. Frankie had never felt anything so soft and warm. He pulled away, breathless, and gazed into her eyes.

Betsey smiled up at him approvingly. "I'll see you tomorrow." Then she got into her car, waved good-bye, and pulled away.

Frankie could feel his heart pounding as if it might jump out of his chest. He watched the car pull away until the taillights disappeared over the hill. He suddenly realized he was standing in the rain. His clothes were soaked clear through. He began to laugh and jogged to his truck. *I think I'm falling in love with that girl!* As he drove home, he inhaled her girlie scent, and this made him smile. He pretended she was still beside him.

As soon as Frankie walked into the house, the telephone rang. "I got it, Mr. D.," Frankie shouted. "Hello."

"Hey, you," a sweet voice responded. It was Betsey.

"Hi," Frankie fumbled. He felt embarrassed, since he had just kissed her a few minutes ago.

"Just thought I'd tell you I think you are a great kisser."

Frankie about dropped the phone in utter bliss. Instead, he responded, "Gee, thanks." He could feel the heat rising up his neck.

Betsey continued. "Actually, that's not why I called. I wanted to ask you something else." She paused, trying to find the right words.

Frankie finally said, "Betsey, you can ask me anything."

With a deep sigh of relief, she said, "Okay. Here goes. Have you ever considered being a huddle leader for the FCA?"

Frankie had been a regular attendee of FCA after he'd accepted Christ last year, but he'd never thought about serving as a leader. He immediately thought of Jimmy. Jimmy was always the leader, and Frankie had always been the follower.

"I hadn't really thought about it. Why?" Frankie asked.

"Your name came up at our first meeting as a great candidate. The group wanted me to ask you if you'd consider serving this year as part of the leadership team."

"Let me think about it," Frankie said hesitantly. "I do appreciate the thought, though," he said sincerely.

"You'd be great, Frankie. And on a more selfish note, I hope you say yes, because it will give us another chance to hang out."

Frankie smiled at the thought of Betsey being by his side. "Well, when you put it that way, how could I say no? Count me in!" Frankie said confidently.

"Hooray!" Betsey yelled into the phone. "I'll see you tomorrow at school. I can't wait to tell Coach Watson you said yes."

"Coach Watson?"

"You bet. He's the one who brought your name up in nomination."

Frankie was honored. "I see," was all he could say.

"Well, I guess I'll be seeing you at school tomorrow."

"Not if I see you first."

"Good night, Frankie DeMotto."

Frankie hung up the phone and sauntered into the living room, where Mr. D. was pretending to read a book. Frankie's smile spread across his face, and he had a dreamy look in his eyes.

"Must have been quite a workout at the Y tonight," Mr. D. teased.

"You have no idea," Frankie swooned.

Mr. D. chuckled as he looked at the smitten boy. "Looks to me like you've been hit by Cupid's arrow of love."

Frankie blushed. "I think I hear my math book calling me." He headed to his room, leaving Mr. D. sitting on the couch, wearing a mischievous smile.

As Frankie sat at his desk, trying to figure out algorithms, he grabbed his journal and wrote, "I had my first kiss. It was amazing. Betsey Bailey has stolen my heart." He closed the book and smiled. Then he prayed silently, *Thank you for bringing me a new special friend, God.*

He grabbed his algebra book, and his thoughts returned to his homework.

*******

By October, Frankie and Betsey had become the "it" couple at Stanton High. He was the football player, and she was the head cheerleader. This stuff was usually scripted only in the movies. Everyone admired this "perfect" couple, because both of them were so humble and kind. Most of the school was happy Frankie had found a new best friend.

October brought homecoming, and it was one of the highlights of the school year. Two weeks before the homecoming dance, Frankie and Betsey were doing their usual walk around the track at the Y.

"Hey, Betts, I've got a question for you." Frankie said.

"I'm all ears," she said. She turned and looked at him, once again wearing that radiant smile.

Frankie stopped walking and took both her hands in his. "Would you be my date at the homecoming dance?" He looked intently into her soft blue eyes, which always seemed to twinkle with joy. He held his breath as he waited nervously for her to respond. He could feel his heartbeat pound in his chest as he waited.

"Frankie, I was hoping you would ask me." She cocked her head to the side, reached over, and gave him a big hug. "I'd love to be your date."

Frankie exhaled in relief and lifted her up off her feet, returning her embrace.

*******

Homecoming week came with a flurry of activities. The entire week was filled with dressing up in costumes, pep rallies, and a dance. Crowning of the king and queen at the dance would culminate the activities. Betsey and Frankie had been nominated for the homecoming court.

The Friday morning of homecoming, Frankie awoke to Mr. D. singing as he cooked breakfast. "You're sure in a cheerful mood this morning," Frankie commented as he pulled up his chair at the kitchen table.

"It's a very special day," Mr. D. replied. "Big game tonight and then the dance. Do you want me to pick up Betsey's corsage at the florist today?"

"That would be great, Mr. D."

"I'll just touch base with you after school to see if there is any last minute details we need to cover before you have your first big date tonight." Mr. D. turned and winked at Frankie.

Frankie gulped down his bowl of cereal. "I don't want to be late for school. I'll see you around 3:30."

When Frankie got to school that morning, the entire building was decorated for the big game. The cheerleaders had put up posters and streamers wishing the team good luck and victory. Each player also had a special message on his locker. Frankie and his teammates were so excited for the game. The day seemed to crawl as everyone was anticipating the fun to be had later that evening. Finally, the last bell rang, and Frankie headed to his locker to dump his books. As Frankie unloaded his books at his locker, Betsey stopped to wish him good luck.

"Good luck tonight," she said as she gave him a quick hug. She looked adorable in her white and red cheerleading outfit. She had a red ribbon holding up her ponytail, and her eyes seemed exceptionally blue.

"Did you know I'm the luckiest guy on campus today, because I've got the prettiest date to the dance?"

"Thanks, Frankie," she said. "I'll see you after the game tonight."

"I'll pick you up at your house as soon as I get showered. See you then."

She gave him one last quick hug and then they departed.

Frankie drove home to have a quick bite to eat and relax. When he walked into the house, he was greeted with a surprise: his mother was sitting at the kitchen table, drinking a cup of coffee with Mr. D.

"Mom?" He hadn't seen her since she'd moved last spring. Their work schedules and football camp had made it impossible for them to meet all summer. He ran over to her and gave her a huge hug.

"It's sure good to see you, son," she replied. She stepped back and eyed him up and down. "My how you have grown. It sure looks to me like Mr. Druthers is keeping you well fed." She smiled in appreciation as she glanced across the table at Mr. D.

"What are you doing here?" Frankie asked.

"Mr. D. called me and told me you were nominated for homecoming court and that parents would be escorting at halftime. I couldn't miss something so special, so here I am."

"You're coming to my game?" Frankie almost shouted with excitement.

"You bet," she replied with a smile.

Frankie looked over at Mr. D., who was sitting at the table. A big smile was on his face.

"Is this another one of your surprises for me?" Frankie asked.

Mr. D. just shrugged as if he didn't know what Frankie was talking about. Frankie went across the table and gave the old man a hug. "Once again, thank you," he said.

"How about if I let you have a few minutes to yourselves so you can get caught up?" Mr. D. asked. "I'll just be in the backyard, raking up some leaves."

Frankie took a seat at the kitchen table next to his mother.

"Well, where should I begin?" his mom said. "I'm staying with my parents and live in the basement of their house. It's really pretty cozy, but for two of us to live there would've been tight. I enjoy working at the grocery store as a checker. I've run into a lot of old friends, classmates, and such. The people in Topeka are really kind. It's actually been good to be back. Other than the fact that I miss you every day."

*She really looks good and happy.* "I'm glad it's working out, Mom. I miss you, too, but I'm happy here. Football is off to a great start, and living with Mr. D. has been fantastic. He's really good to me."

"He's a good man, son," she said as she looked out the window at the old man bent over a pile of brown leaves. "I hear you even have a girlfriend."

"Aw shucks." Frankie blushed.

"So, tell me about her."

"She's so great, Mom. Her kind heart is the best part of her. I want you to meet tonight. Okay?"

"Mr. D. says she's not too bad to look at either, huh?" She reached over and playfully jabbed his arm.

"Prettiest girl in school," Frankie replied proudly.

"Good for you, son."

"Have you heard from Dad since he moved out?" Frankie asked in an almost hushed whisper.

His mom looked down at the table and took a deep sigh. "The last time I saw your father was the day he came to pick up his things. It's really better that way. It helps me to let go of him and move on. How are you doing with all this?" She looked up to meet his gaze.

"It is what it is," Frankie replied. "I've decided to forgive and forget. It does me no good to dwell on what could or might have been."

"You're a good boy, Frankie. I'm really proud of you. Do you know that?" She stood, bent down, and gave her son a loving hug.

"Enough of this hugging stuff," Mr. D. jokingly said as he returned to the kitchen. "Let's eat before my meatloaf is burned to a crisp."

"One more thing, Frankie," his mother added. "I just wanted you to know I've started attending church. Westside Baptist in Topeka to be exact."

"Really, Mom?" He reached over, picked her up, and they twirled in a circle.

Laughing, she said, "Put me down before you hurt yourself. I can't have the star be injured before the big game on my account."

*My mom's attending church! That's the best news I've heard all day!*

Later, as he went into his room to pack his football gear, he said a quick thank-you prayer. *Lord, once again you've surprised me with a blessing. You not only brought my mom here to watch me play a game, but you've also brought her to church. Thank you for answering my prayers.*

Frankie gave his mom and Mr. D. one last hug and then headed out the door for the football game.

*******

Stanton High was playing the Blair Bears. By halftime, it was a blowout: Stanton 24 and Blair 0. Frankie was having a great game, rushing almost eighty yards in the first half. He was so grateful his mom was there to see his success on the field. He was enjoying every second of the night.

Since it was the homecoming game, parents led each candidate for the royal court onto the field. As usual, Frankie was partnered with Mr. D., but tonight, his mom flanked his other side. Frankie wore his grass-stained jersey, and Mr. D. had on his "lucky" red sports coat, which he wore to every game. His mom beamed with pride as she stood by his side and held his arm. She looked beautiful in her red sweater and blue jeans. Her brunette hair was in a bob haircut and held in place by a red headband.

Mr. D. couldn't wipe the grin off of his face as they announced Frankie's name over the PA. The threesome marched proudly out to the center of the field. Applause erupted from the stands as each candidate took their place. The winners would be announced that night at the dance, but each nominee was given a rose and a certificate at the field. Frankie especially enjoyed this, since his mother was there to share the moment. When he received his rose, he handed it to her, and she broke out in laughter. He looked to his left, and Betsey stood next to her parents, a couple people down. Frankie winked at her as their eyes met. She wore her cheer outfit and a radiant smile. His heart warmed as he looked at her and thought, *She's my girl.* As they exited the field, Frankie introduced his mom to Betsey and then headed quickly back to the locker room to catch up with the rest of his team.

Stanton easily went on to victory, 42–10. Frankie had 186 yards in total offense.

He quickly ran home and showered after the game. His mom and Mr. D. congratulated him on his excellent performance. "You are really good," his mother stated proudly.

"Thanks, Mom. I'm glad you came."

"Now have a great time at the dance, " Mr. D. instructed. "Don't forget this." He handed Frankie the corsage he was to present to Betsey. It was a red rose laced in baby's breath.

"This looks so nice, Mr. D. Thanks again for picking it up for me."

Frankie stood by his mom, while Mr. D. took some pictures. Then they swapped places, and Mr. D. stood by Frankie, and Mrs. DeMotto snapped some shots.

"Betsey is one lucky girl to have such a handsome young man picking her up," his mother said.

Frankie looked so handsome in his new suit that Mr. D. had bought for him. It was his first suit, and they had gone to the big department store in Omaha to purchase it. Frankie did one last check in the mirror, patted down his wet hair, grabbed the flower, and headed for his truck.

"I'll see you a little after midnight," he hollered over his shoulder.

"Have fun!" the two chimed at the same time.

At the dance, Frankie and Betsey were crowned king and queen. As they danced the spotlight dance, Frankie felt like he was living a fairy tale. Betsey looked radiant in her crimson red dress. It fit her like a glove, yet was modest. Her pearl necklace encircled her neck and was a perfect match to her pearl-white teeth. Her hair was pulled back in a chignon, and she looked so sophisticated. Frankie looked handsome in his new suit, and together, they complimented each other.

As the dance wound down, Frankie took Betsey by the hand. He felt like she was his prized trophy. Every time he looked at her, his heart leaped with delight. As the lights came on to signal the end of the dance, the students started heading toward the exit door.

"Hey, guys, a bunch of us are heading to Millie's for a bite. Do you want to join us?" Jason asked.

"I'm beat," Frankie responded and looked at Betsey to see her reaction.

"Me, too. It's been a busy week, but thanks for thinking of us. I think we're ready to call it a night." She agreed with Frankie.

Frankie held her hand in his, their fingers intertwined, and they headed to his pickup. He opened her door and helped her up. She giggled as he easily picked up her 110-pound frame and gently sat her in the cab.

"You are so strong. No wonder those tacklers have a hard time bringing you down," she teased, squeezing his bicep.

Frankie closed the door, smiled, and jogged around to the other door. As they drove, they held hands and listened to the latest pop song on the radio.

Betsey finally broke the silence. "Frankie, tonight was so special. I almost feel like Cinderella, and you are certainly my Prince Charming."

He looked over at her and gave her a huge smile.

The night ended with Frankie leaning over and placing a gentle kiss on his beloved's mouth. They sat in the pickup for a few more minutes of kissing. Then breathlessly, Betsey reached for the door handle. "I better get in before my parents come out to check on me."

"I'm not sure I'm ready to run from your dad because he's caught me kissing his little girl," Frankie teased. He opened his door and walked around the cab.

He politely opened Betsey's door, and they walked to her front door. "Good night, Prince Charming. Thank you for the best night of my life."

They exchanged one last hug, and Betsey disappeared behind the door. Frankie felt as if was walking on air as he headed back to his truck. *I've never been happier!*

\*\*\*\*\*\*\*

"And that's when I knew Betsey Bailey was *the* one," Frank told Oliver Hadley.

"I can sure see why, Prince Charming," Oliver teased. Then the two men chuckled as they gazed up at the picture hanging on the wall.

# Chapter 12

# SENIOR YEAR

That evening, as Frank got ready for bed, he took a framed picture off his nightstand. He gazed at it lovingly and caressed the picture tenderly with his index finger. It was a picture snapped at his wedding. It showed him and his lovely bride as they were exiting the church on the day of their wedding. They looked elated and brimming with love as they stepped into the crowd waiting to throw rice over them. It was Frank's all-time favorite photograph.

It was his nightly ritual to end each day with a kiss to his beloved wife. It had begun on his wedding night, and he continued that tradition, even though she was gone. He held the photo to his parched lips and whispered, "Good night, my beloved." Then he gently returned the frame to its spot on his nightstand.

Frank closed his eyes and, once again, allowed his mind to move to happier times.

*******

The football team had decided to dedicate this season to Jimmy. Frankie had been voted team captain, not only because he was Jimmy Watson's best friend but also because his coaches and teammates respected him for his hard work.

Frankie's senior year was starting out even more successful than his junior year. He was averaging 8.3 yards per carry on offense and a whopping 22.5 yards on kick-off returns. He even had two punt returns for touchdowns. UNL had offered him a scholarship, and he had given them his verbal commitment. He was really looking forward to making it official on national signing day in November. Then came their last regular season game. They were one victory away from an undefeated season. Frankie knew some of the UNL coaches would be in the stands, and he was excited to show them his skills on the field.

They entered the game 10–0 and were playing their crosstown rivals, the Genoa Dragons. They, too, were having a good season, with the record of 9–1. It would be standing room only, and local sportscasters had dubbed it the "game of the week." Several college recruiters—from UNL and other schools—were in the stands to catch a glimpse of prospective players.

As the team gathered in the locker room prior to taking the field, it was their ritual to kneel in a moment of silence. As Frankie knelt, he prayed, *Thank you, God, for the gifts and talents you've given me on the field. Help me honor you tonight. And Jimmy, this one's for you, my friend. How I wish you could be here to help us on to victory. I can still almost sense you out on the field with me, opening up the holes. Thank you, friend. Jesus, watch over us, protect us, and lead us to victory. I ask it in Jesus' name.*

Frankie stood with a sense of confidence and joy. As Coach called them to huddle up, Frankie yelled, "This one's for Jimmy!" Like a band of warriors storming the field for battle, the team roared a cheer in approval. As they exited the side door, Frankie paused and took in his last home game. The bright lights illuminating the ebony sky, the crisp autumn air, the cadence of the drums, the chants of the student body as they began their revelry, the smell of fresh popcorn emanating from the concession stand: Frankie loved everything about a Friday night football game.

As he stood in awe of all of this, he felt Coach Watson place his hand on his shoulder. He turned, and Coach gave him a knowing wink. "This is your night, Frankie," he said. The team then stormed onto the field, followed by the roar of the home crowd.

The game was a true gridiron classic of two great teams. With 2:39 left in the game, Frankie's team trailed 17–14. The Stanton defense had done its job and held its ground on the last series. As the Genoa punt squad took the field, Frankie stood at the thirty-yard line, waiting to receive the punt. If all went as planned, his team would end up with decent field position.

He heard the clack of shoulder pads as his teammates made contact with the opponents to open holes for Frankie to run through. He grabbed the ball out of the air and tucked it safely in his arms. Like a gazelle, he began to sprint upfield. There was an opening at the forty-yard line. Then Frankie veered right as he crossed midfield. A Genoa player stretched out his arms and grabbed Frankie's left ankle. Frankie lost his balance and stumbled, but he did not go down. But Frankie's momentary loss of balance allowed another Genoa player to gain momentum on him.

All of a sudden, Frankie felt as though a truck was running over him, and his knees buckled. He heard a loud pop. As he hit the ground, he felt a searing pain roaring through his left leg. The cleats from his shoes had done their job and stuck in the ground. But on impact, they remained stuck, while Frankie's knee buckled. The result was a tear in a ligament in his left knee.

Frankie lay in the fetal position on the ground. The Genoa player quickly scampered away. The hit was clean, but he knew Frankie was seriously hurt. The crowd gasped, before a hushed silence fell over the entire stadium. All Frankie could do was close his eyes and pray. The pain was unbearable. Every player backed away and took a knee as trainers from both sidelines raced onto the field.

Coach Watson sprinted over and knelt beside his star player. With a calm voice he said, "Look at me, Frankie." Frankie had his eyes squeezed shut, and tears streamed down his cheeks. He was clamping his jaw to keep himself from screaming. Even his teeth hurt from this pressure. He heard his coach's voice and opened his eyes.

"I'm not going to leave your side, son." Coach Watson grabbed Frankie's hand. Frankie gave it a squeeze as if to say, "Thank you." He couldn't talk because of the intense pain.

An ambulance raced onto the field, and several men removed a stretcher. Mr. D. had now come from the stands and found his way onto the field. He, too, knelt alongside Coach Watson and spoke to Frankie. "I'm here, my boy. We'll get you taken care of right away. You just hang in there." Frankie nodded and just looked up at his two mentors. Sheer terror was reflected in his eyes.

Gingerly, the men placed Frankie onto the stretcher. Mr. D. climbed into the back of the ambulance alongside the stretcher. Frankie lifted his head from the stretcher and hollered at Coach Watson, "Finish this for Jimmy!" And with tears streaming down his face, they closed the back of the ambulance.

*Instead of heading into the end zone on the winning score of the game, I'm headed to the emergency room,* Frankie thought. Sirens blared as they raced off the field. Frankie felt one of the ambulance attendants inject something into his arm. "This will knock him out and help him not have to endure the pain."

Frankie surrendered to the weight pressing down on his eyelids. He closed his eyes, and soon, the drone of the siren was no more.

*******

Frankie came to in a hospital bed. Mr. D. was sitting in a chair by his head. Mary and Mark Watson were standing at the foot of his bed, and Betsey was on his left. She was holding his hand. As his eyes came into focus, he saw his knee covered in a brace that extended from his ankle to his thigh. His leg was elevated in a crane-like device. Frankie couldn't move, but the pain had dissipated due to medication.

The first words out of his mouth were, "So, did we win the game?"

Mr. D. stood at the sound of his voice. Coach Watson patted his healthy right foot and said, "Yes, sir, we sure did, thanks in part to you getting us great field position on that punt return. We scored with twelve seconds left in the game and won 20–17."

"That's good," Frankie mumbled in his drug-induced state. His tongue felt thick and as dry as a desert.

"You need to rest, my boy," Mr. D. said sympathetically. "Your fan club is here, praying for your recovery and rest."

Betsey gave Frankie's hand a squeeze. "You gave everyone quite a scare," she commented. "Even the Genoa fans were somber after you went down."

Frankie could feel the love of everyone in the room. Between that and the drugs, he was drifting back to sleep. He thought, *Maybe when I wake up, this will all be a bad dream.*

*******

The doctor reported that Frankie had shattered his left kneecap and torn his ACL—a major knee ligament. His football season, and possibly his entire football career, was coming to a crashing halt.

His mom came to stay with him as soon as Mr. D. called. Mr. D. gave up his bed and offered to sleep on the couch as long as she wanted to stay. If it weren't for the love and support of his friends and family, Frankie was sure he would've just wanted to die. But everyone's constant encouragement, Betsey's beautiful smile, and all the love he felt helped keep up Frankie's spirits.

After spending three nights in the hospital, Frankie was released to go home. Mr. D. and his mom picked him up in his truck. They had packed a twin-sized mattress into the back, so Frankie could sit with his leg extended. They drove Frankie home, where Mark Watson was waiting for them in front of the house. Both men helped Frankie carefully get down from the bed of the pickup. Frankie was still getting used to walking on crutches, and since he could not put any weight on his left leg, balance was an issue. So, Coach Watson and Mr. D. walked alongside him up the front steps and into the house; Mrs. DeMotto followed behind with Frankie's duffel bag. Coach and Mr. D. escorted Frankie all the way into his room, until he landed on the bed with a heavy thud.

His room was filled with cards, balloons, flowers, and various gifts from the community. "Wow, look at all this," Frankie said as he took in the sight.

"You've got a lot of people praying for you, son," Coach Watson said. Frankie just closed his eyes as the medication began to take over once again.

Frankie slept for several hours, and when he woke up, Mr. D. and his mom were standing at the end of his bed, deep in conversation. At first, they weren't aware of Frankie's consciousness.

"When do you think I should tell him?" his mother asked Mr. D.

"Tell me what?" Frankie asked.

Both heads turned immediately at the sound of his voice. Both faces wore a look of alarm.

They approached Frankie's side. His mom looked at Mr. D. Finally he spoke, "Well, son, we got a call from Coach Watson while you were asleep. It seems as if he spoke with the University of Nebraska coaches today."

"Yeah, I know they were at the game," Frankie interjected. "Did they like my punt return?"

An awkward silence hung in the room. Suddenly, Frankie sensed something just wasn't quite right. "Well ..."

"Son, it seems as if they are very concerned about your injury. Most times when players take a hit like yours, they don't recover. They believe your football playing days are over," Mr. D. said sadly.

"What?" Frankie screamed. "Are you telling me they don't want me to play at Lincoln anymore?" Panic spread across his face.

His mom reached over and soothingly patted his arm. Frankie yanked it away, as if her touch was a branding iron on his skin. "Get out!" he shouted. "Get out, and leave me alone!"

Mr. D. replied, "Listen Frankie, it's going to be—"

"I said get out! I mean it. I really need a minute to myself," Frankie interrupted. He looked like a trapped animal: hopeless and helpless.

They nodded understandingly and slowly walked out the door.

There was his journal and Bible. He reached over for the notebook and began to write: "Well, God, this is strike two. You've taken my best friend. You've stolen my dream. One more strike, and you're out!"

Angrily, he closed the book, put down the pen, and threw the journal across the room. It hit the closet door with a loud bang. The noise brought Mr. D. running into the room. "Everything all right in here?" he huffed breathlessly from his sprint. "I was afraid you fell out of bed or something."

Frankie responded by pulling his covers over his head. *I don't want to talk to anyone at the moment.*

Mr. D. was not deterred. He walked over and sat down on the side of the bed. Frankie stayed under the covers, but Mr. D. spoke gently. "Listen, son, I know you're feeling pretty down right now. Who could blame you? Heck, I'm down, too. Let me tell you something I've learned along the way. We don't always get to pick the script God gives us. But you know what? God knows what He's doing. It doesn't always feel or seem like that to us. But someday, somehow, we will see His perfect plan. Frankie, trust me on this one. It's all going to work out."

Frankie listened to Mr. D.'s soothing voice but stayed hidden under the covers. He didn't want Mr. D. to see the hot tears streaming down his face.

Mr. D. patted Frankie on his good leg. "I'm here for you. Let me know if there's anything I can give you."

*I'm lucky to have these people here by my side. I know Mr. D.'s always right, and I want to believe him.* Frankie stuck his right hand out from under the covers and gave him a thumbs-up signal. Mr. D. got the message. He smiled and patted the boy lovingly.

"We're going to get through this together, my boy. And the good news is, you've got your mom by your side, too!"

As if on cue, Frankie's mom came in carrying a tray of food. "I thought you might be hungry," she said. Frankie popped his head out of the covers at the smell of the grilled cheese sandwich.

"Smells good." He smiled weakly.

She sat the tray containing tomato soup and the sandwich on a stand next to the bed. Then she took a seat in a folding chair by Frankie's side. "Listen, Frankie, I know you feel like your world has been tipped upside down. No one knows how that feels better than me. But you know what I've learned in the past six months? God meets us where we are. Remember all those times you invited your dad and me to church, and we just ignored you? Well, now I go every Sunday in Topeka. Who knows, but if it weren't for the fact that your dad left, I still might be sitting in the house across the street every Sunday, reading the paper just like I used to. Difficulties come to us in this life, Frankie. What I've learned is to run to God during tough times rather than rejecting Him."

Frankie sipped his tomato soup as he listened intently to his mother's words. "Thanks, Mom," he said quietly. "It's just so hard to have my dream shattered."

She reached over and held his hand. Tenderly, she looked into his eyes. "I get it, son. But trust me: something better is going to come along. You just keep your eyes on God and see how he can turn this mess into something miraculous."

Frankie nodded. His mom lightened the mood. "How about some music to cheer you up?" She brought in the radio, and they listened to the pop station give their top-ten hits of the week. They sang along and laughed.

At the sound of their singing, Mr. D. popped his head through the door, smiling. As he watched, he prayed: *Thank you, Lord, for meeting this boy where he needs you.*

Later that night, as Frankie lay in his bed thinking about the words he had heard from Mr. D. and his mother, he realized once again he'd been at a very important crossroad. Once again, he had a choice to reject God in anger and disappointment or run into His arms to find comfort and strength in his time of need. "Thank you for your comfort and mercy for me, Lord," Frankie whispered into the dark room. "Help me get through this new trial, because I won't be able to do it without you."

He reached over to the nightstand and opened the drawer. He dug under a pile of books and magazines and found the shiny penny Betsey had given him at his friend's funeral. He held it gently in the palm of his hand. "Help me trust you in the hard times, God," he whispered. "Help me stay on the path with you."

He closed his eyes and felt the warm peace of the Lord envelop his body like a warm blanket. He knew he'd had the chance once again to choose which way he would travel. And he chose the road of the cross.

*******

Two weeks passed. Frankie stayed home from school, because he couldn't maneuver Stanton High's halls well. His mom served as his tutor and helped him stay caught up with schoolwork.

Finally, Coach Watson found a wheelchair for Frankie to borrow and delivered it so Frankie could go back to school. "Our church loaned this to you, because the doctors felt it would be easier for you to get around the halls using this rather than your crutches. They feel it would be best to have someone push you in the hall between classes, so you don't accidentally bump your extended leg."

"Thanks, Coach," Frankie said. But his body language spoke disappointment.

"It won't be for long, Frankie," Mr. D. interjected. *I can tell that Frankie isn't thrilled with being in a wheelchair at school.*

"I hate being so helpless," Frankie scowled. "It's so frustrating!"

"I'm sure it is," Coach said, "Trust me, Frankie. Getting back to a normal routine will help you take your mind off this injury."

"I agree, son," his mom chimed in. "It's time I head back to Topeka tomorrow morning. I think my time here as your nurse has run its course. I'm leaving you in Mr. D.'s good care."

"Besides," Mr. D. teased, "I think I know a pretty young lady who would be happy to be your chauffer."

A smile finally appeared on Frankie's face as he pictured Betsey Bailey steering him through the halls of Stanton High.

The next morning, Mr. D. delivered Frankie and his wheelchair to Stanton High. Betsey was waiting at the front door, along with several of Frankie's teammates. They cheered as Mr. D. rolled Frankie up the front steps. Frankie felt like a victim and didn't return anyone's gaze. He felt like an animal at the zoo everyone had come out to stare at. He wished he could just go home and crawl back into his bed, pull the covers up, and escape this nightmare.

Betsey opened the front door to the school. "Let the designated driver take over," she beamed, smiling at Frankie and Mr. D.

"Hope you have better luck putting a smile on his face than I had this morning," Mr. D. admitted. "Good luck." He stepped in front of Frankie's chair and said, "Make the most of your day, Frankie. It's time to start making some lemonade with your lemons." He gave Frankie's right knee a pat and headed back to his truck.

A group of the football players rallied around Frankie, trying to cheer him up. He just sat sullenly, while Betsey rolled him to his first-period math class. "See you in forty minutes," she said cheerfully as she wheeled Frankie under the table in the back of the classroom. "I'm off to art!"

Frankie sat gloomily staring at the chalkboard, while Mr. Smith, his math teacher, explained the latest algebra assignment. Ten minutes before the bell rang, Betsey reentered the room. She was carrying her pom-poms and a poster. "I thought your wheelchair needed some decorations," she said as she began to apply her items to the back and sides of his chair.

Frankie ignored her. He sat stone still and gloomily stared straight ahead.

"The poster says, 'Caution, slow moving vehicle.' I put a big smiling face under that," she reported to Frankie.

Frankie didn't respond.

Sensing his crabbiness, Betsey handed her pom-poms to Molly, a fellow cheerleader, and whispered, "Put these in your locker. I'll grab them after school."

She gently rolled the wheelchair out from under the desk. "Off to second period. History, here we come."

Frankie gazed at his lap the entire trip. Finally as they neared the door, Betsey stopped. She leaned forward and whispered into his ear, "Frankie, I know this must be hard. Try to make the best of it, okay?"

He spouted, "Easy for you to say. You're the one doing the pushing."

Betsey backed away, as if his tongue was a whip that had just lashed her. Without another word, she rolled him into the back of the history classroom and left.

Frankie rarely smiled the entire first day of school. He constantly stared at his lap and ignored everyone who passed him in the hallway.

Finally, the last bell rang at 3:15. On the way out to the parking lot, Betsey stopped the wheelchair. She angrily stormed to the front and knelt so she was at eye level with him. "Listen to me, Mr. Frankie DeMotto. Yes, your world has changed. Yes, your dreams may have been altered. But guess what? You still have a lot to be thankful for. You can either continue to sit there, grumbling, complaining, and feeling sorry for yourself like a little victim. Or you can decide to make the best of a bad situation and live like a victor. Whichever attitude you choose, you will still be sitting in this chair for the next four to six weeks. But if you want me to continue to push you around, the bad attitude has to go, and I mean now."

Frankie had never seen Betsey be so bold. *She's right.* "You're right." he sighed. "I'm really sorry for taking this out on you." He reached for her hand and gave it a squeeze. Betsey leaned over, gave him a quick hug, and said, "We're in this together. Okay?"

"I wouldn't want to do it any other way." He smiled sheepishly, and she stood. She pushed him to where Mr. D. was waiting beside his truck.

"So how's my patient doing today?" he asked.

"I'd say, he's made a remarkable recovery," Betsey chimed in.

Frankie turned and looked at her, smiling. Mr. D. winked at Betsey.

When Frankie arrived home from school, he immediately hopped into the kitchen using his crutches and picked up the telephone. He dialed the Watsons' number, and Mary answered. "Hi, Mrs. Watson. This is Frankie DeMotto."

"Frankie," she said, surprised. "You've sure been on my heart. How are you doing these days?"

"Let's just say I've had better ones. Hey, the reason I'm calling is that I've been thinking. I think I have an idea for our next FCA meeting. Would it be okay if I give my testimony?"

"Sure, Frankie. I think that's a fantastic idea," she replied excitedly.

"Great then. I'll prepare something to share, and I'll see you Wednesday night."

"I'm looking forward to it already. I'll let Mark know."

Mark was sitting in the kitchen and overheard his name. "Let me know what?" he asked as she hung up the phone.

"Well, that was Frankie DeMotto. I think we're going to be in for a real treat Wednesday night. Frankie asked if he could give his testimony at FCA."

"Really?" he replied with raised eyebrows.

"Really." She reached down and gave her husband a big hug. "I can't help but think Jimmy must be smiling down from heaven right now."

Mark squeezed her hand, and tears quietly slid down their faces.

# Chapter 13
# FCA MEETING

The FCA met twice a month during the school year. Meetings usually took place in the school gym, but tonight, they were meeting at the home of Mary and Mark Watson, their leaders.

Beginning around 6:45, cars began to pull up to the Watsons' home. Soon, about twenty-five students had assembled. Cars and trucks surrounded the house like bees at a honeycomb. At 7:00, Mr. D. pulled his truck into the driveway. He jumped out and helped Frankie descend.

Betsey was waiting and ran over and greeted Mr. D. "Good to see you again, Mr. D.," she said warmly.

"Right back to you, Betsey," he said.

"So, are you ready?" she asked Frankie as they walked to the front door.

"He's been practicing for me all evening," Mr. D. replied. "He's got it down to a science." He patted Frankie on the back.

Frankie, using his crutches, and the others made their way into the main living room, where the students had gathered. As they came in, a hushed anticipation fell over the room. Mark Watson extended his hand and greeted Mr. D. "Thanks for dropping him off."

"My pleasure," he responded.

"Would you like to stay?" Mark asked.

"No, thank you. I've been Frankie's practice audience for the past couple of days. I've got some errands to run, so I'll head out. I know you're going to enjoy it. I'll pick him up about 8:30."

"See you then," Mark replied. Then he turned to face the room of teenagers. "Paul, why don't you get us started?"

Paul Werner, one of the seniors on the basketball team, said, "Hey, everyone, let's gather up." The small talk ceased, and people found places to sit on the floor, sofa, or folding chairs.

Paul opened with a prayer. Then Mary Watson stood and walked to the front of the room. "I got an interesting phone call a couple of days ago," she began. "Someone requested to have the floor tonight." She smiled as her eyes focused on Frankie's face.

Frankie tentatively stood on his good leg. He grabbed his crutches and hobbled to the front. Mary grabbed a stool and sat it at the front of the crowd. Frankie laid his crutches beside the stool and took a seat.

Betsey stood beside Frankie, holding his Bible. She spoke first. "Let's turn in our Bibles to Romans 8:28." The sound of ruffling pages filled the quiet room as students began to flip through their Bibles. "Would someone like to read what it says?"

Mary Jones spoke up. "It says, 'And we know that in all things God works for the good of those who love Him, who have been called according to his purpose.'" She paused and looked at Betsey and Frankie.

Frankie said, "As you know, it's been a rough couple of weeks for me." Several heads in the crowd nodded in response. "When I first woke up in the hospital and realized my knee was a mess, I was angry at God. I thought, *Lord, if I'm living for you, how could you let this happen?* I was mad. I was disappointed. Then I began to get bitter and resentful. My anger was eating me from the inside out. I was becoming a very grouchy, sarcastic, and negative person."

Frankie paused, looked over toward Betsey, and smiled. She said, "Now let's look at Romans 8:31–32. Mary, would you keep reading for us?"

"Sure," Mary replied. "'If God is for us, who can be against us? He who did not spare his own son, but gave him up for us all—how will he not also, along with him, graciously give us all things?'"

Frankie continued. "I've been a Christian for about a year. I love to learn about God. I love to read His word. When my accident happened, I realized it was time for me to really put my faith into action. I had to ask myself, *Do I really believe this stuff I'm reading or don't I?* So, one night I grabbed my Bible and my journal. I wrote the following questions:

(1) Is God really going to work my messed-up knee for His good according to His purpose?

(2) Even though my dream of playing football at UNL seems to be a broken dream, is God really for me?"

Frankie paused again and looked over at Betsey. She spoke, "Let's finish by reading Romans 8:37–38."

Mary continued to read. "In all these things we are more than conquerors through him who loved us … and nothing will be able to separate us from the love of God that is in Christ Jesus our Lord."

Betsey walked over and sat beside Mary on the couch. Her part of the presentation was over. Frankie had the stage to himself.

He continued. "I'm not going to lie. Having a messed-up knee stinks. But having a rotten attitude along with it and playing the victim is worse. Somehow, with Christ's power and the love and support of friends, I know I will be able to move forward. So, through this trial, I've come to discover answers to my questions. Yes, God is really going to work for good according to His purpose.

And yes, God is really for me—even though my dream may be changed. And most important, yes, God loves me.

"Would I like to play football again someday? Sure, I would. But I've surrendered that to the Lord. I do know one thing. First and foremost, I am a Christian. Football does not define me. It's a game I play. I really don't know if I'll ever set foot on a field again, but I have peace God will show me the way.

"Isaiah 55:8 (NIV) says, 'For my thoughts are not your thoughts nor your ways my ways, declares the Lord.' I take that to mean God has a plan I may not completely understand. But one thing I know is that I can trust Him. My point is this: we can call ourselves Christians, but the bottom line is a true Christ follower does just that: follows. And that means we must read His word, listen to what He tells us, and obey.

"Betsey, would you read what Matthew 19:26 says?" Frankie asked.

"Sure," she replied.

"Let's all flip over there," Mary Watson chimed in.

Betsey read, "Matthew 19:26 (NIV) says, 'With man, this is impossible, but with God all things are possible.'"
Several students nodded.

Frankie continued. "My plea tonight is that we, as Christians, will determine to live as more than conquerors; that we will choose to live as victors and no longer victims. Will you join me on this new journey to trust God at a new level; to ask Him to move the mountains in our lives and show us His glory?"

James Franco, a junior basketball player, shouted, "Amen, Frankie!" Several students clapped their hands in agreement.

Frankie smiled. "Let me close by sharing with you one of my new favorite verses. It is found in Psalm 56:3 (NIV)." Frankie paused as he heard the flipping of Bible pages searching out the psalm. By heart, he recited the verse: "'When I am afraid I will trust in you.' My hope is that you will learn to trust God, no matter what is going on in your life."

He looked over at Coach Watson. "Well, that's all I've got." Frankie leaned over and grabbed his crutches. As he leaned on them, the crowd clapped their hands in approval. Frankie humbly smiled. Betsey jumped up and gave him a big hug. Mary and Mark Watson followed her, and soon, everyone in the group was congratulating Frankie on a job well done.

The rest of the evening was spent in small groups, praying for their classmates, teachers, and families.

Later, as the crowd dispersed, Frankie and Mary sat side by side on the couch as he waited for Mr. D. to arrive. "I was so proud of you tonight," Mary beamed. "You really scored a touchdown for Jesus!"

A horn honked as Mr. D. pulled the truck into the driveway. "Thanks," he replied.

Mary leaned over and gave him a big hug. She whispered, "I know Jimmy was smiling down on you from heaven."

Frankie just smiled at her and then hobbled to the door.

"Way to go, son." Coach Watson patted him on the back. "You did a great job tonight."

"Thanks, Coach. I'll see you tomorrow at school."

On the drive home, Frankie shared with Mr. D. about the evening. Mr. D. just smiled, listened, and drove. "I think you've got it, my boy."

As Frankie crawled into bed, he felt exhilarated. He reached for his journal and wrote in big capital letters, "VICTORY!" With a smile on his face, he laid down the book and crawled under the covers. For the first time since his injury, Frankie slept soundly without the assistance of any medication. He was saturated by the love and peace of Jesus Christ. That was all he needed!

Chapter 14

# NEW BEGINNINGS

The sun was beginning its descent behind the looming mountains, and Frank sat, staring out the window. The darkness was beginning to cloak the valley in its blanket of black. Frank couldn't get his mind off his glory days of high school. Then he remembered.

Frank rose from his recliner, grabbed his walker, and shuffled to his bedroom. He opened the closet door and turned on the light. Sure enough, there on the top shelf was the box. Frank stood on his tiptoes and reached as high as he could. His fingers grazed the side of the box, but it did not move. Frank reached over to a cane that lay beside his bed. He grabbed the cane and used it to push at the box. On the first nudge, the box slipped over the ledge, and its contents spilled out on the floor. Lying in a heap was a well-worn scrapbook, a pile of letters held together by a thick rubber band, his black journal, and his Bible.

Frank stood, gazing at the items. He bent down, retrieved the scrapbook, and shuffled back to his recliner. As Frank gazed down at the cover, he remembered how Mr. D. had presented this book to him on the day of his college graduation. Mr. D. had spent years collecting various news clippings, photos, and awards Frank had won. He compiled them into this book and given it to Frank as a surprise.

Even now, as Frank flipped through the worn-out pages, yellowed by time, he could almost hear the roar of the crowd and the cadence of the drums as he stood waiting to catch the ball and run it in for a score.

*Those were sure the days,* Frank said to himself. The room grew dim with the setting sun. Frank flipped through the memory book. He finally closed the cover and then closed his eyes. Another day was done.

*******

Ever since Betsey's pep talk, Frankie was like a new man. Even the doctor commented about his new attitude and effort. "If you keep this up, Frankie, you'll be back on the field in no time," he encouraged as Frankie sat atop the table at his latest checkup.

Part of Frankie's rehab included swimming. Once again, he and Betsey began their nightly routine of meeting at the Y at seven. But now, instead of running laps, they enjoyed swimming laps. By February, Frankie's recovery was complete. He was able to lift weights again, and he soon began to regain his strength. At his last doctor's appointment, he'd been given the okay to play football again. Frankie was elated.

With the green light, Frankie began sending college applications to local Division II schools in hopes someone would offer him a football scholarship. Coach Watson even helped by sending out letters highlighting Frankie's skills on the field. He also included information about Frankie's knee recovery.

One March day, Frankie arrived home from school. There were only two months until graduation, and he hadn't made a college decision yet. He was beginning to think his dream of playing football in college was just that: a dream. Maybe it was time for him to just give up and enroll at UNL as a student.

Frankie opened the kitchen door and found Mr. D., sitting at the table. He was wearing a mischievous smile.

"Okay, Mr. D., what's up with you?"

Mr. D. held up an unopened letter. It was addressed to Frankie and the return address was from Kearney State College Athletic Department. Frankie quickly grabbed the letter. He held his breath and tore it open. Mr. D. sat wide-eyed at the table as Frankie read the letter out loud:

Dear Mr. DeMotto:

Your success on the football field has not gone unnoticed by our coaching staff. Congratulations on your fine season.

We were sorry to hear about your injury. However, we feel you would still be a value to our program. We would like to set up a meeting with you and your family to discuss the potential of a football scholarship to KSC.

Please call us at your earliest convenience to set up an appointment. I look forward to hearing from you soon. I truly believe you will add a powerful force to our offense.

Sincerely,

Coach Jim McDonald

Head Coach Kearny State College

Mr. D. slapped his leg and shouted, "Whoppee!"

Frankie just stared at the letter in his hand. Just moments before entering the house, he was about ready to toss in his dream of playing college football. Then here came the letter.

"Wow!" Frankie exclaimed. "They want me with my bad knee and all."

"Listen to me, son," Mr. D. interjected, "you've worked hard at your recovery. Doc gave you the thumbs-up to play again. Why wouldn't they want you? They know talent when they see it. Most of all, God opens doors that no man—in fact, no injury—can shut!"

Frankie stared at the letter. Suddenly, it was if he heard a soft whisper speak into his ear: "Remember, you've earned this." He smiled. Those were the exact last words Jimmy had spoken to him right before he left for camp.

He quickly grabbed the phone and dialed his mom. *I can't wait to tell her this big news!*

\*\*\*\*\*\*\*

A week later, Frankie, Mr. D., and Coach Watson hopped into the coach's car and headed to Kearney, Nebraska. It was about a three-hour drive west of Stanton. The three men talked about football and enjoyed the flat plains along I-80 as they drove. At around one, Mr. D. knocked on the Jim McDonald's office door at Cushing Coliseum.

"Come on in, it's open," a husky voice bellowed from inside.

Coach Watson led the trio into the office. A huge man stood behind a cluttered desk. He was wearing khaki pants and a blue polo shirt with the KSC football mascot over his heart.

Jim McDonald extended his massive right hand and said, "Welcome. I'm so glad you are here. Have a seat." All three men shook hands and then sat down. Frankie sat in the middle.

"Let's get right down to business," Coach McDonald said. "I know UNL offered you a scholarship but then retracted when you were injured. The way I look at it, their loss is our gain." He chuckled as he gazed at them.

"As you know, we pride ourselves with quite a winning tradition here at KSC." He stood and turned to face the wall behind his desk. "These are just a few of our outstanding conference champion teams and some of our All-Americans."

Frankie gazed up at about six framed photos of athletes dressed in their blue and gold uniforms.

"Frankie, we believe you are an asset to our program. We'd like to offer you a full ride to Kearney State. We would pay for your tuition, books, and room. How does that sound, son?"

Coach McDonald looked intently into Frankie's eyes. Frankie was intimidated by the man and looked over to Coach Watson. Then he returned his gaze to Jim McDonald. "It would be a great honor to play for you. I'll gladly accept your offer." Frankie stuck out his hand.

"I was sure hoping you'd say that." Coach McDonald chuckled. He retrieved a pen from his desk drawer and handed it to Frankie. "Let's just make this official. You can sign right there." Frankie took the pen, and with a shaky hand, he signed his name.

Coach McDonald came around to the other side of his desk. "Welcome to our program, son. I know none of us are going to regret this. We will be out at Stanton High next Friday, and I'll have our people notify the press. That way, it will be official." He picked up a blue and gold baseball cap with the KSC insignia across it and handed it to Frankie. "Welcome aboard."

Frankie placed the cap onto his head. It was a perfect fit: just the confirmation he needed.

As they drove home they chatted like excited squirrels. Frankie commented, "Wasn't that campus amazing?"

"I sure wish I had that practice facilities and weight room for my athletes at Stanton High," Coach Watson replied.

"That Jim McDonald is a good guy," Mr. D. quipped. "Frankie, I believe you will be in good hands with him at the helm." The conversation bantered on and on the entire trip home.

Frankie ran straight to the phone as soon as he entered the house. His first call was to his mother; his second was to Betsey.

That night, Mr. D. made a special dinner of Frankie's favorites: fried chicken, mashed potatoes, gravy, and green beans. He even splurged and went to Millie's Diner and bought an apple pie. Betsey joined them, and they celebrated Frankie's scholarship.

"I'm so excited for you, Frankie," Betsey said across the table.

"God's will be done. Never forget it," Mr. D. commented. He wiped his greasy fingers on his napkin and then walked over to grab the pie. "Save room for dessert, you two."

"Don't worry about me, Mr. D.," Frankie quipped. "I've always got room for Millie's apple pie!"

Mr. D. returned to the table, carrying three large slices of pie.

"With graduation only a month away, it sure is exciting to hear what our classmates are planning," Betsey commented.

"I hear you accepted an academic scholarship from Creighton University," Mr. D. said to Betsey. "Well done. That's quite a reputable institution."

"Thank you, sir. I'm excited. They have an excellent nursing program."

"You will make a great nurse someday. You certainly got a great start rolling ol' Frankie around this past year," Mr. D. teased.

Betsey chuckled at the old man's ribbing. "Thanks Mr. D. I appreciate the compliment—and the great meal."

Frankie was excited for his friend. *God, you certainly are working your plan for our lives.*

That night as Frankie lay in bed, he wrote in his journal, "Thank you, God, for showing me your goodness." As far as Frankie could see, his future looked pretty bright. He smiled and closed his eyes. *Life was good, indeed!*

# Chapter 15

# COLLEGE DAYS

There was a festive mood at The Haven; today was the big football game between Notre Dame and Michigan. Frank and Oliver had decided to watch it in the recreation room on the big screen television. Oliver popped some popcorn, and Frank brought some diet Cokes in a cooler. The two friends pulled up some chairs directly in front of the TV.

Other residents began to congregate to watch the game. Oliver was dressed in green from head to toe. He wore a "Fighting Irish" T-shirt, kelly-green dress pants, and a Notre Dame baseball cap.

"You look like a leprechaun or something," Frank teased.

Frank, just to be ornery, picked Michigan to win. He looked around the room; it was evenly divided between those wearing Notre Dame green and Michigan blue. *Maybe this place isn't such a bad place to live, after all.*

The room was filled to capacity by game time. For the next four hours, the residents hooted and hollered as if they were actually at the stadium. When the final second ticked off the clock, the scoreboard read: Notre Dame 24 and Michigan 21.

"Hooray for the Irish!" Oliver squealed. "That would be $5 you owe me, Mr. DeMotto. Once again, the green and gold prevailed!"

Frank rolled his eyes as he handed Oliver an imaginary five-dollar bill. "Good thing we don't bet real money, or I'd be pretty darn broke."

Oliver slapped his friend's hand and then lifted his arms in the sign of victory.

"I'm ready for some peace and quiet," said Frank. "Time for me to head back to my room."

As he entered room 105, the warm sunshine was beaming in through his patio door. He sat in his chair and allowed the sunbeams to radiate heat down on his tired old frame. *I feel like a cat ready to take a snooze.* In no time, Frank's eyes were closed, and once again, he drifted off to sleep.

*******

Today was the big day. Frankie was moving into his dorm; it was time for preseason football at Kearney State. Mr. D. and Frankie had been up since seven, loading the truck. Frankie had to report to his first team meeting at three o'clock.

Betts had stopped over to give him a quick hug and wish him well. She dug into her purse and said, "I made something for you." She pulled out a card. "I made this for you. It has all your favorite scripture verses. I thought it might keep you motivated and pointed in the right direction." She handed it to him and smiled.

Teasing, she pointed her finger at his heart. "Now, don't lose your focus. You've worked too hard for this." She reached up around his neck and gave him one last hug.

Frankie squeezed her hard and then looked her eyes. "Thanks, Betts. It's great, and so are you. I'll call you tonight, okay?"

"That sounds great. I can't wait to hear about your first day on the field. Good luck today." She turned and headed to her car.

When Frankie and Mr. D. arrived on campus, they headed to the men's dormitory, where Frankie had been assigned a room. There, Frankie received his room key and a packet full of information. He and Mr. D. headed back to the truck to start unloading his things.

As they were starting to unpack boxes and arrange the furniture, there was a knock on the door. Mr. D. went over and opened the door. Standing in the doorway was a young, slender boy, around 6′1″ tall and 180 pounds. He had slicked-back hair and wore dark sunglasses. He had on jeans with a white T-shirt and Chuck Taylor high-top tennis shoes. He reminded Frankie of James Dean in *Rebel Without a Cause.*

"Hey, you must be my roomie," he said as he sauntered into the room. "This dump might actually have some potential," he commented as he gazed around the dorm room.

Huffing, puffing, and carrying armloads of boxes, a man and a woman appeared next. "Do you think you maybe could lend a hand, Sean?" the man asked in disgust. He walked to the middle of the room and angrily dropped the box with a thud. Then, without another word, he left. A meek-looking woman entered next and gently laid her large box on top of the unmade twin bed.

"Whew!" she sighed. "It's hotter than I realized."

"Oh, stop complaining, Mom," Sean shot back at her disrespectfully.

She looked at the floor as she wiped the sweat from her face with her sleeve. "Come on, Sean. We'd better go help your dad with the next load, before he has a heart attack." She quickly raced out the door and back to the car.

Sean rolled his eyes in disgust. "Meet my parents," he replied mockingly. Then he, too, disappeared out the door.

Neither Mr. D. nor Frankie had spoken a word since the intruders walked in. They both just stood and stared at each other in disbelief. Finally, Mr. D. broke the silence. "It might be a long semester," he said.

Frankie looked at the pile of boxes that had been dumped in the middle of the room. He wondered, *What have you gotten me into now, Lord?*

Frankie and his new roommate were polar opposites. Sean was a quarterback recruited from Kansas City. He had grown up in the large city and was street smart. His idol was the new screen star, James Dean. Therefore, he donned a white T-shirt, jeans, black Converse tennis shoes, and a black leather biker's jacket. He wore his hair slicked back and even carried a pack of cigarettes rolled up in his T-shirt sleeve.

In contrast, Frankie was the clean-cut, small-town boy. He wore a buzz haircut and had high moral standing. His idol was Jesus Christ. Frankie had never even tasted alcohol nor smoked a cigarette. He had a feeling that wasn't the case for his new roommate.

As Sean began to unpack, he unloaded several beer mugs, shot glasses, and an ashtray. He noticed Frankie staring at him and said, "Hope you don't mind if I smoke."

"In here?"

"Is that a problem?"

"Well, I don't smoke, if that's what you're asking. I'd appreciate it if you would not smoke in our room."

"Whatever."

Frankie walked out and gently closed the door. He stood in the hallway and stared at the door. *This guy is certainly going to be a challenge.*

*******

At 2:30, Frankie asked Sean, "Do you want to walk over to the team meeting together?"

Sean popped his head out of a box full of clothes. "Sure. Just give me a minute." Sean threw off his jeans and T-shirt and quickly changed into workout gear. He grabbed a duffel bag off his bed. *At least we have football in common*, Frankie thought. He closed their door, and they headed off to their first team meeting.

As they walked over to Cushing Coliseum, Frankie made small talk with his new roommate. "How big was your high school in Kansas City?"

"I graduated with about five hundred in my class. How about you?"

Shyly, Frankie replied, "Eighty-five."

"Eighty-five!" Sean replied. "What a hick-town you must have grown up in. If you hang out with me, I'll show you a thing or two."

*That's what I'm afraid of,* Frankie thought. Sean talked incessantly the rest of the way to the coliseum, bragging about his drinking escapades and wild living. *Lord, help me,* Frankie prayed.

Finally, they arrived and found where the team was gathering for its first meeting. The boys saw several football players loitering in the hallway. Sean and Frankie headed toward the group. A large offensive lineman named Jed saw them coming and said to the boy on his right, "Look here. We've got some fresh meat."

Sean coolly stood nose to nose with Jed. "Excuse me?"

Frankie, on the other hand, was trying to make himself invisible.

"You heard me, tough guy," the offensive lineman replied. "You got a problem with that?"

Suddenly, Coach McDonald poked his head out of the classroom. "Is there a problem here, gentlemen?" he asked gruffly.

"No, sir," Jed replied sheepishly.

Sean crossed his arms in front of his chest and stood his ground. His eyes never left the face of the upperclassman.

"I'd suggest you both step outside with me to grab some fresh air." Coach McDonald grabbed both boys by the elbow and led them toward the front door of the building.

Sheepishly, Frankie entered the classroom by himself. *I don't need to be associated with Sean if that's the kind of trouble he gets himself into on the first day!* Frankie quickly scanned the room. Windows lined the classroom. They were wide open to allow fresh air into the stale, hot, room. The smell of chalk mixed with floor polish emanated in the air. Several upperclassmen talked casually to each other. Frankie saw that freshmen were assigned seats in the front row. Each player had his name taped to a seat, and on each seat was a stack of papers. The seats were arranged by the players' positions. *Sean will have to sit with the quarterbacks,* Frankie happily thought. He then spotted his name written on a seat in the middle of the running backs, two sections away from Sean. The veteran players strolled in, joking and laughing with each other as the freshmen entered quietly. The new boys quickly found their seats and nervously started thumbing through the packet.

"This certainly isn't high school anymore," a boy sitting beside Frankie whispered. Frankie turned. Sitting next to him was a boy about his size. He was blond, with freckles across his nose and cheeks. He, too, had a clean-shaven haircut, and best of all, a large smile covered his friendly face.

"I'm Joel Cunningham. I'm a running back from the St. Louis area."

"Glad to meet you," Frankie responded. He stuck out his hand, and they exchanged handshakes. "I'm Frankie DeMotto. I live about three hours east from here: in Stanton, Nebraska."

"I heard about you. Word has it you had an offer from UNL first but then blew your knee," Joel said.

"Where'd you hear that?"

"Several of the upperclassmen were talking when I came in. One of them mentioned the DeMotto kid. I guessed that must be you. So, how's your knee?"

"I've been working hard, and it should be good to go."

A sudden hush fell over the room as all the coaches strolled in the door. Head coach Jim McDonald led the way. Sean and Jed brought up the rear. *Sean doesn't look quite as cock of the walk,* Frankie observed as he watched the boy slink into his marked seat. The coaches stood facing the team, and Coach McDonald stepped forward.

"Welcome, men." He paused. "Today is the beginning of our new season. It's good to have you upperclassmen back, and it's good to see some new faces. I'd like to get some things straight right off the bat. Here at Kearney State we live by some simple rules: no alcohol or tobacco—hence, stay out of trouble, pass all classes, and give me your best. We expect you to succeed off the field as well as on the field." The other coaches eyed the players like a mother hawk does her children.

Frankie listened intently as the coach continued. "Our coaching staff believes in discipline. Believe me, if you choose to break any team rules, there will be consequences. Any use of alcohol or tobacco will result in immediate suspension from this team. Is that understood?"

"Yes, sir," the team bellowed in unison.

"Good. Now, I'd like to introduce you to the rest of my coaching staff." After each coach was introduced, the players were dismissed by positions and followed their assigned coach into another classroom.

The running back coach was Spencer Jackson. Frankie and the other running backs followed his thick frame as they walked down the hallway. Frankie could remember reading Spencer's name in the paper when he played for Nebraska a few years ago. Spencer was fit and looked like he could still play.

When they had gathered in the meeting room, Spencer shut the door. He passed out a thick spiral bound book that contained all the offensive plays. "Welcome, running backs," he said with a smile. "As you know, we are the main workhorses of the offense. If we can't run the ball, chances are we won't win. It's imperative you memorize this playbook. Study it as if you were a doctor getting ready for med school. I want you to know every play inside and out. Got that?"

All heads nodded.

Spencer walked them through a few other details and then said, "Let's head to the locker room. I want you boys to suit up and meet me on the field in fifteen minutes."

The boys raced to the locker room to change. The rest of the day was spent going through rigorous conditioning drills. By six, every muscle in Frankie's body was screaming in pain. Some of his teammates had thrown up because of over exhaustion. He was thankful he had worked so hard at conditioning during the summer.

The freshmen players soon learned the older players considered them the scrubs on the team. It was a rude awakening after being the king of the hill in high school. After practice, the newbies were assigned to collect all balls, pick up any trash, and get all supplies loaded on a truck. Each section was responsible for its area, and today, Frankie and Joel stayed to put away the tires they had used for drills.

"Welcome to college," Joel said sarcastically as he bent over and grabbed the first tire and threw it into the supply truck.

Frankie smiled and grabbed another tire. Sweat dripped off his face as he bent over. "Boy, that shower is going to feel good," he commented.

"Dinner will taste pretty good, too," Joel chimed in.

Cleanup took an extra ten minutes. By the time they got to the locker room, the showers were full. Joel and Frankie took off their sweaty gear, wrapped a towel around their waists, and sat on a bench in front of their lockers. They leaned back against the lockers and closed their eyes in utter exhaustion. Finally, the crowd began to clear, and they made their way into the steamy shower. The hot water soon began to soothe away their tight muscles, and they emerged refreshed and ready to eat.

"Want to grab a bite to eat with me?" Joel invited.

"Sounds good to me," Frankie replied.

Frankie and Joel enjoyed their first meal by reminiscing about high school and reliving their first day as a college football player. *It feels as if I may have met a new good friend.*

After they finished eating, Joel said, "I'm really pooped. I'm ready to call it a night. It was nice talking to you today, Frankie. I'll see you tomorrow."

"Ditto," Frankie replied.

It was now nine o'clock. Frankie stood in front of his dorm room, exhausted from the hard day's work. He was so tired he almost fell through the door. Suddenly, he remembered, *I promised Betts I would call her!* Frankie walked into the lobby, found the phone booth, and dialed Betsey's number. He let the phone ring eight times *She must be at work,* Frankie surmised. Disappointed, he put down the phone and walked back to his dorm room.

Frankie could hear Sean rustling around inside. He popped his head in the door in time to see Sean take a huge pull off of a Coke bottle. Sean also looked spent.

"Wow, that kicked my butt," he groaned as he replaced the bottle on the desk by his bed.

"You can say that again," Frankie said, and he turned on the radio. The weekly top-ten hits were being counted down. Both boys plopped onto their twin bed and, without another word, they both closed their eyes and quickly fell asleep.

*******

The alarm clock blared its wake-up call at six o'clock. Frankie's body screamed in pain, because his muscles were sore from the previous day's practice. Groggily, he crawled out of bed and headed down the hall to the shower. He quickly hopped into the warm water, hoping it would soothe his aching muscles.

After the shower, he threw on some workout clothes and grabbed his cafeteria card. He was ready for some breakfast. He could hear Mr. D.'s voice in his head, saying, *Breakfast is the most important meal of the day.* He smiled.

Sean was still in bed. "Morning," he grumbled in a sleepy voice.

"Good morning to you," Frankie responded merrily. "The shower will do your sore muscles some good," he encouraged.

"I sure hope so," Sean replied, and he pulled the covers over his head.

"I'm heading over to grab some breakfast. Hope you make it on time to practice."

Without responding, Sean rolled over and turned his back to Frankie.

Frankie rolled his eyes, closed the door, and thought, *I'm glad I'm not your mother!*

On his walk to the cafeteria, Frankie thought about how different he was from his roommate. *Sean is abrasive, cocky, and tries to act so tough. I tend to be quiet and shy.* He quickly shot up an arrow prayer: *God, please give me the patience and grace to live with this new roommate you've given me.*

Frankie arrived at the cafeteria and scanned the room full of hungry football players devouring their food. His eyes caught sight of Joel, who waved him over to a table. Joel was already sitting by two other young men.

"This is Marty and Dave," Joel introduced the other players sitting at the table. "Marty plays defensive line, and Dave is a split end."

"Hey," Marty replied. He stuck out his hand, and Frankie shook it. Marty was larger than him. He had larger biceps and a huge hand; he also resonated a tough edge. *Definitely a defensive player.*

Next, Frankie extended his hand to Dave. "Nice to meet you."

"Ditto," the skinny boy responded. Dave was taller, blond, and very tan.

"Marty is from York, Nebraska, and Dave is from North Platte," Joel continued.

The other two boys looked up from their plates of food and nodded. "Grab a seat," Joel told Frankie.

"Thanks." Frankie put down his tray and sat opposite of Joel.

"How you feeling today?" Joel asked.

"A hot shower never felt better. Let's just say, I could sure feel those drills from yesterday." The others nodded in total agreement.

During breakfast, the boys exchanged stories. They talked about where they went to high school and what they were majoring in. As Frank sat and listened, he thought, *It sure feels good to have some new friends.*

## Chapter 16

# TEMPTATIONS

Friday night became card night. Two other residents of The Haven—Mike Dunlap and Anthony Merrill—joined Frank and Oliver. Mike had lived at The Haven for a year and a half. He had been a widower for almost five years. His children and grandchildren lived in the community, so they had moved him to be closer. He was a large man in size and personality. His 6′4″ and 260-pound frame earned him the nickname "the Giant." His booming voice could be heard around the hallway. He often wore bib overalls, which always made Frank think about Mr. D.

Anthony, on the other hand, was a quiet, gentle soul. He usually wore a cardigan sweater, which earned him the nickname "Mr. Rogers," from the television series. He wore wire-rimmed glasses and reminded Frank of a college professor. Nightly, he could be found on the back patio, smoking a pipe.

Each Thursday after supper, the foursome would collect their spare change and head to the recreation room. It soon became fondly known as "poker night." Frank actually enjoyed this male camaraderie. Mike was in charge of bringing the poker chips, Anthony would bring the deck of cards, and Frank and Oliver were in charge of the refreshments; popcorn and diet soda were the norm. The pot usually ranged about $2.50, because they played with quarters.

On this particular night, the men began to swap stories of their wilder days. Frank sat, quietly listening to the other men tell the tale of their first experience with beer. Mike shared about his first time smoking a cigarette. None of the men had ever had any real issues with addiction, and it was funny to recall their youthful mischief. Finally, it was Frank's turn to share his story.

"So, Frank," Oliver chided, "what's your story?"

"Yeah, Frank. Did you ever get into trouble?" Anthony teased. "Or have you always been a saint?" All the men chuckled at that thought.

Frank looked up from his cards with a sly grin. He remembered his first bout of trouble as if it were yesterday.

*******

Classes were now in full swing at KSC. Frankie was barely keeping pace with his hectic schedule. He was carrying twelve credit hours plus football. He practiced everyday from three until seven. By the time he showered and grabbed a quick bite to eat, it was eight o'clock before he could hit the books.

One night as he was bent over his book at the desk in his room, Sean poked his head into the door. "Seriously, DeMotto, you're killing me," his roommate drawled. "You are taking this school thing way too seriously. Why don't you lighten up a little and join me for some fun?"

Frankie didn't even lift his head and ignored Sean's comment. *I wouldn't call what you do fun.*

Sean entered the room and stood beside the desk. Nonchalantly, he placed a pack of cigarettes next to the open book. "Listen, buddy, feel free to take one and live a little. All this Goody Two-shoes stuff is killing me." Sean began to snicker and walked to the door. "Don't bother waiting up for me," he continued, looking back over his shoulder. Then he winked, chuckled, and walked out of the room.

Frankie stared at the cigarettes sitting on his desk. The only people he'd ever been around who smoked were adults. His parents were smokers, and the smell always disgusted him. Feeling a bit mischievous, he opened the pack and peeked inside. Stacked tightly together were filtered cigarettes. The aroma of tobacco lingered as he inhaled the contents of the box.

His mind went immediately a discussion he had with Mr. D.: "Just stay away from tobacco, son," Mr. D had pounded into his brain. "Nothing good ever comes from sucking tar into your healthy lungs."

Frankie closed the lid on the pack and put it on Sean's desk. Then he refocused his attention back on the biology book.

*******

Frankie woke up with the stiffest neck of his life. He had fallen asleep at his desk while reading biology. He gazed at the clock: 2:25 a.m. He looked over at Sean's bed, which was empty.

Frankie slowly rose from his chair and stretched his aching body. As he walked to the door, he heard the voices of several people coming from the hallway. He slowly opened the door, like a private investigator trying to remain unseen, and discovered Sean, another boy, and two girls sitting in the hallway. They giggled drunkenly.

Frankie threw open the door and whispered loudly, "Sean. What's going on out here?"

"Hi roomie," Sean slurred in his drunken stupor. Then the rest of the partiers joined in with giggles. "Come on and join us," he offered as he picked up a paper sack with a bottle sticking out of the end. He thrust it toward Frankie.

"You heard Coach. No booze! It's one of our team rules," Frankie scolded.

"Ooohhhh!" the entire group mimicked. "It's not like anyone is going to find out. Right, Frankie?" Sean hinted.

"Seriously, Sean. Security will be doing their hallway checks. You better get your friends out of here before all of you end up in trouble."

"You're not my dad." Sean slowly tried to stand. "Let's move this party somewhere a little more fun," he said, and he reached down to help one of the girls get to her feet.

Frankie just stared at the group, and without another word, he shut the door. He lunged back onto his bed and pulled the pillow over his head. His mind was racing with thoughts of Sean causing trouble. Plus, he had piles of homework.

After what seemed like hours, he looked at the clock: 4:00 a.m. Exhausted, yet unable to settle his mind, he decided he might as well get up. *My biology test is just a few hours away, so I might as well get up and cram. I can't sleep anyway.*

Frankie saw an open bottle of Coke next to Sean's empty bed. He needed some caffeine, so he thirstily gulped it down. The soda burned more than usual as it slid down his throat. Plus, it tasted strange. *Probably because it's warm,* he thought. He sat down at his desk and tried to refocus on his biology book.

Within five minutes, Frankie had downed the entire bottle of Coke. All of a sudden, he felt queasy. *I need some fresh air.* He threw on his jacket, grabbed his biology book, and opened his bedroom door. When he stepped into the hallway, he discovered Sean and the rest of his party passed out and lying on the floor.

He gingerly tiptoed over the sprawled out bodies and made his way to the front door. The cool morning air blasted at his warm face. It felt shockingly cold, as if someone had just dumped cold water onto his face.

"Brrr!" he said. But his stomach was so nauseous he knew the fresh air would do him some good. He trotted through campus and found a gas station open on the corner of campus. He headed inside and grabbed a large coffee. Then he sat in a booth and opened his book to study some more. Unfortunately, his head was spinning, and his mind wouldn't focus. His legs were bouncing up and down under the booth, and his heart felt like it would pound out of his chest. His was dizzy, and the room even seemed to spin. He thought about the Coke back in his room. *What in the world did I drink?*

Frankie finally gave up trying to study. He grabbed his book and headed back to his dorm room. *Maybe I can grab a couple hours of shut-eye before class.*

The campus was still dark, because it was only five o'clock. On his way back to the dorm, he passed the football stadium. *Maybe if I just jog a couple of laps it will help clear my head, and this dizziness will cease.* He jogged over to the locked gate, dropped his backpack, and quickly leaped up on top of the wire fence. He easily maneuvered over the fence, as if he were a cat burglar, and dropped to the other side with a thud. *A jog is definitely what I need.* Slowly, he began to jog around the track.

Before long, a car pulled up next to the locked gate, and a beam from a large flashlight shone down on his book bag. "Who's there?" a voice called from behind the beam.

Frankie was on the other side of the field when he heard the voice. He stopped dead in his tracks and panted heavily. "Frankie DeMotto," he answered. "I'm a football player."

"It's a little early for practice, isn't it, son?" the campus security officer asked.

Frankie wasn't quite sure how to answer, so he just trotted across the field and toward the gate.

"What do you think you're doing?" the security guard asked, annoyed.

"Just trying to clear my head before my first test," Frankie answered honestly.

As Frankie drew nearer, he felt really dizzy. All of a sudden, it was like he was in a fun house at a carnival. The entire football field felt like it was tipping, and everything around him began to spin. He fell to the ground and sat in a daze. The guard pointed his flashlight directly at Frankie and squinted.

"Are you okay?" the officer asked concerned.

"Uh huh. I think so. Just out of breath," Frankie stammered.

"I'm unlocking this gate and coming in. You stay where you are. No sudden moves. You hear me?"

"Yes, sir," Frankie replied politely.

The officer made his way over to Frankie. By now, Frankie had put his head between his legs in an attempt to stop the vertigo.

"You don't look so good," replied the officer. "Let's get you to my car," he said as he hoisted Frankie to a standing position. "Are you drunk?" He sniffed Frankie as he hoisted him up.

"No, sir."

"You sure are acting funny."

Frankie thought again about the Coke bottle back in his room. *What if there was something in that Coke? It sure did taste funny when I drank it.* "I did drink a bottle of Coke a few minutes ago. I couldn't sleep; I have my first big test this morning. That's probably it. I have a queasy stomach, because I'm nervous for my exam."

The officer took out a pocket flashlight and shined the little beam into Frankie's pupils. "I think you're going to be okay. The fresh air probably did you some good. I suggest you get back to your room and not take anymore laps around the track."

"Thank you, sir. I agree."

"Get in the back of my car, and I'll give you a ride to your dorm."

Frankie stooped in to get into the rear of the car. His entire world suddenly began to spin. The vertigo kicked into high gear, and without warning, he vomited. Brown liquid sprayed over the entire backseat of the security officer's car.

"What the heck!" the guard screamed. "Move away from my car!"

Frankie continue to heave onto the grass. The officer opened his trunk and grabbed some rags. He threw the rags at Frankie. "Clean that mess up now," he ordered.

"I'm so sorry, sir," Frankie apologized as he began to wipe up his mess in the backseat. The smell of the puke made him vomit again.

Frustrated and angry, the officer grabbed the rags. "Let me just take care of this myself."

Frankie lay curled in a fetal position on the grass. He closed his eyes in an attempt to stop the vertigo. After a couple of minutes, the dizziness subsided.

The officer closed the rear car door. He turned to Frankie and asked, "Are you sure you haven't been drinking?"

"No, sir. Just a Coke back in my dorm. I swear."

"I think it would be the best idea for you to walk back to your dorm. There's certainly no need to have any more mess in my backseat."

Frankie stood, his legs a bit wobbly. "Yeah, I'll be fine."

"I hope I don't ever catch you on the track during off hours," the officer said.

"No, sir, you won't. Is there any chance we can keep this between us? I'd rather not have my football coaches know about this."

"Since this is your first offense, I'll let it ride. But let's not have a next time."

"Thank you, and no, sir, there won't be a next time," Frankie promised. And he really meant it.

He gathered his backpack and slowly started walking to his dorm. The officer slowly pulled away but gave Frankie one final stern look: *I've got my eye on you, kid.*

Five minutes later, Frankie was back to his residence hall. He fumbled in his bag for his key. Finally, he unlocked the door to his dorm. Sean was now sound asleep on his bed, and the rest of the party was nowhere in sight. Frankie stormed straight to his desk and grabbed the empty bottle of Coke. He lifted it to his nose. A strange smell drifted from the empty container. He marched over to Sean's bed and dropped the glass bottle on top of Sean's comatose body. The bottle landed on Sean's gut.

"Hey, what's that for?" Sean asked groggily.

"What was in this?"

"Just a little whiskey. Why?"

Frankie's head was throbbing from being sick, his lack of sleep, and the scary encounter with security guard. "Do you know how sick that made me? I can't believe you, Sean," Frankie said angrily.

"Well, you didn't have to drink it," Sean spat back. "It wasn't your bottle in the first place."

*I guess he's got me there.* Frankie just rolled his eyes and flopped down angrily on his own bed. *I will* never *drink another drop of whiskey, that's for sure!*

*******

That was my only experience with whiskey, Frank said to the group around the poker table. Everyone chuckled. Oliver said, "Seriously, Frank, you really were a saint!"

Frank replied, "I didn't get into trouble with my coaches. But it certainly taught me not to drink hard liquor."

189

## Another Near Miss

Toward the end of poker night, the men brought up the subject of interesting encounters with females. Mike shared a crush he had on the school nurse in Middle School and how he faked being sick almost weekly just so she would touch his head to feel for a fever. The old men laughed hysterically to think of the smitten adolescent getting sweaty palms from the touch of a woman in a nurse's cap.

Anthony told about his piano teacher, who smelled like baby powder and lilacs. "My mother never had to drag me to piano lessons. I was always waiting in the car, ready to go every Thursday after school. Sometimes, I would purposely miss a note just so she would place her soft hand on mine and help me correctly hit the chord."

"Those were sure the days," Mike replied.

Frank said, "I never even kissed a girl until my junior year of high school. I was always so focused on football and shy. There was only one gal I ever loved. However, there was a time when another young woman caught my eye …

*******

The leaves were changing color in the beauty of fall. The brown, gold, and rust colors adorned the trees that surrounded the practice field. The team crunched through the fallen leaves as they made their way onto the field. Frank loved this season not only because of football but also because of the natural beauty. Even the air smelled of bonfires.

It was now October, and he was in his tenth week of football. He had worked himself up to the third-string running back position, which was pretty good for a freshman. The strength—along with his mobility and speed—had returned to his knee. Frankie felt as good as new.

Today, he was serving on the "scout" squad for the first team. As he took a handoff and headed up field, one the of the senior linemen tackled him from behind, and his knee twisted awkwardly. He slowly got up from the ground and hobbled back to the huddle.

The injury didn't go unnoticed by Coach Jackson. "DeMotto," he hollered, "front and center."

Frankie left the huddle and gimped toward his coach, trying not to grimace with each step he took on his left leg. When he got to the sideline, Coach Jackson asked, "So on a scaled of 1–10, with 10 being my knee is torn, where you at?"

"Six," Frankie replied and swallowed hard to try to drown out the thundering pain.

"Hit the training room pronto," Coach Jackson commanded.

"Yes, sir," Frankie replied. A student trainer came over, put his arm around Frankie, and helped him hobble to the training room.

Once he arrived, the trainers placed bags of ice on his left knee and secured them with an Ace bandage. As Frankie lay on the training table, trying to focus on the ceiling and not on the pain, he heard a sweet voice from across the room. "What's your damage?"

Startled, Frankie looked around and saw there was only one other person present—and it was a she. In fact, she was a pretty brunette, wearing a blue T-shirt, gold shorts, and a great tan. Her flirtatious smile was directed right at him.

Frankie blushed. "I've got a bum knee. How about you?"

"High ankle sprain," she replied. "I'm on the cheer squad, and I'm probably out for a week. What a way to start the season!"

Frankie looked away. He almost felt like Betsey's eyes were looking over his shoulder—or worse yet, reading his lustful thoughts.

"I'm Melissa Roberts. Everyone calls me Missy," she said with an inviting smile.

"Hi, Melissa. I'm Frankie DeMotto. I'm a running back on the football team." Once again, he quickly looked away.

Missy didn't back down. "I'm a junior, and I live off campus. We have postgame parties after every home football game. Why don't you and some of your football friends join us this Saturday?" She grabbed a pad sitting on a nearby table and jotted something on the paper. She hobbled over on one foot and handed it to Frankie. Meekly, Frankie took the note. "Call me," she said.

She took off the ice bag, threw on her sock and shoe, and headed for the door. "I've got to get to my class. Nice meeting you, Frankie."

Frankie's hands were sweating as his eyes lustfully gazed at her beautifully sculpted body. She was fit and toned, like an athlete in top form. "Sure," he replied. Again, he felt the pangs of guilt as the thought of Betsey entered his mind. Ignoring his conscience, he stuck the note with Missy's number into his duffel bag.

It was a ritual that every Thursday night at eight o'clock, he would talk to Betsey on the phone. Tonight was her turn to call, so when the phone rang promptly at eight, Frankie knew who was on the other line. His stomach flipped, and he stared at his duffel bag, which contained Missy's phone number. The phone rang a third time, and he finally picked up.

"Hey you. How's your day?" she asked cheerfully.

"Actually, I hurt my knee again," Frankie said sullenly.

Betsey's voice changed immediately to concern. "How bad is it, Frankie?" she asked with compassion.

"I'll live."

"You must really be down. I wish I could come over and cheer you up in person."

"That's nice of you, Betts, but I'm okay. I've got to go and study. I'll talk to you tomorrow." He quickly cut off the conversation and placed the phone back in the cradle. Guilt panged at his heart as he stared first at the phone and then at his bag, holding the number of Missy Roberts.

With resolve, Frankie unzipped his duffel bag and withdrew the phone number of the enchantress he'd met earlier in the day. Quickly, before he could change his mind, he ripped the yellow note to shreds. He brushed it off his hands and into the trash. Frankie felt like a thousand pounds had been lifted off his heart and that he had dodged another major temptation bullet. *Betsey is my one and only girl.* He certainly didn't want to do anything that would jeopardize their relationship in any way.

He reached into his desk drawer and pulled out the card Betsey had made him. He recited the scripture verses and then prayed out loud, "Lord, I confess my lustful thoughts toward Missy Roberts. Please forgive me. I don't ever want to do anything to hurt Betsey." Peace began to fall upon his soul.

*Whew!* He sighed. Frankie grabbed the phone and quickly dialed Betsey's number.

"Hello." Her sweet voice filtered through the phone like the voice of an angel.

"Hey, it's me. Sorrow about being so rude," Frankie said sincerely.

"No problem. I'm sure you are very disappointed with your injury. You're forgiven."

Frankie could almost see Betsey's twinkling blue eyes and beautiful smile. "Do you know I'm the luckiest guy on earth to have such an amazing girlfriend?"

They continued to catch up for about twenty minutes. When Frankie hung up the phone this time, he knew in his heart no other girl would ever be able to take the place of Betsey Bailey. She was his one and only.

*******

Oliver spoke first. "So, let me get this straight. You only dated, kissed, and knew one girl your whole entire life?"

"You got it." Frank beamed. Even the thought of his beloved Betsey still brought a smile to his face and warmed his heart.

"Well, I'll be," Oliver continued.

The other men rolled their eyes, and Anthony teased, "Saint Francis DeMotto sits among us men." Then they all began to chuckle.

Chapter 17

# PROPOSAL

Frank was showered and dressed when he heard the knock on his door. "Coming," he called.

When he opened the door, Oliver Hadley stood smiling. "Smells like pancakes and bacon to me, Frank. You ready to join me for some breakfast?"

"Come on in. I've got to take my pills first." Frank motioned him into the room.

Oliver stepped into the doorway, and once again, the beautiful picture of Betsey Bailey caught his eye. Frank turned the corner and caught his new friend gazing at the photograph on the wall.

"She was as pretty as a picture, huh?" Frank asked.

"You bet," Oliver replied.

"How about you? Did you marry the love of your life?"

"Margaret O'Hanlon. A true Irish Catholic. A match made in heaven, " Oliver proudly reported.

The two men headed down the hall toward the smell of breakfast. As they hobbled down the hallway, they shared their love stories.

*******

The next four years flew by at warp speed. Frankie's tweak of his knee didn't cost him his career. It just held him up with a couple of weeks of rehab on the stationary bike. By his sophomore year, he was the second-string running back and saw lots of playing time.

Joel Cunningham was now his roommate. Frankie had heard through the grapevine that Sean had been kicked off the team for breaking the code of conduct and had returned home. *No big surprise there,* Frank thought.

Even though Frankie and Joel played the same position, it did not cause adversity. They helped each other on the field and celebrated each other's success. In fact, they were now best friends. Joel was a Christian, too, and each Sunday they attended church together. Afterward, they would head to the local café and order high stacks of pancakes.

Frankie and Joel were both scheduled to graduate in May. Joel was majoring in engineering and Frankie in business. *Someday, I want to own my own lawn business. All those years of mowing yards weren't for nothing!*

Betsey was on schedule to graduate in May, too. This spring she would be taking her nursing boards. She had just finished her internship and been asked to interview for a job at Methodist Hospital in Omaha.

Frankie figured he would be heading back to Stanton following graduation. He and Betsey had maintained their relationship in spite of the long distance. They grew as friends, and they talked every Sunday on the phone. Both of them felt Jesus had allowed this separation to help protect their purity. Being so far apart physically had allowed them to grow closer emotionally. Frankie was head over heals in love with Betsey.

It was Easter Sunday. Joel had ridden to Stanton with Frankie. They planned to spend the long weekend with Mr. D. Frankie also had a surprise up his sleeve that only his best friend knew.

As they were getting ready for church, Frankie said to Joel, "Today's the special day. I'm going to drive and get Betts myself.

You can catch a ride with Mr. D., and I'll meet you both at church."

"Sounds good to me." Joel winked. "See you there."

About ten minutes later, Frank pulled up to Betsey's parents' house. She, too, was home for spring break. When Frankie pulled the truck to a stop, she was sitting on her front steps. *She looks so pretty*, Frankie thought as he gazed at her. She was wearing a pale pink spring sundress and white sandals. She carried her Bible as she walked to the car. Frankie jumped out of the car and ran over.

"You are a beauty to behold," he exclaimed as he picked her up and twirled her around.

"It's great to see you, too," she said. "Thanks for picking me up. Happy Easter!"

"Happy Easter to you, too," Frank responded. He reached over and opened her door. She climbed into the truck and they headed to church. They rolled down their windows to enjoy the warm spring morning. They each got lost in their thoughts as they took in the day's beauty. When they pulled into the church parking lot, Frank put the car in park. "Hey Betts, would you grab my Bible out of the glove box?"

"Sure," she replied, and she opened the metal compartment. Sitting inside was a small, square box with a ribbon wrapped around it. "What's this?"

"It's an Easter surprise for you," Frankie answered with a coy smile.

"May I open it now?"

"Not until you answer my question." He shifted in the driver's seat and turned to look directly into her eyes. He took both of her hands in his, and with a husky voice, asked, "Betsey Bailey." He gulped nervously. "Will you marry me?" He gazed intently into her sparkling blue eyes.

Betsey's eyes got as wide as a deer in the headlights. "Oh, my gosh, Frankie. Are you serious?" She beamed.

"Totally serious." He held his breath.

Without another word, she lunged toward him and kissed him passionately on the mouth. Breathless, they pulled apart and gazed into each other's eyes.

"Yes, oh yes, Frankie DeMotto. I'd love to marry you."

"Well then, I guess you get to unwrap your surprise," he teased.

Betsey quickly tore off the wrapping paper to reveal a black felt box. She carefully lifted the lid and gazed at the treasure awaiting her inspection. Inside was a beautiful quarter-carat solitaire diamond ring. It sparkled brilliantly as the morning light streamed through the windshield. The round diamond was set on a gold band.

"Oh my gosh, Frankie. It takes my breath away."

Frankie took the box from her shaking hand and removed the ring. He placed it between his fingers and said, "I've been saving up for a long time to give you this, Betsey Bailey. Many yards were mowed on your behalf." He gently placed the diamond onto her finger.

Tears of joy streamed down Betsey's face as she stared at the beautiful gem. "Frankie, I think this is the happiest day of my life!"

He jumped out of the car, strode over, and opened her door. As they walked to the front entryway of the church, arm in arm, they heard applause. They looked up to see Joel, Mr. D., and Betsey's parents cheering.

"So everyone knew but me?"

"Well, I did have to ask your dad for permission."

The crowd surrounded them with hugs and gave its approval of the beautiful ring. Excitement was in the air as the elated group headed into the church service.

During the service, Frankie and Betsey sat with their fingers intertwined. The love they felt was palpable to everyone in their midst. During the first worship song, Frankie looked down the row at the group seated at his pew. His heart swelled with love. God had been so faithful to him, and he felt like the happiest man on the earth.

The message that day was on new beginnings. *How appropriate,* Frankie thought. *I am at another crossroad. A new adventure is about to begin with the love of my life!*

Chapter 18

# THE WEDDING

Saturday morning meant it was time to catch up on all the pregame hype for college football. Frank and Oliver studied the sports page as if it were the Holy Grail. Each man was determined to come out as the winner in today's game pool. Oliver's daughter was going to pick him up at five o'clock. Once a month, she would pop in and take him out for dinner. It was the highlight of the month for him.

"Tonight, I'm in the mood for barbecue," Oliver said as he gazed at Frank over the top of his spectacles.

"Hmmm," Frank replied without putting the paper down.

The two men and never talked much about their families. Oliver sensed this might be another topic Frank didn't want to discuss. He assumed Frank didn't have any family that lived close by, because, to his recollection, he'd never seen Frank leave or have any visitors.

"Just out of curiosity," Oliver asked hesitantly, "do you have any family nearby?"

Frank didn't speak, but shook his head. Once again, his eyes never left the sports page. Sensing Frank wasn't in the mood to talk, Oliver picked his paper back up.

"I never had any kids," Frank spoke softly into the newspaper.

"Oh," Oliver replied gently.

Finally, Frank gently laid his paper down and gazed intently across the table at Oliver. "I think it's time I shared this story with you," he said as though he were about to reveal something very near to his heart.

Oliver quickly laid the paper down and gave Frank his full attention. "I'm all ears, my friend," he encouraged with a warm smile.

Frank let out a deep sigh and then slowly looked out the window.

*******

Frankie awoke with so much joy, he felt as if his heart might explode. Today was his wedding day! He jumped out of bed and headed to the kitchen, where he could hear Mr. D. and his mother chatting excitedly and banging pots and pans. He sauntered into the kitchen. Mr. D. looked over his shoulder. "Good morning, Frankie. I hope you're up for your last bachelor breakfast … Tada!" He put a plate full of scrambled eggs, bacon, and wheat toast on the counter. "I couldn't have the groom faint from starvation now, could I?" he teased.

Frankie's mom gazed at her only son. "How did you grow up so quickly?"

"Oh you two, don't be getting all mushy on me today," Frankie replied, and he grabbed his plate of food.

"Mom, I 'm so glad you could take time off to come and be a part of my big day," he said with a lump in his throat.

"Son, I wouldn't have missed this for the world!"

Then Frankie looked at Mr. D. "Thanks for all you've done for me," he said solemnly

"Frankie, it's been my pleasure. Thank you for giving me the honor to serve as your best man." Mr. D. flexed his muscles to lighten the serious mood. They all laughed.

After breakfast, Frankie said, "I'm going to go for a jog. It might do me some good to release some of this nervous energy." He jumped up and headed out the front door. As he ran, he could hear the birds chirp. He began to hum the hymn "How Great Thou Art." He lifted up praises to the Lord. *I love you so much, God. Thank you for everything you've blessed me with.*

He regained his focus and noticed the wrought iron fence of the Ridgeview Cemetery looming ahead about half a mile. He picked up his pace and was soon on the gravel road that looped through the cemetery like a winding river. He instinctively knew where his heart was leading him: Jimmy Watson's grave.

He had visited this place many times. The white bark of the birch tree always served as his landmark, before he caught sight of Jimmy's headstone. He slowed his pace and ambled toward the marble headstone with his friend's name chiseled into it. "I wish you were here, my friend," he said into the air. "I bet you'd be my best man."

He approached the headstone and knelt on one knee. He noticed a dried flower arrangement that had blown over in the wind, and he set it aright. He dug inside the pocket of his running shorts and found the once-shiny penny Betsey had given him. "In God we trust," he read out loud as he gazed at the penny lying in his palm. "I've tried, my friend. Thank you for helping me discover Jesus."

He gently placed the penny atop the grave marker. A tear slowly trickled down his cheek, as he thought of the what-ifs of Jimmy still being there to share in this special day. Suddenly, he felt a cool breeze. He took a deep breath and inhaled the fresh air. Peace began to override his sorrow, and he smiled. "Put in a good word for Betts and me." He smiled at the gravestone. Then he placed the penny back into his pocket, turned around, and picked up his pace to return home.

At 1:30, the trio headed toward the door. Mr. D. and Frankie grabbed their tuxedo bags. Mrs. DeMotto, already in her new dress, paused at the door and said, "This certainly feels like a Kodak moment to me." She grabbed her camera. "Gentlemen, would you please do me the honor?"

Quickly they laid their garment bags on the sofa and stood arm in arm. Mrs. DeMotto took a few shots, and then Mr. D. asked, "How about one of the groom and his mother?"

"That would be wonderful," she remarked, and she handed Mr. D. the camera. She smiled lovingly at her son, and as he placed his arm around her, she said tenderly, "I'm so happy for you, son. You know I love you, don't you?"

Frankie enveloped his mother in a hug. "You bet I do, Mom."

"Come on, you two. We're going to be late. Let's get this photo taken," Mr. D. commanded.

Finally, with the last click of the camera, the trio headed out the door. The professional photographer was to begin at 2:00 at the church. On the way, Mrs. DeMotto began her mother-of-the-groom checklist:

"Ring—check. Hotel confirmation—check. Marriage license—check. Wallet, money—check."

Mr. D. glanced out of the corner of his eye at Frankie. Small sweat beads glistened across Frankie's forehead as his mother spoke.

"Relax, my boy," Mr. D. said reassuringly. "You've got it all covered. Just take a deep breath and try to relax."

Frankie inhaled deeply and felt some of his stress depart as he exhaled. Finally they arrived at the church, and Mr. D. pulled the truck into the rear parking lot. The Baileys' red Cadillac was already parked. A station wagon with the words "Make Photography" also took up a spot.

The trio hopped out, their arms full of tuxedos, and they rushed to the rear entrance of the building. They could hear voices buzzing as they entered the door.

"You lead the way, Mr. D.," Frankie said excitedly. "I don't want to ruin the surprise and see Betsey in her dress until it's time."

Like a soldier on a lookout mission, Mr. D. went ahead and poked his head into the hallway. "The coast is clear."

"I'll meet you in the sanctuary," Mom said. She gave Frankie a quick peck on his cheek and then brushed off her ruby red lipstick smudge with her thumb. "Sorry." She smiled.

The two men strode quickly through the back hallway and found the church library, which would be used as the groom's room. Both men were in the process of putting on their tuxes when Joel walked into the room, already dressed to the nines.

"Wow, you clean up darn good!" Frankie teased as he shook hands with his best friend.

"Not too bad yourselves," Joel replied as he inspected the other two men.

"These darn shoes are going to kill my bunions," Mr. D. scoffed.

"I give you permission to take them off if you are in the back row during pictures," Frankie offered.

Just then they heard a knock on the door. The men turned their heads as Mr. Bailey—Betsey's dad—poked his head through the door. He, too, was dressed in his black tux. His blue eyes sparkled, just like his daughter's.

"Well, gentleman, they're ready for us," he said, smiling. He extended his hand to Frankie and then gave him a hug. "I know my little girl is in good hands." Then he patted Frankie on the back.

The men walked toward the sanctuary of the church. "Let's do this," Frankie said. Mr. D. gave him a knowing wink of confidence.

As Frankie turned the corner, his eyes first caught sight of the stained-glass windows that encircled the main sanctuary. The light reflected off the sun-drenched windows, making the colors look as if they were dancing. Frankie stood in awe at the beauty. A swooshing sound caught Frankie's attention, and he turned his gaze to the side doorway. Molly and Brenda, Betsey's bridesmaids, entered the sanctuary first. Their soft pink chiffon dresses rustled as they walked.

Mrs. Bailey stood in the doorway and held it wide open. Like Cinderella entering the ball, Betsey Bailey made her entrance. Her blond hair was swept up into a soft ponytail. Her floor-length lace veil trailed behind. A hoop slip made her white satin dress billow. She looked like an angel. Frankie stared at his beautiful bride and swallowed the lump in his throat. *She looks so radiant.*

"Wow," he managed to speak. "You look amazing." He walked over, took Betsey's hand, and gazed lovingly into her sparkling blue eyes.

"Thanks," she said, "You look pretty darn good, too." She reached up and gave him a kiss on the cheek, and he gave her a big bear hug. Their parents and Mr. D. took out tissues and dabbed at their eyes.

"It's going to be an amazing day," Frankie's mother stated.

Frankie squeezed Betsey's hand lovingly, and they headed to the stairs at the front of the church to begin the photo shoot.

The wedding began promptly at four o'clock. The entire ceremony only took about forty-five minutes. A cake reception was held in the church fellowship hall. An hour later, Mr. and Mrs. Frank DeMotto exited through the front doors of the church amid the rice thrown by their guests. The photographer snapped a candid photo of them running down the steps. It revealed their true love for each other in a perfect click of the camera.

Frankie opened the door of the truck and helped Betsey stuff her long train into the vehicle. Then he merrily jogged to the other side. A poster stating "JUST MARRIED," was taped in the rear window. A string of cans dangled off the back of the truck. Happily, the newlyweds pulled away from the church saluted by the applause of their family and friends and the clanking of cans.

*Today is the first day of the rest of our lives*, Frankie thought. He reached over and grabbed his bride's hand. They smiled contentedly.

# Chapter 19

# NEWLYWEDS

Oliver noticed Frank was unusually quiet this morning as they sat at their usual table. He put down his newspaper. Frank was staring out the window as though lost in thought.

"Hey, buddy, what's going on in that mind of yours?" Oliver asked gently.

Frank turned and looked at his best friend. Tears were brimming in his eyes. "Oliver, today is the anniversary of the worst day of my life."

Oliver pulled up his chair so he could get closer to hear his friend. Frank began to unload his story in a choked voice almost drained by the weight of the pain.

*******

Frankie and Betsey's first six months of marriage were like a fairy tale. Betsey worked as an RN at Clarkson Hospital, and Frankie started a commercial lawn-mowing business. They lived in a small, two-bedroom rental cottage in the Dundee area of Omaha. It was only a few miles from the hospital where Betsey worked. They were also only about an hour away from her parents and Mr. D.

"Life doesn't get any better than this, " Frankie said to Betsey one night as he lay in bed, holding her close.

"Yes, it does." She leaned on her elbow and gazed into his face. "It would if we had a baby to join us."

Frankie bolted upright. "Are you telling me what I think you're telling me?" he asked excitedly.

"Mr. DeMotto, you're going to be a daddy," Betsey said proudly.

Frankie held Betsey's face in his hands and looked at her tenderly. He gently placed a kiss on her lips and whispered, "Betsey Bailey, I love you more than you'll ever know. I can't wait to have a baby together."

*******

Betsey was in the eighth month of her pregnancy. One day on her rounds at the hospital, she began to feel faint. She quickly found a chair at the nurse's station and sat down. Pains from her swollen belly caused her to groan and double over.

"Are you okay?" Karen, Betsey's coworker, asked.

Betsey couldn't answer. The pain in her abdomen took her breath away. Suddenly, a pool of blood collected onto the chair. The blood began gushing from between her legs, as if a garden hose had been turned on.

"Oh my!" Karen gasped in shock. Her nursing mind quickly kicked into gear. "Hang on, Betsey. I'm getting you a wheelchair, and we're heading down to the ER."

Frankie was at work when the phone on his desk rang. "Frank's Place. How can I help you?"

"Frank?" A female voice he didn't recognize answered. "This is Karen at the hospital. I work with Betsey. Listen, she's here in the ER, and the doctors are checking her out right now. I found you as her emergency contact and wanted to call you immediately. I really think you need to get down here as quickly as you can."

"Why? What's happened?"

"I'm not exactly sure. She's in good hands, but you need to get here quickly."

"I'm on my way," Frankie said frantically. He quickly dialed Mr. D. and explained Betsey was in the emergency room. He asked him to call the Baileys and to try to get to the hospital as quickly as they could. Frank grabbed his keys, locked the front door, and ran to his car. He had no idea what he would face when he walked into the emergency room doors.

All the way to the hospital, Frankie pleaded with God. "Lord, please don't take my baby. Please be with Betsey and protect her body. Please be with the doctors and give them wisdom." His adrenaline was racing, and his heart was pounding so fast it felt as if it might leap out of his chest.

It took Frankie twenty minutes to weave through traffic and get to the ER. When he finally arrived, he frantically ran through the door and straight to the check-in counter. Breathlessly, he said, "My wife is Betsey DeMotto. Where is she?"

The receptionist quickly picked up the phone as Frankie stood in a panic. His throat felt constricted; his heart felt like it might shatter from the pain and fear he was feeling. He was overwhelmed with worry. *All I want to do is see my wife.*

"She's in room B," the receptionist stated. "Go through that door." The door buzzed as she hit the button that allowed Frankie entrance. He scanned the brightly lit hallway for room B. The shiny floor was slippery, and Frankie almost skidded past the doorway as he ran.

When he arrived at room B, he found a nurse posted at the closed doorway. "Is that where they have taken my wife? I'm Frank DeMotto."

"Yes," she said. "I'm the person who called you. I'm Karen. I work upstairs with Betsey."

"What's going on in there?" Frankie asked fearfully.

"I really don't know for sure. All I do know is that Betsey's in good hands. I got her down here as quickly as I could." Karen began to sob.

"I'm sure you did," he replied kindly. "Tell me what happened." He searched Karen's face for an answer.

"It was just a normal day, as far as I could tell. But all of a sudden, Betsey staggered over to the nurse's station and slumped over in the chair. A pool of blood started gushing between her legs. That's when I grabbed the wheelchair, and I ran her down to the ER as fast as I could. The doctors were checking her out within minutes of us arriving. I think she was unconscious by the time I got her down here. Frank, I moved as quickly as I could." Her voice trailed off, and she began to sob again. "I'm really sorry."

Frankie gently placed his hand on her shoulder. As he stood next to her, he peeked through the small, rectangular window of the door. He could see a team of doctors around the bed. He couldn't see Betsey, but he could see the doctors working frantically.

Frankie felt a tidal wave of fear overtake him. He looked away from the window, took a deep breath, patted Karen on the back, and collapsed in a chair across from room B. He put his head into his hands and he began to pray silently: *Lord, I feel so helpless. Please be with my wife and child. Guide the doctors and give them wisdom as they work on her.*

Suddenly, the door to room B opened, and a doctor in olive green scrubs and wearing a mask stepped out. His scrubs were splattered with blood. He took off his mask, and it revealed a tan face and serious eyes.

"Are you her husband?" he asked as he looked across the hallway at Frankie.

"Yes," Frankie replied shakily. He jumped out of his chair and approached the doctor.

"I'm sorry, son. We did all we could," the doctor said flatly.

"Did she lose our baby?" Frankie asked, pain oozing from his voice.

The physician paused and looked at the ground. With a heavy sigh, he muttered, "Son, I'm afraid we lost them both. I'm so sorry."

Frankie's knees buckled at his words, and his head began to spin. "You lost them *both!*" Frankie screamed. "What do you mean?"

"I'm sorry, son. I'll do my best to explain. Unfortunately, your child incurred a placental abruption. This means there was a premature separation of the placenta from the uterine wall. As a result, the baby is not able to survive. This then caused disseminated intravascular coagulation in your wife. Blood clots formed throughout her small blood vessels and blocked the flow of blood to her organs. Due to this and her rapid drop in blood pressure, we were too late. We did all we could do. I truly am sorry for your loss."

As the doctor spoke, Frankie felt the hallway begin to spin uncontrollably. Karen ran and grabbed Frankie just as he was about to go down. She maneuvered him carefully back to the chair. *My world has collapsed.* He gasped for breath and sobbed hysterically.

"Nurse," the doctor shouted down the hall. "We need some help here." A male nurse came running. "Give Mr. DeMotto a sedative please," the doctor instructed. Then he spoke to Karen. "We will get Mrs. DeMotto cleaned up and allow him to have some time with her. Are there any other relatives present?"

Frankie looked up. "Not yet, but they're on the way."

The male nurse returned with a syringe and injected a tranquilizer into Frank's bicep. He just rocked back and forth in the chair, head in his hands. *Lord, please let me die, too. I don't think I can go on without her.*

Then Frankie heard the clicking of shoes headed toward him. He lifted his head from his hands and saw the Baileys and Mr. D., running.

"Frankie," Mrs. Bailey screamed, "where's my Betts?"

Frankie looked helplessly at Mr. D. Nurse Karen walked over to the threesome. She recounted the tragedy as they all stared in shock. Tears, moaning, and gasps for breath emanated from the shocked family. The three of them staggered over to Frankie, who had not moved. They wrapped their loving arms around him, and together, they swayed in a slow, rhythmic dance of grief.

Thirty minutes passed. The sound of the hallway clocked ticked loudly in the eerie silence of the death chamber. Finally, the doctor's soothing voice broke the quiet. "You can come in now. Take as much time as you'd like."

Frankie slowly stood and led the entourage through the open door of room B. Betsey looked like she was sleeping peacefully on the pillow. Her blond hair cascaded around her face. Frankie reached for her lifeless hand and let his face fall onto her shoulder. His sobs were uncontrollable as he took in the scent of her shampoo. *What am I going to do without you?*

Betsey's parents stood on her other side. Her mother gently stroked her daughter's beautiful blond hair as tears cascaded down her face. Her father stood stoically beside his wife, attempting to be her pillar of strength. Mr. D. sat on a chair at the foot of the bed, his shoulders hunched.

About an hour later, a nurse poked her head into the room. "I'm very sorry to bother you. I need you to sign this paperwork before you leave. It's hospital policy." She handed the stack of papers and a pen to Frankie.

He grabbed the paperwork and angrily snapped, "Are you kidding me?" He threw the papers to the ground.

Mr. D. came to his side. "Listen, son, she's just doing her job." Mr. D. bent over and retrieved the pile. "We'll take care of this," he calmly said to the nurse. "How about if I drop them off at the front desk in a little while."

"I'm sure that will be fine." Quietly she exited the room, leaving the grieving family to say their good-byes.

Frankie continued to stare at his unmoving, lifeless wife. *How do you expect me to go on living, God? My life might as well be over.* Once again, Frankie faced a crossroad. *As far as I'm concerned, this one leads only to a dead end.*

*******

Oliver sat in stunned silence as he listened to Frank's story. *No wonder Frank has such a calloused heart and is angry with God. This is sure a good example of the saying, "Hurting people hurt people."*

"I never remarried," Frank spoke barely above a whisper. "And I've never forgiven God for taking away the best thing in my life." Tears began to stream down Frank's face. Oliver reached for a clean napkin on their table and handed it across the table.

"Thanks for sharing this with me, " Oliver said sympathetically.

"Today's the anniversary of her death."

Oliver took his friend's hand. "You know what, Frank? You and me are going to finish this race of life together. I'm here for you."

"Yeah, I know. Thanks, Oliver. I was sick of being so lonely. I truly hated who I had become: a bitter, grumpy, lonely old man. I really think you've saved me from myself. Who knows, maybe you're my angel."

"Ha!" Oliver chuckled. "Who are you kidding?"

For the first time that day, the two men laughed.

Chapter 20

# A TIME TO LIVE

Frankie woke up with a start and bolted upright in his bed. He was covered in sweat and gasped for air as if he were a drowning victim.

"Where am I?" he said, and his voice almost echoed eerily back at him in the darkness of his bedroom. He glanced over to his right. Betsey—his beautiful wife—usually slept peacefully by his side. The only thing there now was an indention from where her body once fit. His eyes caught sight of the clock on the nightstand; it blinked 5:45 a.m. on its face. Tears began to stream down Frankie's face. Betsey was dead. She had died at the ER the previous day. Unfortunately, his reality was now his worst nightmare.

"Oh God, " he wailed into the dark room, "why?"

He could feel the rage and the bitterness boiling inside his body. *God, if you truly loved me, how could you allow this to happen?* It felt as if his rage was squeezing the life out of him. Suddenly, it was if God nudged him gently, and his inner voice whispered, *Remember the dream.*

At that very instant, twenty-three-year-old Frankie DeMotto remembered the dream he just had—a dream of being a grumpy, lonely, old man living in some retirement home. It was if he were

Scrooge from *A Christmas Carol. I think I may have just visited with my past, present, and future ghosts.*

He grabbed a glass of water sitting on his nightstand and gulped it down. *God, were you showing me a glimpse of what my future would look like if I allow this anger, bitterness, and hatred to callous my heart?* Frankie searchingly prayed. Tears streamed down his face.

Silence was his only answer.

He turned on the small light on his nightstand. He caught a glimpse of his Bible, resting beside the framed photo of Betts and him, exiting the church on their wedding day. It was his favorite picture. New hot tears stung Frankie's eyes as he gazed at the picture. As if the Holy Spirit were speaking, he heard the words, *I Peter 1:6, 7* resonate in his head.

Quickly, he grabbed the Bible and flipped the pages rapidly the back of the book. When he came upon the verse, he read out loud, "You have been grieved by various trials, that the genuineness of your faith being much more precious than gold that perishes though it is tested by fire, may be found to praise, honor, and glory at the revelation of Jesus Christ."

Frankie laid the opened book on his lap. As if a lightning bolt had struck him he had the thought, *This is the most important crossroad of my life. The question is which way will I turn? Will I head down the path of bitterness, or will I choose to follow the Lord?* He knew that Jesus' way led to the path of life. His dream showed him where the road of bitterness may lead him.

"Oh my God, please help me," he sobbed. He walked over to Betsey's jewelry box and opened the lid. Propped up on the ring holder was his special penny. He stared at it and then gingerly placed the penny in the palm of his hand. He gazed intently at the words, "In God We Trust" engraved on the coin. The memory of

Betsey handing him this penny at Jimmy's funeral flashed into his mind. Again, fresh hot tears streamed down his face.

All of a sudden, the song of a morning glory bird brought him to the present. The first rays of a new sunrise had begun to seep through his window. Frankie stood up and opened the shade. A gentle breeze entered the stale, dark room. He slowly inhaled, and it was as if the fresh air was bringing him back to life.

*Today I choose you, God. I know the only way I'm going to get through this is with you by my side.* He stood gazing out the window and listening to the bird. *Help me to keep living. Please don't allow me to become a grumpy old man with a bitter heart. Help me, Jesus.*

He held up his hand, like a little boy reaching up for his daddy. He lifted his eyes to the sun, peeking over the horizon. Then he recited his personalized version of Psalm 121:

> I lift up my eyes to the hills—where does my help come from? My help comes from the Lord, the Maker of heaven and earth. He will not let my foot slip—He who watches over me will not slumber; indeed, He who watches over Israel will neither slumber nor sleep. The Lord watches over me—the Lord is my shade at my right hand; the sun will not harm me by day, nor the moon by night. The Lord will keep me from all harm—he will watch over my life; the Lord will watch over my coming and going both now and forevermore.

Frankie prayed aloud, "God, I don't know any other way to do this. I need you now more than ever. Please hold me close."

He looked again at the bird perched on the limb outside of his window. Tenderly, Frankie placed the special penny in his pocket.

The smell of fresh coffee caught his nose. He remembered now that Mr. D. had driven him home from the hospital. The old man had even stayed overnight. *Good old Mr. D. is always here when I need him most.*

At that moment, Frankie realized he would not be alone in this new storm. God would again provide people to comfort him, to be with him in his grief, and to love him through this latest tragedy. He grabbed the doorknob, turned the handle, and sighed. *Today is the first day on my new road. God, please lead the way.*

He took his first step out into the hallway filled by the light streaming in from the kitchen. It was as if the darkness and the bitterness of his soul were dissolving with each step. When Frankie closed the bedroom door, it was as if the door of his heart was being closed to the bitterness.

"Today I choose life," he whispered, and a blanket of peace fell upon him. It was as if God himself were in the hallway, standing there beside him, covering his hurts and healing his heart.

A small smile crept upon his face. He headed toward the light. *Life will go on.*

# AUTHOR'S NOTE

Many of us have been handed a tragedy of some kind: death of a loved one, a major illness, or a divorce. To you who have suffered, I truly say I am sorry for your pain.

As a believer in Christ, I am often reminded we are not guaranteed an earthly life of bliss. Jesus told us in John 16:33 (NIV), "'In this world you will have trouble. But take heart! I have overcome the world.'"

In John 14:27 (NIV), Jesus says, "'Peace I leave with you; my peace I give you. I do not give to you as the world gives. Do not let your hearts be troubled and do not be afraid.'"

I have discovered my life often is not what I have scripted. Many times, God and I have a conversation like this: "This is *not* what I signed up for, God." At times like these, I am reminded of my Lord and Savior, kneeling in agony and prayer in the garden of Gethsemane. It was here that Jesus prayed to His Father: "'My soul is overwhelmed with sorrow to the point of death … My Father, if it is possible, may this cup be taken from me. Yet not as I will, but as you will'" (Matthew 26:38–39 NIV).

Jesus can sympathize with our weaknesses, and He invites us to approach the throne of grace with confidence, so that we may receive mercy and find grace to help us in our time of need. (See Hebrews 4:14–16.) My prayer for you, my reader, is to discover the true love, grace, and peace of God. That you, like Frankie DeMotto, will find freedom and grace to help you attain your crossroads.

And if you, by chance, are that grumpy person imprisoned by a hardened heart of bitterness, may I say to you, today is a new day! Today, choose life!

Ephesians 4:31–5:2 commands us, "Get rid of all bitterness, rage and anger, brawling and slander, along with every form of malice. Be kind and compassionate to one another, forgiving each other, just as in Christ God forgave you. Be imitators of God, therefore, as dearly loved children and live a life of love, just as Christ loved us and gave himself up for us as a fragrant offering and sacrifice to God."

I encourage you to "put off your bitterness" by saying the following prayer:

1. Father, today I choose to forgive _____ for the following things he/she has done to hurt and cause me pain. (Name each one the Lord reveals to you. Speak each item out loud, and say I forgive him/her for …)

2. Father, I also choose to forgive _____ for all the hurt and pain I have experienced because of these things he/she has done to me because it made me feel (speak out loud the emotion you felt with the offense):

| Rejected | Hopeless | Angry | Judged |
|---|---|---|---|
| Abandoned | Helpless | Bitter | Guilty |
| Unwanted | Out of Control | Rage | Unclean |
| Lonely | Distrustful | Hate | Dirty |
| Unloved | Anxious | Sad | Ashamed |
| Resentful | Fearful | Depressed | Ugly |
| Unprotected | Betrayed | Used | Fat |
| Failed | Dumb | Stupid | Worthless |
| Inadequate | Inferior | Insecure | Condemned |
| Trapped | Jealous | Defeated | Victimized |

3. Father, please forgive me for my sin against you because of my bitterness and unforgiveness toward _____. Thank you for forgiving me. I receive your forgiveness and cleansing from all unrighteousness, and I choose in faith to forgive myself.

4. Lord, I release _____ and things that he/she did to me to your perfect justice. I choose not to hold any of these wounds, hurts, and pain against _____ any longer. Father, thank you for setting me free from the bondage of my unforgiveness and bitterness. I Ask you to heal me of my painful memories, wounds, and hurt.

In Jesus' name, Amen.

My prayer is that you will truly discover Christ's deliverance from your bitterness and unforgiveness. And that you will walk in the freedom Christ died for you to have.

"So if the son sets you free you will be free indeed" (John 8:36 NIV).

May you discover the road of the cross and live loved!

# BIBLIOGRAPHY

*The Holy Bible, New International Version*®, NIV®. Copyright ©
1973, 1978, 1984, 2011 by Biblica, Inc.™ Used by permission. All
rights reserved worldwide.

*New Revised Standard Version Bible: Anglicized Edition*, (NRSV).
Copyright © 1989, 1995, Division of Christian Education of the
National Council of the Churches of Christ in the United States
of America. Used by permission. All rights reserved.

CPSIA information can be obtained at www.ICGtesting.com
Printed in the USA
LVOW130003200412

278312LV00001B/2/P

9 781449 743390